I Know Where She Is

I KNOW WHERE SHE IS

S. B. CAVES

San Diego, California

 Canelo US
An imprint of Printers Row Publishing Group
9717 Pacific Heights Blvd, San Diego, CA 92121
www.canelobooksus.com

Printers Row Publishing Group is a division of Readerlink Distribution Services, LLC. Canelo US is a registered trademark of Readerlink Distribution Services, LLC.

This edition originally published in the United Kingdom in 2017 by Canelo.

Published in partnership with Canelo.

Correspondence regarding the content of this book should be sent to Canelo US, Editorial Department, at the above address. Author inquiries should be sent to Canelo, Unit 9, 5th Floor, Cargo Works, 1–2 Hatfields, London SE1 9PG, United Kingdom, www.canelo.co.

Publisher: Peter Norton • Associate Publisher: Ana Parker
Art Director: Charles McStravick
Senior Developmental Editor: April Graham
Production Team: Beno Chan, Julie Greene, Rusty von Dyl

Library of Congress Control Number: 2021953454

ISBN: 978-1-6672-0126-9

Printed in the United States of America

26 25 24 23 22 1 2 3 4 5

For my wife

Part One

1

Francine didn't notice the letter until she was on her way to the kitchen for another glass of vodka. She spotted the white envelope standing out against the grey carpet and automatically assumed it to be a fast-food flyer. She picked the envelope up, turned it over. It was unmarked, no stamp, and the fold hadn't been glued down but tucked inside. She took it to the kitchen, set her glass down on the counter and removed the small sheet of lined paper from inside. Five words were scrawled in jagged chicken scratch:

I KNOW WHERE SHE IS.

It took a second for the sentence to calibrate in Francine's mind. She inhaled sharply and traced her eyes over the writing again to ensure she hadn't misread it. Then she opened the envelope and tipped it upside down as though an explanation might fall out, like a vital piece of the trick missing from the magician's hat. She realised she could hear herself panting, and was suddenly burning inside her blouse. The moisture evaporated from her mouth.

She folded the paper up and placed it delicately back inside the envelope, then padded to the front door and swung it open. Barefoot, she stepped out onto the cold concrete and looked around. Nobody there. She walked over to the balcony and peered down into the vacant courtyard below, her eyes searching for movement in the shadows. She turned and saw light through the door panes of number 40. She rang the bell, could hear the muffled blare of their television from within.

A small Chinese lady opened the door and stared up at her blankly.

'Hi,' Francine began, unsure as to whether the woman even spoke English. 'Sorry to bother you. I live next door.' She pointed at her apartment, despite crossing paths with the woman almost every day. For six years they'd maintained an unspoken treaty with one another. I won't bother you with small talk or empty pleasantries if you will extend me the same courtesy. Up until now, it had worked just fine. 'I got a letter through my door today. It didn't have a name on it or anything. I was wondering if you saw someone come by my place.'

'No,' the woman replied with a small shake of the head.

'You haven't seen anyone hanging around the building? Anyone you don't recognise?'

'No,' she repeated, defensively this time.

'Okay, thanks.' Francine walked to number 36 and pressed the bell, conscious of the Chinese lady still watching from her doorstep. When nobody answered after three rings, Francine cursed and went back inside her own apartment. She poured herself another inch of vodka and stared at the envelope. How could someone write such a vague message and leave no way to get in contact with them? As she gulped from the glass she sloshed vodka down her blouse but didn't bother to dab at the

4

damp patch. She turned the conundrum over in her mind, trying to make sense of it. The vodka had dulled her body somewhat, but she was still able to think rationally. What it really came down to was this: the author of the note was either pulling a hurtful prank or telling the truth. Perhaps some kids had found her address, knew about what had happened and had decided to venture out in the pouring rain to deliver the letter. The chances of that scenario being plausible slimmed when she considered that they wouldn't even have the joy of seeing her reaction as she read the message. She hadn't been bothered by anyone in years, not since she moved to this apartment. Could her address have leaked on the internet? She wasn't sure how that could be possible, not with the measures she'd taken to prevent such a thing from happening.

No, this felt different. There was a disturbing vagueness to the note. In her experience, if someone wanted to pick open the scab, they didn't tiptoe around it; the sick bastards went into explicit detail, spilling every sordid scenario they could think of to hurt her.

So what was the alternative? She trudged to the living room and snatched her cell phone off the sofa. Her fingers, clumsy from the alcohol, located Will's number then hovered over the screen for a moment before dialling. She paced the living room, waiting for him to answer, biting her thumbnail and hearing the click of her teeth inside her skull. It rang six, seven, eight times before it went to voice-mail, and she tasted blood from her thumb. She hung up and redialled, the phone slippery in her palm. Again the dial tone droned on, and for one fleeting, terrible second she thought she was going to get the voicemail again. But then he answered, his voice distant with confusion.

'Francine?'

'Yeah, it's me.' She cleared her throat. 'Yeah, hello. It's Francine.'

'I got that. Um… how are you?'

'I think it might be a good idea if we talked, like face to face. Can you come over?'

'What?'

In the staccato silence that segmented their dialogue, Francine could hear Sheila hovering close by, muttering, meek and curious.

'Look, can you come over? Right now, tonight. I have something I need to show you.'

'What is it?'

'I don't want to do this on the phone, Will. I wouldn't be calling you if it wasn't important.'

He paused, exhaled. 'We might not have the same opinion on what's important at eight o'clock at night when it's pissing down with rain,' he said, and ever so faintly, Francine heard a squeak from Sheila.

Heat flared through her chest, a ring of fire burning the nape of her neck. She felt sweat trickle down her back. 'You won't have to be here for very long, I promise. I just…' She faltered, her skull heavy as a cement mixer. 'Can you come or not, Will?'

He took a few breaths to consider her question, or to receive instruction from Sheila, Francine wasn't sure which, and then said, 'Is it some kind of emergency?'

'Yes, I think it is.'

'And you can't tell me what it's about?'

Now it was her turn to hesitate, knowing that he would recoil, that he would berate her, or maybe hang up. 'It's about Autumn.' She was going to leave it there, but the

6

vodka told her the sentence needed an exclamation mark. 'Obviously it's about Autumn. Why else would I call?'

'I see.'

'Right. You see. So can you come over?'

'Why can't you come to me?' At this, a flittering whisper protested, but Francine couldn't pick out exactly what was said. She heard muffled sounds, presumably as he covered the phone to say something to Sheila. Then he added, 'I mean, I can meet you somewhere. It doesn't seem fair that I should drive all the way over to you.'

'All right.' Francine swept a clammy hand down her face. 'I'll leave in ten minutes and phone you when I'm near. Will there be a diner open or something like that?'

'I'm not staying to have coffee and doughnuts, Francine. I've got things to do here.'

'Fine. We'll just go sunbathing then, shall we?' She felt the anger rise in her throat like bile. She swallowed it down before continuing. 'I meant a diner where we can go to be out of the rain. What do you think I'm trying to do here, lure you into some kind of date?'

Sighing, he said, 'We can talk in the car, surely?'

The muscles in her jaw tensed. 'Works for me. I'll be there in an hour.'

'Don't keep me waiting around for you.'

He hung up before she could retort, and childish as it was, she resented that he'd had the last word, knowing that he'd done it to spite her. No, maybe that wasn't completely true. He might have done it for Sheila's benefit, and this thought only made the ropes of tension tighten across her neck and shoulders.

She went to the bathroom and splashed her face with cold water before swigging a capful of Listerine. In the

7

mirror, she saw that her eyes were glassy and bloodshot, but she could pass that off as exhaustion if he mentioned it.

She changed into a baggy sweater and a pair of unflattering jeans that gave her a white momma ass – a phrase she'd picked up on one of the numerous trashy reality TV shows she cycled through. In truth, her ass wasn't as flat as the jeans made out, and anyway, today was Thursday, which meant she was allowed pancakes for breakfast and vodka for dinner, but tomorrow would be five miles on the treadmill, squats and that godawful rowing machine.

The more she walked around her apartment, the drunker she felt. 'I'll end up killing someone,' she murmured to herself, and decided to make a Thermos of instant coffee.

She put the letter in her jeans pocket and kept her hand on it as she descended through the apartment complex. She wanted to be able to feel it at all times, to stop it from sprouting a pair of wings and flying off into the night. As she stepped out of the lobby and into the snarling wind, she was pelted by freezing rain that had started up. She jogged across to her car, rummaging for her keys, and was drenched through by the time she was behind the wheel. At the very least, the cold shock of the downpour managed to chase away some of the lethargy. Rain tattooed the roof of the car as she turned on the engine and waited for the heater to warm up. She unscrewed the lid of the Thermos and sipped coffee, hoping it would battle the chill.

When she pulled out of the parking lot, she had to turn the wipers on full speed, the rubber squealing rhythmically. She drove slowly and carefully, her chest squashed against the wheel as she leaned in close to peer through the bleary windscreen. When she stopped at a light or behind a row of cars in traffic, she could feel the wheels gently pulling away from her until she applied more pressure to the brake pedal. It would be easy to skid and spin out of control, slick as the streets were. She made sure she kept her distance, gauging the other cars by the smudged red spheres of their brake lights.

It was easier driving on the freeway, where she didn't have to stop and start so much. Lightning crackled over the mountains in the distance, leaving witchy after-images in the sky. The thunder sounded like the world was tearing in half. Francine began to feel apprehensive, but she knew it was the letter and not the weather that had frayed her nerves. She drank some more coffee to still the squirming snakes in her stomach.

With her mind drifting, she nearly missed the exit to Sycamore. She'd only been to Will's house twice since he'd moved there, and only once since he got together with Sheila. It was, in her opinion, a town with a lot of nothing going on, where the six-screen cinema was the height of excitement and the bowling alley served as the venue of choice for date nights because it did 2-for-1 beers on weekends. It was a place where things took their time to change, if they changed at all. Francine understood why he liked it.

She pulled into the parking lot of a brightly lit drive-thru restaurant called Clucky's Chicken and Waffle and dialled Will's number.

'Stay where you are,' he said, sounding bored. 'I can be there in fifteen.'

The two inches of coffee left in the Thermos was luke-warm, but she drank it down in one go, then crunched on some mints from the glove box. The rain was now a misty spray, but the wind maintained its aggression. In the parked car adjacent to hers, a teenage couple, maybe seventeen, were laughing as they ate chicken out of a bucket. She could just about make out the muted rhythm of the music from their stereo. The girl got out of the car and walked into the front of the restaurant, and as she waddled back waving a handful of napkins at the boy, Francine noticed that she was heavily pregnant. *So young*, she thought. At that age, the girl probably still believed in the myth of undying love; that what she and her partner had was unique enough to deflect all the hardships the world would throw at them. But there was nothing unique about them. That fierce animal lust would lose its potency, and with time, their fascination with each other would wither and crumble to silence. That was when you could be sure that you truly resented someone: when you could no longer summon the emotion to shout.

That's not strictly true, though, is it, Francine? Father Time didn't kill you and Will, did he? The vodka had a habit of turning her thoughts to poison, which was why she only ever drank at home, where she could project all her bitterness at the TV. She rubbed her face with her hands in an attempt to massage the dregs of drunkenness away.

Light flooded the car as Will pulled into the parking lot. She opened the door to get out but saw that he was one step ahead, jogging over to her passenger side. She unlocked it for him and he got in, wiping his hands on his chinos.

'How are you?' he asked without looking at her. His words, unguarded by his keeper, were already noticeably lighter. He'd grown a neat beard and his hair was longer. He was wearing glasses too, but she suspected his vision was just fine. Perhaps he was going for a Steve Jobs look; probably one of Sheila's bright ideas.

'I'm fine. And you?'

'Yes, busy. September is always a busy time of year for us.'

'How's Sheila?'

'She's fine,' he answered quickly. 'We're both fine. So… what was it you wanted to talk about?'

Francine turned on the interior light and handed him the letter. He removed the piece of paper, read it, then glanced up at her. 'I don't get it.'

'Someone put that through my door tonight.'

'Who?'

'I don't know. They must've delivered it and left. It wasn't there when I came home from work.'

He handed the letter back to her. 'That's it? That's what you've called me out for?'

'*I know where she is*. They're talking about Autumn.'

'It's a prank.' He shrugged. 'I mean, I'm assuming there's nothing more?'

'No. It was just this letter. But it's clearly about Autumn. What if the person who wrote this is telling the truth?'

He inhaled and released an exasperated breath. 'Francine, you're chasing shadows. Look at the writing. It's like some four-year-old scribbled it. It's nonsense.'

She'd anticipated this response. His role within their dynamic had always been that of resident sceptic. She was the one who sought the counsel of mediums and researched the alternative meditation techniques that might allow her to create a psychic link to Autumn. She would try anything, no matter how ridiculous it seemed or how crazy it made her appear for contemplating it. It had to be better than ignoring the whole thing, training your mind to forget that Autumn had ever existed in order to cope with the pain. That was the weak thing to do and a large brooding part of her hated him for it.

'I haven't had any pranks since I've lived in Morning House. Nobody's tried to reach out to me about the case and my number isn't listed. I don't think this is a prank, Will. I know that sounds stupid and you think I'm just grasping at straws, but this could really be something. Don't you think so?'

He removed his glasses, rubbed his eyes with thumb and forefinger. 'It's going to be ten years in December. There might be things on the news, articles in the paper. I'm scheduled to appear on breakfast TV for a small segment about it myself. They're going to have a reconstruction of what she might look like now.'

'And you didn't want to tell me this?'

'It's a five-minute thing,' he said irritably. 'I'm not exactly relishing the idea of seeing what our daughter might look like as a young woman, Francine, but if it brings anything up in the public eye, I'm willing to do it. I didn't mention it to you because I knew it would be too much for you.'

She snorted. 'Too much for me? What are you talking about? You don't have any idea.'

'Look, the whole point of the segment is to bring Autumn back into the minds of the public, to refresh their memories. If you go on there and have a breakdown on live TV then that's all they'll report about. They'll forget Autumn, they'll ignore what we're trying to achieve.'

She leaned back into the seat and gripped the steering wheel to occupy her hands. 'I've done all the crying I'm likely to do. I'm all dried out. But I want to be kept in the loop with these things, Will. I *mean* that. You don't get to dictate what I can and can't be involved in when it comes to our daughter. I don't care what kind of media training you've had. Just don't shut me out.'

'Point taken. If anything comes up in the next couple of months, I'll let you know. Now, is there anything else we need to go over?'

'Well, I haven't finished going over this,' she said, holding the letter up. 'You think it's all bullshit, that's fine. But shouldn't we at least check it out? We could take it to the police station and have it tested for prints…'

'Stop, stop, stop.' He waved his hands. 'Francine, just get a grip, will you. Listen to what you're saying. You want to take a piece of paper to the police station to dust it for prints? This is madness.'

'But what *if*, Will?'

He shook his head. 'May I?' He held out his hand. She passed him the letter again. 'Let's assume this is from someone who knows where Autumn is. Let's just put aside the fact that they've taken almost ten years to get in contact. And let us also assume that the purpose of sending you this message was to help you find her. Am I thinking along the same lines as you so far?'

'It's a possibility,' she replied stubbornly.

'You're right. It's highly improbable, of course, but it is a possibility. So this person wants you to know that *they*

13

know where Autumn is after all these years,' he pinched the envelope at the corners and held it up like an exhibit of evidence, 'yet they leave no way for you to contact them. Of course, they could've just tried knocking on the door, but why go to the trouble? So the envelope,: there's no phone number, no email address and no stamp. It makes you wonder why they bothered getting an envelope at all, doesn't it? And then we have the handwriting. I'm obviously no forensic expert, but it doesn't take a genius to see that whoever wrote this was either a child or mentally… *impaired*. I'm guessing a child, who probably giggled the whole time they wrote this crap. Or maybe they used their left hand to disguise the handwriting. In any case, it's stupid, Francine. You're projecting something on to it that isn't there.'

'Fine.' She reached out to snatch the envelope and he pulled it away. 'Can I have it back?'

'Not yet.'

'Give it to me.'

'Not *yet*,' he said, sterner this time. 'I need you to see reason. What you do regarding our daughter affects both of us, do you understand? Sure, you could take this letter to the police and they'd probably indulge you for a little while, but when you'd gone they'd laugh at you. They'd extend you the courtesy of not making you into a complete joke to your face, but there are others that won't be so kind. Do you have a computer at home?'

'Yeah.'

'All right. Well tomorrow, go online and type in Autumn Cooper-Wright. There'll be a bunch of videos on YouTube, things like "Top 10 Mysterious Disappearances". Then, of course, you have the blogs and the conspiracy websites, all with their own ideas of what happened to her, ranging from alien abduction to the possibility that you and I killed her and buried her in the hills.'

'Jesus Christ. Just stop it, would you? You think I don't know all the horrible things they say about her online? I've seen more than I can stand.' She looked away from him, and for a moment she was sure she was about to cry. She took a deep breath and the emotion passed. 'I do my best to keep away from it.'

'Look, all I'm saying is that if you want to go out there chasing shadows, there'll be plenty of people willing to help you. And none of it will do either of us any good.' He placed the envelope carefully on the dashboard and the two of them sat there, the silence swelling. Rain flecked the windscreen, and the skinny, leafless trees swayed on the sidewalk. Eventually, Will said, 'I should get back. Will you think about what I've said?'

'I'll think about it,' she replied.

'Good. If you want, I can let you know when that TV thing is going to be. I don't have a date just yet.'

'Sure.'

'Okay. Well, drive safely.' He opened the door and got out. Just before he closed it, Francine leaned over the seat.

'If I get any leads on this thing, shall I call you?'

He shook his head and laughed mirthlessly. 'Why does it always have to be like this with you, Francine?'

'I won't ever stop looking, Will. You can lecture me until you're blue in the face. But I won't ever stop.'

'Fine. Then I'd rather you didn't call me up and get me involved in this ridiculous crusade you're on.'

'Finding our daughter is ridiculous to you?'

'There's a right way and a wrong way to do things, Francine.'

'And nothing has worked yet, has it?'

His fingers drummed a loose pattern on the roof of the car. 'Drive safely,' he said again, and closed the door.

She watched him jog back to his car and waited for him to pull away before she turned her ignition on. As she drove off, she passed the car with the young teenage couple. Through the steamed windows, it looked like they were laughing.

2

At five a.m., a full two hours before her alarm was due to sound, Francine kicked out of the twisted sheets and got dressed. She wasn't sure whether she'd dozed at all, but guessed that she'd probably managed to snatch a few minutes of shallow sleep. Her mind had whirred incessantly, the caffeine and anxious excitement making it impossible for her to switch off.

It was still pitch black as she drove to the gym, but it had stopped raining. It wasn't unusual for her to put a shift in on the free weights before work, but today she'd given herself enough time to swim too. The pool didn't open until seven, so she did the rounds on the cross-trainer, the treadmill – upping the incline almost vertically – and her usual dumb-bell routine. All the while she'd been eyeing the punchbag. She'd always wanted to use it but couldn't trust herself not to scream as she unloaded on it. She wasn't really sure how to go about hitting the thing, but the place was virtually empty, so she could afford to look silly. She picked up a pair of gloves that lay by the side and slipped them on, then gave the bag a few jabs for practice. It felt good. Once she'd settled into a rhythm, the volume of punches increased, as did their ferocity. Soon her arms were throbbing and her lungs flamed inside her.

She punched until she could no longer lift her hands, her slick forehead resting against the bag.

Afterwards, she swam for an hour without stopping. She couldn't remember ever having done that before, especially after such a strenuous workout, but she wanted to push her body until she'd burned all that anxiety to cinders.

Her body was a patchwork of pain by the time she sat down at her desk. It was as though she'd given her mind a spring-clean, sifting all that sludge, and now she could focus. She worked solidly through to lunch, processing invoices and sending out reminders, only stopping to confer with colleagues where absolutely necessary. All of the six employees crammed into the tiny back office of Worldwide Golfing Supplies knew Francine's story, and they had never tried to engage her beyond routine chit-chat. That suited her fine. When she'd first started, one of the other accountants, a divorcee named Henry who drank lots of black coffee and ate neatly cut ham sandwiches for lunch, asked her if she would like to go for a drink some time. Francine offered him only sincerity in her reply: no, she didn't want to go for a drink – not now, not ever. She hoped her expression would dissuade any future attempts at courtship. He didn't ask again.

As usual, she left her desk and went for a stroll during her lunch hour. She stopped at Starbucks for a cappuccino and bought a newspaper from the corner store before walking to her car. She liked having lunch in her car, comforted by the notion that at any second she could turn on the ignition and drive away forever.

She began skimming the newspaper, waiting for her cappuccino to cool. Quite suddenly, the lack of sleep and the exertion of her morning workout seized her. She could feel her eyes losing focus on the page, her head dipping. She placed the cup in the holder and closed her eyes. Very soon, she was out.

When she woke, her coffee was cold and a girl, maybe eighteen years old, was standing in the centre of the parking lot, staring at her. The wind whipped the girl's hair about her face, tugging at her frumpy dress. She had scrapes and scabs lining her legs and was drowning inside a man's bomber jacket. Francine yawned, looked at the clock, then back at the girl, who still hadn't moved.

She got out of the car and stretched. The girl turned on her heel and cut briskly across the parking lot, casting glances over her shoulder before vanishing through the automatic doors of the small indoor market.

Francine returned to her desk ten minutes late from lunch, but nobody seemed to notice. While she was in the middle of composing an enthralling email to their suppliers regarding low stock on fluorescent golf tees, it began to rain again. The first drops plinked against the window, and then a low rumble of thunder distracted her. She stopped typing and looked out into the parking lot. The girl in the baggy bomber jacket was standing next to her car, peering curiously inside like a child at an aquarium. Francine stood up and watched as the girl cupped her hands around her eyes and pressed herself up against the car window for a better look, before walking round to the passenger side, idly running her finger along the bodywork, then scoping out the back seats.

'What's she doing?' Francine muttered to herself. She walked out of her cubicle and left the office, hurrying down the corridor before taking the stairs two at a time.

Pushing through the double doors of the reception, she marched toward the car. 'Excuse me? Can I help you?'

The girl had been looking through the back window when she snapped upright at the sound of Francine's voice. From a few yards away, Francine thought she saw something amiss in the girl's expression. It was only as she neared that she noticed that she was severely cross-eyed, her pupils pulling away from one another like magnets. *Kermit the Frog*, Francine thought. *She has eyes like Kermit the Frog.* Given the distraction they presented, those eyes made it impossible to tell whether the girl was pretty or not. She appeared gaunt, birdlike almost, her hair a blonde so dull it bordered on silver.

'I said, can I help you?'

'I put a letter through your door. Did you get it?'

Francine stopped in her tracks, so suddenly that her feet splashed down in a puddle, soaking her ankles. 'It was you?'

The girl backed away, still running her finger across the car's wet metallic surface, her pupils not committing to any one object. 'Yes, ma'am.' Her voice was deep, with a guttural tone that came from her belly. 'I didn't know what else to do.'

'*I know where she is,*' Francine said. 'You know where *who* is?'

'Melody,' the girl said, edging around to the front of the car as Francine neared. It was as though the two of them were playing a tentative game of musical chairs. 'Mel… Your daughter.'

'My daughter's name is Autumn.'

'I know her as Mel,' the girl said, raking the wispy hair away from her face. 'Nobody calls her Autumn.'

Francine's throat squeezed closed, locking in a pocket of air that had simultaneously tried to rush out of her lungs. She choked, pain rocketing through her stomach. She felt light-headed. 'Wait… hold on a second, please hold on…' She took a minute to compose herself, to try and get her breathing back on course. Thunder boomed overhead. Taking shallow sips of air, she said, 'My daughter's alive?' Her voice almost fractured with desperation. 'Where is she?'

'Not close.' Without turning, the girl pointed behind her. 'Long way off.'

'How do you know all this?'

'I just made it out myself, and first thing I did was find you. People maybe think we've been dead a long, long time. A lot of us are still alive.' After every few words the girl's mouth tugged to the side, some kind of facial tic that made it look like she was wincing in pain.

Francine wiped her palms on her trousers. 'So you know my daughter, do you?'

'Yes, I do.'

'And I'm just supposed to take your word for it?' She made every effort to give the words authority, but her voice betrayed her.

'*If you're tired, little girl, close your eyes and go to sleep, close your eyes and go to sleep, close your eyes and go to sleep. If you're tired, little girl…*'

An icicle stabbed Francine in the heart. 'Where'd you hear that?' she whispered. The lullaby had strangled her, stealing her breath. 'Did… did Autumn sing that to you?' Again she tried to approach the girl, and again the girl shied back. 'I'm not going to hurt you, I promise.' She could feel panic rising in her. One wrong step and this bird

21

would flap away forever. There were too many questions clogging her mind, too much adrenalin pumping in her blood. 'Shall we get out of the rain? We can go back to my place?' She saw the girl's odd eyes widen, her mouth tugging into a grimace. 'Or a restaurant? If a restaurant is better, I can get you some dinner. I can understand if you're nervous.'

The girl looked away, staring off at the cars whooshing down the wet freeway in the distance. Very slowly, her head began to sway, like she was feeling the vibe of a tune only she could hear.

'What's your name?' Francine asked, hoping to conceal the desperate edge in her voice.

'Lena,' the girl replied, using her index finger to doodle on the wet hood of the car. Francine saw that her brittle hands were covered in scabs, the nails chewed down to the quick.

'Lena, I can help you. If you're in any danger, or you're scared of something, I can help. You tell me what you want to do.'

'I'm very hungry,' she said. 'I haven't eaten nothing good for a long time.'

'All right, that's a start. Would you like to grab a hamburger and a milkshake? Or something else? Anything, you can choose.'

She shrugged, ever so slightly. 'Burger.'

'I could go for a burger, too. There's a McDonald's about five minutes away. We can drive there or walk. Whatever you're comfortable with.'

'I'm not getting in the car.'

'Walk it is, then. Let me just get my umbrella.' Francine unlocked the car door, reached into the back and withdrew the umbrella. She opened it out and held it high above her head. 'You must be freezing. You could come under here if you like.'

Lena's lower lip was quivering and the tip of her nose had reddened, but despite this, she gave a short, definite shake of the head. Francine shrugged and led the way out of the parking lot and across the street to the small strip of stores that preceded the McDonald's. All the while she ensured that she kept stride with the girl, slowing down to match her pace, anxious that at any moment Lena could change her mind and bolt off like a spooked horse. She thought about making small talk for the journey, but it didn't seem appropriate, especially over the crash of the rain. No, it was better to walk in silence and let Lena dictate how and when she would drip-feed the information.

'There's a Pizza Hut too, if you'd prefer,' she said, pointing over at the red and black logo opposite the golden arches.

'McDonald's please,' Lena replied, staring down at her feet as she walked. She wore strange white and pink sneakers that instead of laces had three straps of Velcro. Francine almost expected to see the heels light up as she walked.

The automatic doors slid apart and the oily smell of French fries wafted over them in greeting. The luminous green booths were mostly empty, yet the tables still bore the greasy remains of the lunch-hour rush. They went to the counter and Francine saw the young clerk's eyes drift over Lena. Once he'd taken in her unusual attire and odd disposition, her brow furrowing as she stared open-mouthed at the menu, his face grew wary.

'Lena, what would you like to eat?' Francine asked. When the girl didn't immediately answer, she offered some help. 'Did you want a Big Mac? A cheeseburger?'

It was difficult to tell which part of the menu she was looking at. For all Francine knew, each eye could be reading a different section simultaneously. 'I changed my mind,' she said with a seriousness that momentarily unbalanced Francine. 'I want nuggets.'

Francine ordered a quarter-pounder meal for herself and a nugget meal for Lena. The clerk put the food together on a tray, watching Lena closely as though she were a wild dog that'd somehow got free of its leash and could attack at any moment.

They went to the closest and cleanest booth, although the surface of the table was flecked with crumbs and dotted with a rogue splodge of ketchup. Francine smiled at Lena and pushed the nuggets towards her. Lena's ugly fingers scurried out, flicked the box open and selected one. She held it up to her nose, then pressed her lips against it as though testing its warmth before nibbling it. Francine removed the greaseproof paper from her own burger and took a bite in an attempt to put Lena at ease, though she could have quite happily tipped the whole meal in the trash. Her stomach felt watery and loose, the food becoming a flavourless lump sticking to the roof of her mouth. Something about the rodent way that Lena ate made her even queasier, so she set her burger down and sipped her soda.

'How're the nuggets?'

Lena licked crumbs from her lips then sucked her finger. 'I thought they tasted different.'

Francine wasn't sure what that meant exactly. She let Lena dissect another three nuggets, her hand whipping out like a cobra striking to retrieve individual fries before eating them in three quick bites.

'Where have you come from, Lena?'

'The big house. In the woods. That's where we lived.' She looked up suspiciously, holding a nugget in both hands, then added in a lower voice, 'Me and Mel. And the rest of them.'

'Someone was holding you there?'

She nodded once, very slowly. The strange variation of fast and slow movements only served to unsettle Francine further.

'Who was keeping you there, Lena? Do you know his name?'

'I know all the names of the men at the house.'

'Would you be able to tell the police?'

The girl's lips parted and stretched into a smile, and for a second, both her eyes looked straight at Francine. A low, hiccuping chuckle fell out of her mouth. 'They already know about us. What do you think – we just go missing and nobody knows?'

'Why did you contact me, then?'

'I made a promise to Mel. And she made one to me. We said that if either of us ever got away, we would contact the other's parents. That's what we said.' She paused, cocking her head to the side as though listening to instructions from some unseen adviser, then added, 'It's difficult for me to do this. I'm very scared.'

'Have you not been back to your own parents yet?'

'My mom died of a stroke; not a stroke of luck, I guess. She's long gone. Don't have any other family.' She shrugged, then shook her head. 'I found you in the phone book.'

No you didn't, Francine wanted to say. *I'm not listed*. She decided not to focus on the lie just then, but stuck a little red flag in it for later. If not the phone book, then how?

'I wanted to write everything down for you, but I don't know how to do that sometimes.'

'When did you escape?'

'Must have been...' She held out her hands and began counting off fingers, staring at the spotlights on the ceiling. 'I think two weeks now.'

'And you haven't gone to the police?'

'No.'

'Why?'

'They'll send me back. They know about everything. They're in on it too.'

Francine took a break to let Lena continue eating. She stared at her own food and saw a rubbery orange triangle of cheese hanging down from inside her burger. The girl had lied to her about how she had found her address – that was strike one. But Francine couldn't help but feel there was more that Lena wasn't saying. She sipped cola and thought about it some more.

If you're tired, little girl, close your eyes and go to sleep...

'Can you tell me about the house where you and Autumn were?' She refused to call her daughter Mel. The very notion was obscenely offensive to her.

'It's deep inside the woods. That's where he kept us. There's nobody around, nothing but trees and hills. There's a river that goes nearby.'

'Do you think you can talk me through how you escaped?'

Lena tilted her head to one side and then the other. 'Leslie was saying he felt like he had a stomach ache. I could see he was sick because he kept screwing his face up like this…' She pulled a face, her features changing so rapidly that it startled Francine. In a flicker, it was back to normal. 'I said he should sit up if his stomach was hurting him, because maybe that would help. But he said he couldn't sit up. Then he was like this, doing this.' She gripped her own arm. 'He said he couldn't breathe. Then he just went quiet and I heard him make a mess in his trousers. That's what always happens when people die. Did you know that? They mess themselves. So I guess he was dead.'

'What did you do?'

'I left him there. It was early in the morning so I still had a lot of daytime. I followed the river and it got me through to a clearing. Later that day I came out of the forest and I was on the road. So I hitched a lift.'

'Why didn't you take Autumn with you?'

'She wasn't at the house just then. They took her away for a party a few days before. I didn't get to go because Leslie always has to be at the house and he has to have somebody to keep him company.'

One of the McDonald's employees was going around collecting abandoned trays, spraying antibacterial cleaner on the tables and wiping them down with a roll of blue kitchen towel. He neared Francine and Lena's table, and the girl stopped talking and bowed her head, looking at the employee out of the corner of one eye.

'It isn't safe to be here.' She shook her head. 'They could check here like that,' she clicked her fingers, 'like it's nothing. They could walk in here and sit down and that's it. They won't like that I've gone.'

'It's all right,' Francine said, as soothingly as she could. 'Nobody is going to touch you while I'm here.'

'It's not all right!' Lena slid out of the booth and the tray clattered to the floor, the pink milkshake slopping out of the cup. 'You don't know! They could be waiting for me right now!'

An old man in thick glasses looked round from a booth a few feet away. Francine stood up and put her hands out in front of her in a *don't shoot* gesture. 'Easy, Lena. It's okay.' She heard one of the workers grumbling from behind the counter before appearing with a mop. It sounded like he said, 'What the fuck is this?' but Francine wasn't sure. She turned to the young man and said, 'Please don't do that now. We'll be leaving in a second.' When she turned back to Lena, she saw that the girl was breathing heavily through her slack mouth. Her forehead, now greasy with sweat and lumpy with acne, shone brightly beneath the spotlights. 'Lena? Are you okay?'

'I don't want to be in here.' The girl raised a shaky hand and combed it through her hair. 'I need to get away to a place where they can't find me.' She pointed at Francine accusingly. 'You need to get me away from here.'

'I can do that. But we need to talk some more.'

'I don't want to fucking talk any more!' she roared, her pupils aligning straight again, her throat inflating to accommodate her rage. Francine flinched back, feeling her heart gallop.

Without warning, Lena spun and ran gracelessly out of the restaurant. Francine hesitated for a second and then took up the chase, bursting through the door after

28

her. She was blocked by a wall of flesh – an overweight woman and her brood, paused mid-waddle on their way into McDonald's to watch the drama. Francine huffed irritably and manoeuvred around them, she heard the woman say, 'The word is *excuse me*!' If she'd had more time, she would've liked to point out that those were in fact two words.

Lena zigzagged into the busy road, narrowly escaping a collision with a car, which screeched and fishtailed to an abrupt halt. 'Lena!' Francine screamed, but the girl didn't hear her over the angry car horns.

Francine waited for a break in the traffic before hurrying across the road. She tracked Lena's movements through a residential lane that bisected the backyards of two rows of houses. The girl ran drunkenly, frantic and flailing. Francine could hear her yelping breathlessly, her reedy voice appealing to God.

'I can help you!' Francine yelled, her own voice pinballing off the brick walls. She didn't have anything to use as leverage to halt the girl. When Lena refused to stop, Francine went into a higher gear. Thankfully she was wearing her Skechers, which she always changed into once she was at the office. Arms and legs pumping in unison, she sprinted until she had closed the gap to a stone's throw. Lena wheeled round, saw her and screamed as though she were some axe-wielding maniac instead of the woman she'd been speaking to minutes ago. 'I'm not going to hurt you!' Francine called as Lena's legs buckled beneath her. The girl fell into a heap on the floor, limbs spreading out like a starfish. Francine stopped running, ghostly puffs of vapour escaping her mouth as she panted.

It was only as she bent down to help Lena up that she noticed the girl was giggling.

3

They were locked in the rush-hour traffic, the steady downpour ensuring that the vehicles moved at a crawl.

'We'll need to stop for my bag,' Lena said emotionlessly. It was the first thing she'd said since getting into the car. It'd taken Francine almost an hour to calm her down after she'd caught up with her; then, without any real indication, Lena's mood had changed. There were no more hysterics or random outbursts. She became a mannequin, completely compliant.

'What?' Francine asked. She hadn't been listening, her mind a million miles away. *The house. In the woods.*

'My bag. It has my stuff in it. I hid it by the dumpsters.'

'What dumpsters?'

'Near your apartment. I've got clothes in there; woman at a thrift store let me go through a whole bin of stuff, told me to take what I wanted. She gave me some cake, too.'

Francine listened as Lena began to hum under her breath. She hadn't thought about that lullaby in a very long time, and hearing the melody float from the girl's lips was like a kick in the stomach. Thinking back, she couldn't recall how she'd come up with it; whether it was some variation of an existing song or something she'd concocted herself. But she knew the tune didn't belong in Lena's mouth.

'Lena, I think it might be a good idea for you to see a doctor.'

A long, exasperated sigh escaped the girl. 'No,' she said drearily. 'No, no, no.' She lifted a foot and pressed it against the dashboard. Her knees were studded with tiny pebbles, crimson runners of blood oozing their way down mucky, scarred legs.

She hadn't really noticed it at first, but in the confines of the car, Francine could smell the odour rolling off Lena. The scent of musky sweat, a pungent dampness soaked deep into her clothes, and her sour, undernourished breath. There was something else in the complex mingling of aromas that she couldn't quite define. Her nostrils flared as she tried to separate the smells. Then she realised it was urine.

'You could have injuries. You might be sick from all this running around in the rain.'

'You mean like pneumonia?'

'I don't know. I'm just saying that you should get checked out.'

'Can't go to doctors and can't go to the police. Maybe you don't understand that, but I do, and I'm telling you now I'm not going. I'll jump out of this car while it's moving if you try and force me.' She turned and locked onto Francine. Francine kept staring straight ahead, watching the windscreen wipers arc slowly back and forth.

'I'm not going to force you. I'm just thinking about your health.'

'If you're so concerned about my health, then you should take me away someplace where they won't ever find me.' She barked with laughter; her throat sounded rusty and coated in phlegm. Francine thought that maybe she really was sick. 'Listen to me. They're everywhere. Like him.' Lena pointed at a car inching along in the left-hand lane. 'He could be one. Or him.' She waved at an actor spread across a billboard in the distance. 'He could definitely be one too. Probably most likely is. Fuck's sake, you don't get it at all, do you?' Her hand reached up to her head and pinched out a few strands of hair. She stretched them taut in her fingers and marvelled at them. 'All over the place. Like rats.'

Francine thought very carefully before speaking again. By now she was beginning to understand the verbal dexterity needed to extract information from Lena. Just when she thought a particular line of dialogue was going smoothly, the girl would change pace, altering the trajectory of the conversation. Francine could feel herself losing patience, the anger threatening to bob up to the surface. If there was ever a time she needed to keep her temper, it was now, she thought.

'If you have any ideas about where you would like to go, I'll gladly take you th—'

Before she could finish the sentence, Lena broke in, 'You got a space rocket, huh? You can fly me to Mars?' She chuckled, but her lips weren't smiling.

'No, afraid not.'

'Then I want to go to the big island. Hawaii.'

Without discussing the finer details of the girl's request, such as why she wanted to go there or how she planned to achieve this without a passport, Francine said, 'Hawaii sounds good. I've been meaning to take a vacation. But before I take you anywhere, you have to help me.'

'Help you?' Lena snorted. 'I did help you. I've told you about Mel.'

'You didn't tell me where she is.' Francine could taste the urine stink now, touching the back of her throat. Somehow identifying the smell increased its potency, until the girl's piss saturated the whole car.

'That's because I don't know! A house in the woods, fucking miles away in the middle of fucking nowhere.'

Francine turned the engine off. The traffic wasn't going anywhere. As calmly as she could manage, she said, 'You're lying.'

'Yeah, right, I'm lying. If I'm lying, how come I know so much about Mel?'

'Her name is *Autumn*,' Francine growled. 'Autumn. My daughter's name is Autumn.' Her fingers tightened around the wheel until she was strangling the rubber and could feel the friction burn on her palms.

'We call her—'

'Get out.'

'What?'

'I said get out of my car. And if I see you again, I'm going to call the cops quicker than a heartbeat, do you understand me?' Francine swivelled in her seat, meeting Lena face on. The girl's breath curdled the air between them. 'You think you're going to torture me about my daughter? You think I haven't dealt with a thousand lunatics just like you?'

A collage of expressions contorted Lena's face. Confusion gave way to venom, and then all at once she wore a blank mask. 'I know her real name is Autumn,' she said, docile as a doped-up dental patient. 'But we have to call her Melody. That's all I've ever called her. They gave us all new names. My real name is Cherry,' she added quietly.

'I don't think you're telling the truth, Lena. I really don't.'

'That's fine, I guess,' she shrugged. 'You don't have to believe me. I didn't think you would. All I had to do was tell you, and I've kept up my end of the bargain.'

Francine felt the rims of her eyes sting with the threat of tears. She licked her lips and looked away, blinking until the situation was under control. 'If what you're saying is true, wouldn't you want to help me find her? Wouldn't you want her to be free?'

'Sure. Course I would. I just know it isn't possible.'

'But why? Why wouldn't it be possible? You could show me where she is and I'll collect her. I don't need to go with the cops; I could… her daddy and I could go. We could take guns.' Take guns? What was she saying? *Sure, Francine, you've done a few hours at the shooting range and now you think you're the Terminator.*

'She's in a house in the woods. But sometimes she goes to other houses, too. They take us out sometimes for a few days, but mostly we stay in the woods. That way we don't bother nobody and nobody has to know about our business.'

'So what's stopping me from getting to her?' Francine reached across and without thinking took one of Lena's hands. 'Please, Lena. If you know how I can help her, then tell me. Tell me straight. I know you can. Cut out the riddles and the crazy talk and just *tell* me.'

'You bring guns, but they've got plenty of guns,' Lena said after a long pause. She sat there watching the rain speckle the windows, her hand limp and cold inside Francine's. 'You wouldn't even make it near the house.'

A car honked behind them, momentarily bamboozling them both. The horn blared again, holding the note of anger, until Francine saw that there was a gap in the traffic.

'So what are we going to do, Lena? You need to make a decision, here and now.'

'I can't go back there. You can't ask me to.'

'Then what exactly do you expect me to do for you?'

'Take me somewhere far away.'

'Hawaii.'

'Yeah. Or somewhere further.'

Francine exhaled slowly, a screwdriver grinding in her heart. 'It's not going to happen, Lena. You have to understand that. I think you've been through a lot and I want to be as straight as I possibly can with you. But I'm not going to help you unless you can prove to me that you're telling the truth.'

Lena groaned petulantly. 'But I can't prove it unless I go back, and there's no way I'm doing that. Isn't there any way for me to help you without going there?'

'There might be,' Francine considered. A drum began beating in her skull; the onset of a migraine causing sparks of pain to shoot down her neck. 'But you have to tell me everything. And I don't want any more antics. Got it? Lena, look at me. Got it?'

'Yeah. Sure.'

'That tune you keep humming. Autumn sang that to you, didn't she?'

'Not to me,' Lena said sadly, fiddling with her hands. 'When the new girls get there, they're all scared. They cry a lot, especially at night. And when they make a fuss,

36

it turns into trouble for all of us. So with some of the younger ones, Mel would... *Autumn* would sing to them. She was good with the new ones.'

'Jesus Christ,' Francine whispered. Her throat closed to a pinhead, denying her air. She rolled the window all the way down, gasping. 'Lena, I need to know more. Please... I believe you, all right? I'm sorry I yelled earlier. But this is why you need to tell me everything. Why don't you come back to mine? We'll be safe at my apartment. You'll be able to talk freely. I can give you some food and...' she hesitated, knowing it was a huge risk, 'you can stay on the sofa tonight. Does that sound fair to you?'

Lena shrugged.

'And you can take a nice long shower. I bet you're dying for a shower.' Lena continued to stare down at her hands. Francine wanted to hammer that last point home, to insist that the girl bathe, but she didn't. 'If you tell me what I need to know, and you're completely truthful with me, I'll make sure that you reach Hawaii safely. Do you know my ex-husband? No, you probably don't...'

'Will something.'

Feathers brushed Francine's nape. She rolled her shoulders and shuddered gently. 'Will Wright. How did you know?'

Lena shrugged again, and Francine felt the tension bunch in her shoulders.

–

When at last Francine pulled into the parking space of her apartment complex, Lena opened the door and tumbled out while the car was still in motion. Francine pulled the handbrake up and watched as the girl skittered over to the dumpsters and knelt in a puddle, sifting through the mounds of garbage bags. It was collection day tomorrow and the rats would be squeaking, biting through the plastic bags and dragging banana peel down the street.

The girl's jittery, random behaviour had set Francine's nerves on edge. She felt as though she'd just been on a long-haul flight and had stopped off at an unfamiliar airport. This stranger had breezed into her life and drunk the energy right out of her. Now Francine was running on fumes, the hinges of her jaw achy from yawning, every blink chafing her eyeballs. Coffee, that was what she needed, and lots of it.

Eventually, after clambering over trash and rifling through the bags, Lena lifted out a backpack and held it aloft like a trophy. Francine got out of the car, locked the doors and approached her. The sky flashed white and the rain started drilling on the cars so hard it sounded as though pennies were falling from the clouds.

They jogged into the lobby and shook themselves off. Francine looked at Lena's bag. It was something a first-grader might take to school with them: bubblegum pink with a laminated Disney character emblazoned across the zip pocket. It was scuffed, battered and bulging.

They rode the elevator up, Francine covering her nose as discreetly as possible while Lena rifled through her backpack taking a rough inventory: a rumpled navy-blue sweater, a pair of socks, a fork and a can opener.

The doors dinged open and Francine stepped out, but Lena remained crouched, pulling items from the bag and discarding them on the floor beside her.

'Lost something?' Francine asked.

Lena didn't answer but instead tipped the bag upside down and shook it vigorously. A tangled pair of panties, a nail file, some twigs and a few small trinkets fell out. She peered inside the backpack to ensure it was empty before tossing it behind her. The elevator doors began to close, so Francine held them open.

'It's here,' Lena said, fiddling with something in her hands.

'What is?'

She held out a tattered Polaroid, creased almost to the point of obscurity. It had been folded and refolded so many times that there was a hole directly in the centre along one of the fault lines. The picture was blurred, but showed two girls sitting on the porch of a house, one with dark hair, the other blonde. She pointed a grubby finger at the dark-haired girl.

'Mel,' she said. 'Autumn.'

Francine looked at her. She saw those crazy eyes that stared off in opposite directions. She tried to speak, but tripped over her tongue.

Gathering up her scattered belongings, Lena said, 'That's me and Autumn. Our friend Tammy took it.'

The picture was too wrinkled to make out anything other than a vague impression. Francine held it close to her face and began walking toward her apartment, but the floor had lost its solidity, like she was stepping on sponge. She reached the door but couldn't take her hands off the Polaroid to get out her keys. 'Is that you, baby?' she whispered, and suddenly had to cover her mouth to stifle the sobs. She didn't want Lena to see her like this. It would make her too easy to manipulate. After all, it might just be a photo of two completely different girls. She couldn't even say for certain that the blonde one was Lena, though perhaps if she looked closely she could see a resemblance.

A yell from the elevator distracted her. Lena was using her foot to keep the doors open while she packed her things away, muttering incoherently. Once she was organised, she stumbled out of the elevator and started down the corridor.

'You see the flowers in her hair?' She stood next to Francine and pointed at the white garland sitting in the mass of dark curls. 'I made that for her. She looked pretty in it. She was always prettier than me.'

Francine nodded, swallowing a dry lump in her throat. She coughed, dug out her keys and opened the door.

The apartment shrank with Lena inside it, as though the girl's presence caused the shadows to stretch across the walls.

'Do you drink coffee?' Francine asked, setting her keys in the little bowl atop the kitchen counter. She saw that the girl had become distracted by her new surroundings; her hand testing the texture of the wallpaper, running her fingers over the glass of the framed ship painting that'd been hanging there since before Francine moved in. 'Lena? Would you like a drink?'

Lena's head swivelled slowly. 'You have hot chocolate?'

'Yeah.' Francine opened the cupboard doors above the counter, thankful to be distracted from the girl's gormless face. 'I'll make you some.'

'You mind if I use your toilet?'

'No, of course not. It's just there.' She pointed to the door on Lena's left. Lena opened it cautiously, a few inches at first, and then wider. She reached inside and fumbled for the switch on the wall, waiting until there was light before entering.

With Lena out of sight, Francine hunted for the bottle of vodka that she kept in the fridge, twisted the cap off and took two large slugs. She went to put it back, then decided on one more mouthful for luck. The alcohol did little to calm her. She steadied herself using the kitchen counter for support and stared down at the Polaroid. The girl in the photo was nothing more than a blurred face, her features indistinguishable, yet still Francine gazed, hoping some resemblance would swim into focus.

She'd started setting up the cups for the drinks when she heard a muffled noise from the bathroom. She froze, her hand hovering over the spoons in the drawer. It sounded as though Lena was talking to someone. Herself? Francine certainly wouldn't put it past her. Yet the cadence sounded different to what she had heard previously; there was a start-stop rhythm to it as though Lena were engaging in a conversation. Was she on the phone?

Treading softly, Francine approached the bathroom door, cocking her head in an effort to decipher the dialogue. The girl's garbled speech reverberated off the tiles, distorting the syllables. The only words Francine could make out were 'sure, sure' and 'no, not tomorrow, tonight'. Then there was silence. She stared down at the floor and saw Lena's shadow filling the portion of light spilling out from beneath the bathroom door. Then there was a gentle bump and the door trembled. An image of the girl standing with her ear pressed against the wood popped into Francine's mind. The thought – and the silence – was abruptly broken by Lena's loud cackling. Francine covered her mouth to stop herself screaming out in fright and quickly scooted away. She flicked the kettle on, then drew a knife from the block and placed it next to the breadbin.

The toilet flushed and Lena emerged with her hair slicked back away from her face, her ears sticking out like jug handles. Francine forced an awkward smile. 'Take a seat there,' she said, gesturing at the stool by the counter as she stirred milk and cocoa powder into a cup. 'You didn't eat much back at the restaurant. Are you hungry at all?'

'No.' Lena shook her head, seemingly fascinated by the cube pattern of the kitchen counter.

Francine heated the cocoa up in the microwave; when it was piping hot, she set it down in front of Lena. Lena picked up the mug and said, 'Cheers,' before clinking it against Francine's, slopping coffee and cocoa in the process.

'So,' Francine began, warming her hands around her cup, 'you're saying that the girl in this photo is Autumn.' She held up the Polaroid and Lena looked at it as though she had never seen it before. Then she blinked rapidly and comprehension returned. 'You say you were with her in a house in the woods.'

'Mmm,' Lena said, licking her finger. 'Yep. The big house.'

Francine opened her mouth to ask another question but realised she was rushing. She briefly considered whether it might be worth recording Lena on her phone, but decided against it. She suspected the girl might start playing up if she knew she were being recorded. She got up, went into her bedroom and retrieved the legal pad and pen from the bedside table.

Ever since Autumn had gone missing, Francine had been plagued nightly by a mosaic of bizarre dreams. What little sleep she was able to salvage was usually perforated with snapshots of her daughter in a range of scenarios. She was always trying to tell Francine something, as though subliminally – or psychically, as paranormal expert Vikki Clements would have her believe – providing her with clues to her whereabouts. 'Your bond was so strong that on some extrasensory level, she can still reach you,' Vikki would say before pausing and rolling her eyes heavenward, listening to instructions from Felix, her spirit guide. 'She hasn't forgotten your love. She *wants* you to find her.' Then she would ask Francine things like, 'In the dreams, is she talking? What is she saying? Is she pointing at anything, trying to focus your attention on something in particular?' And the answer was always yes. In the dreams, Autumn would speak to Francine as though she had no idea she'd been kidnapped. But Francine knew, and no matter how desperately she tried to relay this to her daughter – that they had to flee, that they had to run and get away from whatever mercurial realm her subconscious had placed them in – the result was always the same: Autumn would not follow her mother to safety.

'Everything you need to find her is right there in your dreams,' Vikki had said, imploring Francine to write the dreams down and make sense of them. So Francine had filled volumes with the details, straining to chase the phantoms from the back of her mind when she couldn't quite remember all the little nuances. She recalled words, phrases, the environment, what Autumn was wearing, who she was with. Then she would make a spider diagram on a separate page and try and shape these dreamscapes into something viable, to reawaken the part of her mind that held the key to solving the mystery. She did this even after the footage went viral of Vikki Clements openly admitting to an undercover reporter that she was a phoney.

–

When she sat back down, Francine flipped to a clean page in the legal pad and said, 'Can you tell me when you first met Autumn?'

Lena nodded, her lips curling into an oddly childish grin.

'Sure. The first time I met her was the day we took her.'

4

Francine's breath tangled in her throat. She coughed, fighting to suppress her sudden nausea.

'What's the matter with you?' Lena asked.

'You *took* her?'

'Not just me,' she said sternly. 'But me and Les did, yeah.'

Francine sipped coffee too quickly, scalding the roof of her mouth as she tried to remain calm. It burned on the way down her throat but washed away that stomach-acid taste. 'Do you remember a lot about that day?'

'Bits and pieces. It was a long time ago.'

'Try for me.'

'Maybe I don't remember any of it.' Lena shrugged.

'I'm sure you can, Lena. You can try for me, can't you?' Francine bit the inside of her cheek until the taste of copper tinged the coffee coating on her tongue.

'We watched you for a long time,' Lena began, scratching her cheek. 'You went into a bunch of stores and we just followed you around. I held Les's hand and pretended to be his daughter even though… shit, we joke about it now, but we don't look anything like each other.' She found this funny and snorted laughter. It sounded like a pig grunting for truffles.

'How did you take her?'

'Are you mad at me?'

Francine clamped her teeth together tightly, the muscles in her jaw bulging. 'How can I be angry with you? You were only little yourself. Can you tell me more?'

'We were waiting for you to turn your back. The way it would've worked – well, if it hadn't worked out the way it did, I mean – was that he was going to get you in the parking lot. That's how we got the others, when they were loading up their trunk and stuff. But that day we didn't have to.' She used her finger to stir the hot chocolate, then sucked it clean. 'She went to the doughnut stand and so Les said to me, you know, go get her.'

Francine closed her eyes for a second. She took a deep breath, the pen quivering in her fist. 'Get her how?' she asked, slowly and coolly.

'I told her they were giving away dolls upstairs.' Lena shook her head, giggling goofily. 'She didn't believe that, though. So I said, "If I'm lying, I'll give you ten bucks," but that didn't work either. She was really smart.'

'*Was*? What do you mean, was?' Francine could feel her lips pulling into a snarl.

'When she was a kid, I mean, that's all. She was smart for her age. If someone had told me they were giving away bars of gold, I would have probably believed that. I don't know. I don't care.' She stood up and walked past Francine towards the window by the sink. She prised the blinds wider with her fingers and squinted out into the gloom. Then she closed them completely.

'What are you doing?'

'I don't want anyone seeing in.' She gnawed the edges of her fingers, her bug eyes widening. 'I don't want them

46

to find me talking to you like this. They could be watching from out there.'

'Nobody is watching us, Lena.'

'You don't fucking know that,' she returned in that low, angry voice she'd used before. The hairs sprang up across Francine's nape. 'You don't even have a gun here, I bet.'

'We weren't followed; I made sure of that.'

'*I made sure of that*,' Lena mimicked. 'You made sure of shit. You don't know anything. But I do.' She stood with her back against the hallway wall, her head turned to the kitchen window. 'I know what they'll do if they catch us.'

'Sit down, Lena,' Francine said with as much bass in her voice as she could muster. She pointed at the stool. 'Sit.'

Lena's face pulled into a facetious smile for an instant then fell back into that dopey, vacant expression.

'So Autumn wouldn't go with you. Continue.'

'I said something about Santa Claus giving out free candy too, and she believed that. I guess that's easier to believe, right?'

The circumstances of Autumn's disappearance had been featured in three books that Francine knew of and God only knew how many blogs online. Lena's version of the story tied into what had already been widely reported in the media. Eyewitnesses had last seen Autumn leaving the Blue Cloud Mall with a man and another little girl. Like one big happy family. It'd been big news back then and Lena could quite easily have researched the facts of the case and added her own unique spin on it. Whatever nonsense tumbled out of her mouth *could* be real… to her at least. There was no way for Francine to gauge when the girl was lying because Lena probably believed every word of it. But that didn't mean Francine could afford to invest in these fantasies, no matter how convincing. She *wanted* to believe that Lena's story was true because at least that would rekindle some small cinder of hope. Dying embers were all she had left.

She stared at the swirl in her black coffee. Her headache had gone, but so had every modicum of strength she had. She felt boneless, a helium balloon.

'This man, Les,' she said. 'What's his surname?'

'I don't know it.'

'You were kidnapped by Les too?'

'Mm.' Lena nodded, peeling chapped skin from her lower lip.

'How many others?'

'I don't know.'

Francine tensed, her heart double-tapping in her chest. 'How many, Lena?'

'A lot.'

'And they all stayed in the big house, is that what you're saying?'

'Mostly. The house has a lot of secret places so we can stay hidden. We go up to other houses that ain't in the woods and they all have rooms nobody is supposed to know about too. They blindfold us when we drive and the journeys take forever.' She shrugged. 'But *our* house, the big house, is in the woods.'

'And what… what happens at the big house?'

'They fuck us,' she replied. 'Put babies in here.' She tapped her stomach.

'Excuse me,' Francine said and slipped off the stool, clutching the counter for support. Her legs trembled uncontrollably as she strode past Lena and hurried into the bathroom. She ran the taps in the sink, then crouched by the toilet. Mouthfuls of sour coffee roared out of her. Once she'd expelled everything she had to give, the dry heaves began and stars exploded in her vision. Her groans echoed around the toilet bowl and she wept – suddenly and sporadically – pillowing her head on her arms. Gradually the sobs descended into breathless moans. Every time the image forced its way back to the surface, she bit down on her hand: Autumn, small and fragile, her face soaked with tears and the sweat of some man. *Les.*

She rinsed her face with cold water. Puffy, bloodshot eyes stared back at her from the medicine cabinet mirror. *Keep your cool, goddamn it, Francine; you keep your cool. If she sees you're rattled, that's it, she'll run all over you.* She flushed the toilet, not bothering to towel her face dry, and went back to the kitchen. She could feel Lena watching her, perhaps savouring the distress she'd caused. She opened the fridge and removed the vodka. Yes, technically it was Friday, but under these circumstances she could break the rule. *Technically* she'd broken it already with the sneaky sips she'd had earlier, but just then she didn't care. She didn't think she'd be capable of getting drunk even if she downed the entire bottle.

'Sorry about that,' she began, sitting back at the counter, blotting rogue tears with the back of her finger. She unscrewed the bottle and took a swig, swirling the vodka around her mouth before swallowing sharply. 'I don't think that McDonald's agreed with me.' Lena didn't reply. 'You said earlier that the police knew about all this. I don't think that's correct.'

'It is.'

'How can you know that?'

49

'Because half the police force used to come up there to the house. They used to take turns on us. It's like a joke that they're all in on, except we don't get it. It's only funny to them, I suppose. We just lie there and let them do what they want. Easier that way.'

Francine drank. 'But what if I told another police department?'

'They'll deny it. What, are you stupid or something?' Lena stabbed an index finger into her own temple and began tapping. 'Anyway, with me gone they probably think I'm going to go blabbing, so they most likely moved her.'

Francine began to doodle listlessly on the legal pad. So far she'd written: *House – woods, Les, multiple girls – other house far away, houses with secrets.*

'You said they took you to other houses. Can you describe them?'

'I'm tired. I want to go to sleep now.'

'Give me ten more minutes, Lena. I know it's been a long day.'

'I'm tired,' she repeated sulkily, elbows on the counter, holding her head in her hands. 'I don't want to do this any more.'

'A little longer. I think you have the strength to do it.'

'No, I don't. Please, just let me go to bed.'

'No.' Francine shook her head. 'Not yet.'

'I'm through with talking.'

'We're through when *I* say we're through,' Francine yelled, her voice booming through the quiet apartment. Lena peeked through her fingers, both pupils acutely focused. It was like some party trick she pulled, training her eyes to look straight on command, her face realigning

50

into something completely different. 'Now, *I* say ten more minutes and then you can have a shower and sleep.'

Lena muttered into her palms as though whispering to some unseen companion. 'What's next then?' she asked eventually.

Francine tapped the end of the pen against the pad. 'Why Autumn? Why specifically her? You said you and Les followed us.'

'I don't know why. I just know they wanted her. Same way they wanted all the others.' She leaned back, scooped the hair out of her face. 'You think I've got like some insider information or something? I'm like Mel. I'm a victim. I don't help them plan these things. I just go as the bait. Mel's done it too. Lots of times.' Lena's shoulders sagged. She shifted on the stool, turned sideways and leaned her head against the counter. 'Mel helped take a lot of girls.'

'The big house. Who goes there?'

'Lots of people,' she replied through a yawn. 'Many, many people. They come so we can make the men feel happy.'

'How often does that happen?' Francine was aware of the gravel in her voice, but could do nothing to soften the words. It was beyond that now; she had heard too much.

'Every month people come to the big house. And sometimes there are parties in other houses and we do things there. I don't go to those ones a lot because I'm too ugly now. But that photo I gave you… that was on the morning of a feast day. That's why Mel looks pretty.'

Francine's skull felt full of sludge. She tried to wade through it to find something else to ask, a strategic question that would bear some fruit, but she was too tired.

She set the pen down and massaged her temples with her fingertips. Even breathing had become a trial. 'All right. I think that's enough. For now.'

'Can I go to sleep, then?'

'Shower first.'

'I'm too sleepy,' the girl groaned petulantly.

'I want you to get cleaned up. You'll feel better. Trust me.' She heard Lena begin to snore. It sounded faked so she slapped her palms on the counter. Lena jolted up. 'I'll show you how to run the shower. Come on.'

She led the girl into the bathroom and turned on the shower, testing the water to ensure it wasn't too hot. 'Take as long as you need,' she began. 'Don't worry about your clothes.; I'll find you something clean to wear.' As she spoke, Lena began undressing. Francine turned away but added, 'I want this door left open a crack. Don't lock it, okay?'

'Sure,' Lena said, stepping into the tub. Francine caught the outline of her scrawny shape in her peripheral vision and then hurried out to fetch some clothes.

Over the crash of the water, she could hear the girl muttering to herself. Sometimes it sounded like she was on the phone again, as though she were holding a conversation. And sometimes there was just cackling, low and sinister.

While Lena showered, Francine thought about the bed situation. She considered having the girl sleep in the same room as her, but she didn't much like that idea. She wanted her close, but not close enough that she could reach out and slit her throat while she slept. Now there was a funny thought: that Francine might possibly be able to sleep after the day she'd had. She didn't doubt that her body would melt into the mattress as soon as she lay down, but her mind was still running at a hundred miles an hour, thoughts and ideas bursting on the surface like fitful camera flashes.

She removed a pair of thin, musty-smelling pillows and a sheet from her utility closet and laid them over the sofa. Then she switched the TV on, just for the background noise, hoping that it would take the edge off the silence in the apartment.

As she sat on the arm of the sofa, staring into the distance, while an actress prattled on a late-night talk show, there was a creak from the doorway. She looked over and saw Lena standing there in a towel, trailing water, steam from the bathroom curling around her.

'I couldn't figure out how to turn the shower off,' she said. Having shed the crust of dirt, she looked a lot less threatening. Her pallor emphasised the raccoon circles around her eyes, but she appeared softer and altogether more feminine.

'That's all right. Do you feel better?'

She nodded, body glistening.

'Good. This sofa is pretty comfy. You can watch TV if you want, or just have it on if you don't want to sleep in silence.'

'Thanks.'

Francine picked up the sweat pants and long Garfield T-shirt she'd fished out of her closet and placed them on the sofa. 'You can wear these. They should keep you warm enough.'

'When can you take me away?' Lena asked, casually removing the towel that was wrapped around her and using it to dry her hair. Her body was scored with a

53

network of faint scars, each one viciously unique. A road map of abuse. An angry weal snaked across her xylophone ribcage; it looked like someone had tried to brand her and she'd jerked away too quickly.

Every instinct in Francine told her to go over and hug the girl, to reassure her that she didn't need to be afraid any more. She wanted to soothe her, to—

If you're tired, little girl, close your eyes and go to sleep...

'That's going to take some planning,' she said shakily. She thought about Autumn, what her body must look like. She couldn't afford to let her feelings get in the way of this. 'Once I have all the information I need, we can work on getting you settled somewhere. Tomorrow we're going to see my ex-husband. He has a lot of connections with charities and things like that. We can place you somewhere anonymously. They'll be able to give you a job, a roof over your head, and nobody needs to know where you are.'

'You said Hawaii.' Lena threw the wet towel on the armchair and stood naked before Francine.

'I want to keep you safe, Lena. We can work out a plan later. But I have no doubt that Will can get you to wherever you need to go.'

Lena nodded slowly and then reached for the clothes.

'Get some rest. We're setting out early tomorrow. If you need anything in the night, just give me a shout; I'll be in the next room.'

As Francine went to leave, Lena said, 'Thank you, Francine. I know I don't always get my words out properly, but I'm just very scared. I want to help you and Mel... sorry, Autumn. She was my best friend.'

Just like that, she seemed to shrivel before Francine, until she was nothing more than a frightened little girl flinching at shadows. And Francine's heart felt that much heavier for having lost patience with her. She shouldn't have shouted, shouldn't have been so disturbed by the mere sight of this girl... this *child*. She could not imagine the humiliation that Lena had suffered, the endless hours of terror and pain.

Above all else, she had to remember that Lena was no different from Autumn.

'Everything will be all right, Lena. You don't need to worry any more.' She smiled, hoping it would be reassuring. 'Goodnight.'

Francine left the living room and went to the kitchen. She got a glass of water and retrieved the knife from beside the breadbin. *Just in case*, she told herself, and headed to bed feeling both lighter and heavier than she had done in almost ten years.

5

Francine's eyes snapped open. For a few dopey seconds, the urgency remained as the residue of the dream slowly faded. She was back in her bed, the sheets cold beneath her body, the grey-lavender twilight filtering in through the gaps in the curtains. She lay still, listening as the tinny TV sounds seeped through the wall from the living room.

The bedside clock told her it was 06:49. She'd managed about four hours of shallow sleep, which was four hours more than she'd thought she would get. Her mind had turned over all the details of Lena's story, and as she'd finally drifted off, she'd had the feeling she'd made a huge mistake believing the girl. But now, in the honest, revealing light of day, she did believe Lena's story. She was also sure that there were details Lena was deliberately omitting. She just wasn't sure why.

She got out of bed, slipped into sweatpants and a hooded top and walked to the living room. She tapped on the door, half expecting to discover that Lena had crept out and disappeared in the night. But she was still there, sitting cross-legged on the sofa, watching a bizarre children's show.

'Morning,' Lena said, keeping her attention on the TV. It cut to the break and a throat-lozenge commercial came on. Lena hummed along with it. They ate breakfast and

Francine found an outfit for Lena to wear. When she was dressed, and had swigged some mouthwash at Francine's insistence, they made their way down to the car.

'Are we going to Will's house now?'

'That's right,' Francine said as they got in. It was Saturday, so she was banking on him being home. If not, she'd have to play verbal gymnastics with Sheila to find him. As she joined the highway, she removed her cell phone from her pocket and considered calling ahead, but then decided against it. A surprise visit would be the best option.

She had two missed calls from work and the voicemail icon appeared in the top right of the screen. She'd deal with all that on Monday; think of some excuse.

When she saw the Clucky's logo, she pulled over and referred to the map in her glove box. She traced the route with her finger, recalling that Will's house was on a long stretch of road that crested into a hill, at the top of which was a barbershop and convenience store – or at least there had been five years ago. Judging by the map, it was only a couple of miles away.

'Don't suppose you're any good with maps, are you?' she asked. Lena shook her head, drawing smiley faces in the condensation of the window. When she pulled away from the kerb, Francine said, 'You must have a good sense of direction at least, especially if you made it out of the woods. You said it took you about two weeks to reach me.'

'Something like that.'

'How'd you get from the woods to my apartment?'

'Hitchhiked.'

'How'd you know where I lived?'

'I looked you up...'

'The truth, Lena. Come on, we're past this now. How did you find my apartment?'

Lena picked at her bottom lip. 'There's a book with your name in it. Everything I need to know about you is right there. That's how I found out my mom died. That's how I know that in 2011 you had your licence suspended for eighteen months for being over the limit. They keep it updated... just in case they need to pay you a visit.'

Francine felt her blood congeal. She became light-headed, and for a second she thought that she might need to pull over to straighten herself out. The dizziness passed, but she asked no more questions. She probably couldn't have even if she had wanted to; her mouth was so dry that she could feel friction between her gums and lips.

She pulled over a couple more times to refer to the map, made a U-turn and did a lot of scouting for signposts. Eventually she rounded a bend that was vaguely familiar and spotted the striped barber's pole. The houses were spread out, with acres of land between them. Lena said, 'Deer,' and pointed out of the window. That was one thing Francine did remember: all the damn deer that sprang out in front of the car; she'd had to swerve to avoid killing one the first time she'd been here.

They pulled up a few yards down from Will's house. It was a rustic two-storey build with wall-to-wall windows. Aside from its size, it was unremarkable; easy to miss or ignore as it was set back from the road and partially concealed by a copse of tall trees. The only things that gave any indication of Will's wealth, to an outsider looking in, were the cars crowding the driveway.

The scent of the trees filled the air. It added to the tranquillity of the quiet street. The quiet house. Francine imagined waking up here every morning, watching the stupid deer hopping along, listening to birdsong in the distance while she sipped her coffee on the porch swing. Would that kind of life bring her some semblance of peace? Could she be happy in a simple place like this, away from the traffic jams, the malls, the cigarette billboards? Was Will happy here? If he was, she hated him for it.

As they neared the porch, she could hear the absent-minded chatter of two breakfast-show hosts coming from inside the house. She heard Sheila call out a question to Will and her jaw clenched. She knocked. Sheila's face appeared in the large window, and when she saw who it was, she leapt back, disappearing from sight.

The door opened cautiously. Will wore a crisp white shirt and chinos, like he was about to power into a presentation and give some inspirational pitch. He probably wasn't even going to leave the house today, let alone do any work. The pretentious prick.

'Francine,' he said, a smirk on his lips. He shook his head as though baffled by her presence on his doorstep. 'What's going on?'

'We need to talk. Right now.'

He looked at Lena, who was scanning the surrounding trees. 'What is this?'

'We need to come inside.'

'Well, Sheila and I were about to go out.' He adjusted his position in the doorway so that his body blocked as much of the view behind him as possible.

'Whatever plans you had, they're cancelled. Now can you let us in?'

'Sorry,' he began, addressing Lena, 'I didn't catch your name, miss.'

'Lena,' she said without looking at him.

'She's the one who wrote the letter,' Francine told him, watching his face, waiting for his reaction. There was no suspicion, no curiosity. Instead, his eyes became flinty behind his spectacles. He looked angry. 'There's a lot we need to discuss,' she continued. 'May we come in?'

Will looked behind him into the house, then back at Francine. 'I've got to tell you, Francine, I don't appreciate you turning up like this out of the blue, bringing strangers to my house.'

'Oh really? She knows where Autumn is. Now can we come in or do you want to do this on the doorstep. Either way, it's happening, Will.'

He laughed mirthlessly. 'I don't know what you're trying to pull here, but this is a very dangerous thing you're doing right now. You do know that, don't you?'

Sheila appeared behind him, snuggled into a padded pink dressing gown. 'Let them in, Will.' She peeked out at Francine and gave her a shy smile. 'Have you eaten breakfast already?'

'Yes. Thanks.'

'Good,' she replied as Will reluctantly stepped back to allow them passage. 'The quicker you say your piece, the quicker you can be on your way.'

It was only as she entered the house that Francine noticed Sheila's stomach.

'I was going to tell you…' Will began, as though it needed explanation. He closed his mouth. There was nothing more to say.

6

The kitchen was long and spacious, with stone walls, black marble floors and oak counters. It didn't smell much like a kitchen, though: no coffee, no bacon grease, not even a whiff of burnt toast. Of course not: one of the first things Francine spotted was a shiny silver cylinder, which after a couple of seconds of assessment she realised was some kind of juicer.

They took seats at a heavy table that looked as though it would take a team of men to move. Sheila hovered by the sink, running the water gently so she could still hear what was being said, giving the pretence that she was actually hand-washing the glasses they drank their green slush from.

'I guess congratulations are in order,' Francine said, staring at Sheila's back, watching her stiffen.

'Thank you,' Will replied.

'How far along?'

'Seven months,' Sheila said.

'Seven months,' Francine murmured. 'I wish you'd let me know the other night, Will. I could have sent a card or brought some flowers.'

Will was looking at Lena, who in turn seemed fixated with Sheila's stomach. 'It slipped my mind. I've got a lot going on at work. Busy time of year.'

'Yeah, you mentioned that the other day.'

'How about we get down to it, then?' Will said, his gaze staying firmly on Lena.

Francine cleared her throat. Just before she began speaking, an absurd thought occurred to her, *You haven't even offered us a glass of water. All this money and still no manners? Shame on you.* 'This is Lena. She's been living these last nine years with Autumn in a house in the middle of the woods. Don't ask me what woods in particular because we haven't quite figured that part out. Lena, like Autumn, was abducted by a man named Les. Two weeks ago, Les had a heart attack and Lena managed to escape. Autumn was moved to another house outside the woods, for… a party of some sort. Now, Lena is very scared and especially wary when it comes to trying to retrace her steps. I think you might be able to appreciate why.'

Will made a steeple with his fingers, still curiously analysing the bewildered young girl sitting opposite him. After a few beats, he said, 'Lena? Over here.' He snapped his fingers to get her attention, and her boggled eyes rolled towards him. 'Where are your parents, Lena?'

'Dead,' she croaked. 'Mom died of a stroke. I don't got anyone else.'

'I see.' He looked at Francine, concern etched in his expression. 'Lena, where do you live?'

'Live?'

'Yes, your address.'

'I don't live anywhere.'

'Were you in some sort of hospital?'

'Hospital?' Her face screwed into a ball of confusion.

'Yes. Do you remember the names of any carers you had? Maybe a nurse?'

'Stop that,' Francine snapped. Will looked up at her blankly. 'Stop trying to confuse her.'

'I don't think I could confuse her any more than she already is. Francine, this girl is quite obviously unwell.' He touched his temple subtly. 'You should've taken her straight to a police station.'

'No!' Lena screeched and jumped off the chair as though it had an electric current flowing through it. 'No police! They know! They'll take me back!' Behind her, Sheila yelped with fright and dropped a glass into the sink. Lena's head whipped towards Francine. 'You promised me!'

'Calm down.' Francine was on her feet. 'Nobody is taking you to the police.'

'I won't go! They know! How many fucking times do I have to tell you?' Lena reached up, grabbed two handfuls of her own hair and pulled at it.

Cradling her bump, Sheila backed away to the window, doing her best not to scream.

'Don't do that.' Francine reached out and grabbed the girl's wrists. 'Stop. Just calm down.' She held Lena against her, restraining her from doing any more harm.

'I won't go,' Lena mumbled into her neck. 'I won't.'

'You don't have to go anywhere. I said I was going to look after you, didn't I?' Francine glared over at Will. 'It's okay now. Easy. There you go. Easy.'

Will stood braced on the other side of the table. He glanced over at Sheila. She was crying silently, one hand on her stomach, the other covering her mouth. He said, 'Honey? Why don't you go upstairs?'

'I can stay... I don't mind,' Sheila replied weakly.

'This doesn't have anything to do with you,' Francine said, slowly setting Lena back into the chair next to her. 'Why don't you do as your husband says?'

Sheila wiped a stray tear away. 'What have I ever done to you, Francine?'

'This isn't about *you*,' Francine said. 'This is about mine and Will's daughter.'

'Our daughter is dead, Francine,' Will said.

Before Francine could dispute his claim, Lena said, 'No she isn't. Mel's alive.'

'Mel? Who's Mel?' Will asked.

Francine shook her head. 'That's what they call Autumn now. They changed her name to Melody.'

'They?' he said flippantly. 'Who are *they*, Francine?' He rubbed the side of his head as though trying to tame the onset of a migraine. 'Look, this is going nowhere. I'd like you and your friend here to leave my house. And in future, I'd appreciate some notice before you think of dropping by.'

'Are you kidding me? This is our daughter we're talking about. Our little Autumn! Doesn't that mean anything to you? What, because now you're gonna have another child, you forget about your firstborn?'

'I should go,' Sheila said, slippers shuffling on the black marble.

'Yes, you should,' Francine intoned.

'No, stay,' Will snapped, pointing to the spot where she was standing as though commanding a dog. 'Any madness Francine wants to spout off about, she can do so in front of you. This is your home and you have every right to be here.'

'Go upstairs, Sheila. No, stay here, Sheila. Can she lie down and roll over too, Will?' Francine regretted it immediately. Sheila, the poor sad thing, held her stomach and frowned, her cheeks blooming with embarrassment. 'I'm sorry. I shouldn't have said that.'

'Goddam you, Francine. You don't come into my house and talk to my wife like that, you got it?'

'I said I was sorry. I'm just… Will, this is different, I'm telling you.' Some sort of carnivorous worm was trying to chew its way out of her skull. She waited for it to settle, reclaimed her composure and spoke clearly and calmly. 'I understand how crazy it all sounds. Do you think I would willingly come here and make an idiot of myself in front of the two of you if I had the choice? But look…' She was speaking with her hands, getting flustered. She took another breath. 'If there was even a chance that this is remotely true, wouldn't you want to do something about it?' The appeal had beaten the wind out of her. She leaned on the chair for support, couldn't quite remember when she'd ever felt this tired just from talking. Maybe not ever. 'Is there no part of you that believes Autumn could still be out there?'

He bowed his head and removed his glasses, then pinched the bridge of his nose, his brow furrowing. 'Francine, the only way I could get past this whole goddam nightmare was by making peace with the fact that I was never going to see my daughter again. It wasn't easy. Now I would love to sit here reminiscing about her, trying to drum up some hope that she's still out there somewhere. But we have to look at it logically. It's been *ten* years, a decade, and not one shred of proof that she's alive.'

A sour film coated Francine's mouth. She wanted to draw phlegm and hock it onto the marble to rid herself of the taste. Or maybe just spit straight into Will's face. 'But they haven't found a body either.'

'And they probably never will.' He swallowed hard, his Adam's apple bobbing sharply in his throat. 'Don't do this to yourself, Francine. Don't do it to *us*. We have to let her go. You and me. We need to move on.'

'Move on,' Francine echoed, and looked over at Sheila's bump. 'Is that what this is?'

All the compassion fled his face and was replaced by a sneer of contempt. 'Why don't you just go home? Take your friend here and go.'

'You're a fucking fraud, you know that? You go around holding your stupid seminars, talking about Autumn, sharing all these little anecdotes, exploring your so-called grief. But all you're really doing is manipulating people with your lies.' She pounded her chest with her fist. 'I never gave up hope. Never. And now we have the best chance in ten fucking years of finding her and you want to shoo me out like I'm some kind of fucking lunatic? You make me sick. You're a real coward.'

Will stepped closer until Francine could feel the breeze from his nostrils, and for a second, she thought he might actually strike her. 'You think what you have is hope? It's not. It's *guilt*. That guilt has poisoned you for years. And if you don't find a way to get rid of it, it'll kill you. You have to learn to forgive yourself, Francine.' After a moment's pause, he added, 'I forgave you a long time ago.'

His words were worse than a slap. He'd held that moral superiority over her like the Sword of Damocles, but had never reached for it until that very moment. In a strange, sick way, Francine had to admire his self-restraint. Even when things had got really messy during the divorce and the arguments that preceded it, he had never openly blamed her.

That was it. Argument over. No more appeals.

Well, maybe one more. She dug into her jacket pocket and produced the Polaroid. 'Here. Look at this.'

Will took it, his eyes flicking to the photo, then back up to Francine. 'Don't say it.'

'That's Autumn.'

'Francine…' He closed his eyes. 'Francine, please…'

She turned to Lena. 'Tell him. Tell him who that is with the flowers in her hair.'

'Mel… sorry, Autumn. Tammy took that photo when we had the big festival.' Lena peeled a shred of skin from her chapped lip and sucked up the blood.

Will looked at the worn Polaroid again, holding it close to his eyes for a better view. 'Francine, this could be anyone.'

'She just told you it's Autumn!' Francine snapped, her voice ricocheting around the kitchen. 'You just heard her tell you that.'

Will held a palm up in Lena's direction like a traffic cop signalling a car to stop. 'How about we cut *her* out of the equation for now? Let's just agree that maybe she isn't the most reliable source of information. If you believe that this is Autumn, then you should go to the—' He halted, obviously remembering Lena's last outburst. 'You should go and inform you-know-who. I'm not going to stop you. That's your right. In fact, it'd be the correct thing to do.' He handed back the Polaroid, as though eager to be rid of the thing. 'I want nothing to do with it, but if they think you're on to something, I'll do everything in my power to help you. How's that?'

7

On the way home, Francine stopped at the liquor store and bought a bottle of vodka, along with an assortment of candy bars for Lena. She planned on forcing herself to eat something substantial before pouring a large measure of the vodka, but she couldn't wait that long, uncapping the bottle in the elevator ride up to her apartment and taking a long hit. It was cheap stuff, but it had a lot of bite and did the trick. Another swig and she could feel it going to work, dissolving the ache in her head, lubricating the knots in her chest.

Once they were in the apartment, she turned the TV on for Lena and gave her the candy bars. 'There's a bunch of tea and stuff in the cupboard above the microwave,' she said, though she wasn't sure it was safe to leave the girl to her own devices with something as dangerous as boiling water. She grabbed a stool from the kitchen and carried it to the landing outside her apartment, where she sat with the bottle, watching the rain cascade and listening as the wind wailed through the complex. Her hair blew into her face and mouth and the force of the breeze pulled tears from her eyes. But the vodka kept her warm. She was well aware that she was drowning any coherent thoughts and killing questions she could pose to her new house guest, but what was the alternative?

As she raised the bottle to her lips once again, she realised that the weight of it felt different. Confused, she inspected it and saw to her surprise that she'd killed almost half of it in less than an hour. That was two days in a row that she'd binged outside of her allotted 'drunk day'. She hadn't had a slip-up like that in probably… how long? Two years? Maybe a little longer. Perhaps three.

–

Francine had long since resigned herself to the fact that she was never going to be completely sober. She wasn't even sure she wanted to be. But she'd found a way to control the drinking on her terms, and that was good enough for her.

When things had started to get really bad, when Will had finally snapped and left her screaming incoherently in an empty house, she had made a deal with herself that had very likely saved her miserable life. She had woken up one Friday morning with a hangover – 10.0 on the Richter scale, with seismic shocks that had continued throughout the day. Up until that point she'd built something of a tolerance for hangovers; they never got any easier, but she had her little tricks to help her get out of bed and shake her ass into gear for work. For some reason that she couldn't fully recall now – or perhaps there hadn't been a reason at all – she had gone completely wild. She'd collapsed in the bathroom and fallen asleep in a puddle of her own vomit.

That incident had put her off whiskey for a while. It had also forced her to make a deal with herself. It wasn't exactly a moment of clarity, more a grudging truth she had avoided facing for too long: there was no sense in drinking herself stupid if it dulled her ability to progress with the search. If Autumn was still alive as Francine believed her to be, then she had to keep looking, and she couldn't do that blind drunk. So she made Thursday evening her drink zone. In hindsight, perhaps Friday or even Saturday would've been better days. This way, though, she could use Friday as her day to recover and spend the weekend working on finding Autumn. And when her pickled brain couldn't produce fresh ideas, when she spent entire weekends staring at the wallpaper with tears in her eyes, she finally joined the gym.

It took her about eight months to get fit.

Mentally, she felt different after a hard shift in the gym. She'd heard somewhere that working out released endorphins in the brain and that a lot of people got over depression through exercise. She wasn't there yet, but when she sprinted on the treadmill it was like a vacuum cleaner sucking the fog away from her brain. She zoned out, her mind too occupied with the aches and pains to throw any obstacles at her. Soon she was at the gym every day, sometimes twice a day – before and after work – with the exception of Thursdays, of course.

–

Now her mouth was dry and she felt a pang of something like guilt needling her. She'd drunk too much, too soon, and no longer felt the relaxing ebb of the vodka. Instead, she felt heavy and sluggish, as though she could collapse on her bed and fall into a coma. It was no good. Maybe she would sit out in the cold a little while longer, let the chill get back into her bones.

An hour or so later, she plodded back into the house and washed her face. Blinking rapidly, trying to refocus her vision, she looked in the mirror and noticed that both eyes were bloodshot. She thought about tipping the rest of the vodka down the sink, but decided against it before the idea made more sense. After all, she'd only drunk half the bottle, and Thursday wasn't too far away.

She poked her head into the living room. Lena sat on the sofa with her knees pulled into her chest, transfixed by a *Seinfeld* rerun. The curtains were drawn and the twitchy light from the TV made their silhouettes dance across the walls.

'How's it going?' Francine asked, perching herself on the arm of the sofa.

'I feel sick. Ate too much chocolate.'

'Well, that'll do it. Did you want a hot drink?'

'I got one.' She reached down and lifted a mug. Francine was mildly proud that the girl had been able to produce the beverage without scalding herself.

'Good.' A burst of canned laughter rattled into the room.

'I don't think he's going to help me, is he?' Lena asked, picking at her lip.

Francine watched the screen. 'I don't know.'

'You said he would, though.'

'I think it might take a bit of time to convince him. You have to understand that this is a shock to him. He'll come around.'

'We're running out of time.'

'What do you mean?' Francine grabbed the remote and turned the volume down.

'I've been gone two weeks. They're already out there looking for me. They'll track me here.'

'That's impossible, Lena. For all they know, you could be on the other side of the country.'

'No. You don't know them. They'll want to keep me quiet. One way or another, they'll find out I came here. They know where you live. That's why we need to move.'

'If they haven't caught you by now, they aren't going to. Maybe they figure you're too scared to go to the police. I mean, that's true, isn't it?'

'They know I won't go to the police.'

'Exactly. So you have nobody to run to. If they're as powerful as you say they are, then why would they be afraid of you?'

She laughed. 'They're not *afraid* of me. They'll just want me back because I belong to them.' She clamped her lip between her teeth. 'In this life, you pay what you owe.'

'If you're that frightened, Lena, then your best chance of freedom, *true* freedom, is to give me something I can work with.' Francine paused and thought carefully about her next sentence. 'If I find Autumn, then you can come and live with me; the two of you, together. I'm sure she's going to need a lot of help, and you're the one who has been there for her these last ten years.' *You're also the one who helped take her away from me...* 'You're pretty much like sisters, right? When I have her back, the three of us can go and live in Hawaii.'

Lena didn't appear to be listening. Francine withdrew her phone from her pocket.

'Lena, come sit by me a second.' Lena did as she was told. Francine opened the map app pointed at the marker

73

indicating their location. 'This is where we are now. You see here?' She traced her finger along the serpentine grey line that dissected the landmarks. 'This is the highway that leads directly to this neighbourhood.' She looked over to see if the girl was following her. 'You see the names of these other places? Do they ring any bells?'

Lena's scabby lower lip drooped as she looked at the screen. She didn't speak for a long time, though her eyes flittered rapidly across the map.

'Lena? Can you read these names?'

'Of course I can fucking read,' she growled, speaking through bared teeth. 'You asked me to look at it and I'm looking at it. Stop rushing me!'

'Okay, all right.' Francine wanted to get away from the girl, to get the vodka. Lena's violent temper made her unpredictable; it was like sitting next to a frothing stray, waiting for it to snap.

A few minutes went by. Then a few more. Lena began muttering under her breath, so quickly that Francine couldn't quite pick up what was being said. She heard 'not tomorrow, tonight' again, and 'pay what you owe'. Eventually Lena leaned back in the sofa and continued watching *Seinfeld*.

'Lena?'

'I don't know any of those places. I don't know the names.'

'All right, but look at this here.' Francine tapped her finger on the light green section of the map that indicated a woodland area. 'Could this be it, do you think? Somewhere in this area?'

'I said I don't know what it's called. I don't know any of it.'

Francine leaned forward and rubbed her head. The wormy veins in her temples pounded. 'Then what good is any of this? Huh? How do you suggest I find Autumn if I don't have the first idea of where to start?' She stood up and blocked the TV screen from Lena's view. 'Look at me when I'm talking to you, Lena. What do you think I should do? If I can't go to the police, then all I have for help is you. And you don't seem to want to help me all that much either. So you tell me, what's my next move?'

Lena stared up at her. Sitting there in the garish light of the living room, her face expressionless, she resembled a faulty doll that had been taken off the assembly line. 'We watch TV.'

'That's your suggestion?'

'Yeah.'

'You're gonna have to run that by me one more time,' Francine said, hands clenching into fists.

'I said we should watch TV. *Saturday Night Splendour*'s on.'

'What?'

'*Saturday Night Splendour*. You know, Glenn Schilling.'

'Lena, I don't give a shit about Glenn Schilling.'

'You should,' Lena said, and then her cheeks dimpled as though she were trying to hold her laughter in. 'Because sometimes, we go to his place for parties…'

8

The limo pulled up into the studio parking lot just before six p.m., the space marked with a sign reading *Mr Glenn Schilling*.

'Now I don't think that's appropriate,' said the limo driver. 'That kiddie will catch a cold.'

Glenn looked at the gaggle of people crowding around the back entrance of the studio, lined up as though they were waiting to enter a nightclub on New Year's Eve. He saw a woman right at the front of the queue holding a squirming toddler in her arms.

'Oh dear. I think you might be right there, Bob.'

'She doesn't even have an umbrella. She's got her cell phone ready, though, you see that, Mr Schilling? Kiddie in one arm, cell in the other.'

'Well at least it's not hammering down, eh, Bobby?' Glenn leaned forward and patted Bob's shoulder. 'Anyway, I'm sure the child is wrapped up warm.'

'I hope so,' Bob said, getting out of the limo. He walked around and opened Glenn's door.

The usual cheer of adulation rose to greet him as he stepped out of the car and waved. The lights from the various cell phones bobbed like fireflies. Glenn was met by a burly security guard who walked him the ten paces to the studio. Someone had gone to the trouble of making a cardboard sign, speckled with glitter and dotted by rain.

'Just this way, Mr Schilling,' the giant security guard said, gesturing to the door.

'One minute,' Glenn said and stopped next to the woman at the front of the queue. He'd seen her in the line a few times but never with her child. Perhaps that was how she'd muscled her way to the front.

'Glenny! Oh my God, Glenny can I get a picture with you?' The woman was late thirties, her cheeks reddened by the cold. Her son, perhaps four years old, seemed too big for her to be holding. 'Would you mind?'

'Of course not,' Glenn said. 'May I?' He took the woman's phone and handed it to the security guard. 'Perhaps you'd be so kind as to take a couple of snaps?'

The guard nodded; the phone looked like a child's plaything in his meaty hands. Glenn leaned in with the woman and put an arm round her shoulders, then smiled at the flash. The guard handed back her phone.

'Thank you so much! Thank you. We love *Splendour*. Jeez, my mom is going to be so happy I got a photo.'

'No problem,' Glenn said, and pinched the boy's cheek. It felt icy to the touch. 'Thank you for coming out to see the show. I've gotta run. It was nice meeting you.' He smiled and waved at the crowd again, ignoring more requests, and then hurried inside. Shirley was there to meet him with a clipboard and a smile. 'How are you, Mr Schilling?'

'I'm just fine, my dear.' The door closed behind him, drowning the babble. 'It's cold out tonight.'

'Well it should be nice and warm in your dressing room.'

77

'Oh that's good. Listen, do you think you could have someone go out there and give those people some hot drinks? It's very chilly.' He rubbed his hands together and shivered inside his clothes. 'That wouldn't be too much bother, would it?'

'No.' Shirley shook her head, unbalanced by his request. 'Course not. I'll get craft services on to it.'

'I'd sure appreciate it,' he said. 'How's your husband's foot, by the way?'

'His back,' she corrected with a smile. 'He's healing up. I think he's loving the fact that I'm running around after him while he gets to lie there watching TV.'

Glenn laughed. 'Of course he is. You'll give him my best, won't you?'

'I sure will.' She opened the door to his dressing room. 'Have a great show, Mr Schilling.'

'Thanks, Shirley.' He shrugged out of his jacket, hung it up on the stand and sat down in the make-up chair, taking a few minutes to compose himself. On the table in front of him were the notes for the show. He skimmed them. Tonight's guests included a French tennis player, a TV chef promoting his new cookbook, and the female comedy sensation Millie Cheeseman. He sighed, set the notes aside and waited for DeeDee to make him over.

Shirley came to get him an hour later, by which time he'd been preened and puffed with make-up, his skin made orange with foundation, his mane of silver hair backcombed into a bouffant. Tonight he sported an electric-blue suit with a black shirt and no tie, as was his trademark. A gold ring with a blood-red ruby on his little finger was the only jewellery he wore.

The music from the house band sailed down the white corridors. He'd been doing the show for twenty-two years and the butterflies had all but died in his stomach, though there was sometimes a rogue fluttering of wings. When the curtains rose and the lights were blinding him and the anonymous audience were cheering him on, he went on to autopilot. The weariness fell away and suddenly he was dancing, clicking his fingers in time with the piano and trumpet rhythm, shimmying up the glossy waxed stage and shuffling his feet. Thirty-odd years ago, his cavorting had been endearing. He had moved gracefully, unrestricted by the rusty suit of armour that old age encased him in. Now he was a parody of himself. He was still able to slide up and down the stage and keep time with the music, but the ovation that followed was almost belittling: strangers who'd grown up with him on TV acknowledging respectfully that a man of his age could still move beyond a shamble.

'Thank you! Thank you!' He smiled and bowed. 'How about a round of applause for the Carlisle Kings?' He waved his hand over to the house band and rode another wave of applause before segueing into his opening gag: an anecdote detailing a trip to the veterinary surgery with his dog Brutus that ended up with them at an undertaker's parlour due to his failing eyesight. When he hit the punchline, he cued his showbiz laugh to prompt the audience. None of them would remember that he'd told a variation of this gag at least five times over the years, always changing the dog's name or the details of the visit.

'Anyway! Moving swiftly along,' he said, removing a comically oversized pair of spectacles from his breast pocket and putting them on to read the cue card – strangling every last giggle out of the joke. 'I've got a great line-up for you all tonight!'

–

'How was the show, Mr Schilling?'

'Just fine, Bob. Just fine.' He dabbed his face with a handkerchief before picking up the large brandy that Bob had prepared for him. 'Cheers, Bob,' he said, and sipped long and deep.

'No worries, Mr Schilling. I'll have you home in a jiffy.'

He sank into the leather seat and closed his eyes. He'd given that studio audience every ounce of his energy, and he supposed they knew it. Wasn't that, after all, the reason his numbers were still so high after all these years? Because he could still out-hustle the scruffy young bucks that sprouted every couple of years like knotweed? These manufactured celebs who made their name on YouTube could have their six weeks in the sun and fade back into obscurity as they always did. He'd already forgotten more tricks of the trade than they would ever know. His charisma could outshine an empty head with a pretty face. His wit was sharp enough to pierce any up-and-coming comedian's ego. He was the king of Saturday-night TV.

And he was tired.

Tired and wired, that was his gig. He'd get home wanting to sleep but be too pent up to doze. He could take some Ambien, he supposed, but he never liked to do that. Cindy ate those things like Skittles and most days she'd fall asleep in her breakfast.

Back in the early days, picking up a coke habit was a necessary requirement for the job. It was the only way you could work such an insane schedule and still resemble a functioning human being. After all those years of grinding out gigs in smoky basement bars, sometimes doing two or three shows a night just to make the embarrassment seem worth the effort, he finally made it. He kicked the coke, beat the pills and found a way to drink responsibly. Now he did one show a week, thirty-two times a year, and was paid more money than he'd ever have a need to spend. He was lauded by the public, praised by his peers and had had dinner with every incarnation of the president from the past three decades. A little insomnia was a small price to pay.

Bob pulled up to the gate and George let him through with a wave. The limo drove down the pebble path, rounded the fountain and stopped in front of the steps. Glenn necked the last of the brandy, said his goodnight to Bob and started towards the mansion. His knees popped at every step, and after sitting down for so long, the top of his spine felt as though it'd curved like a shepherd's staff. 'Old, old, old,' he said and scanned his thumbprint on the front-door sensor. The door opened with a click and he entered the cavernous reception area.

Cindy would be asleep in the bedroom. He briefly considered curling up next to her and watching some TV. Perhaps there would be a decent movie on, or one of the reality cop shows that he strangely enjoyed. With a deep sigh, he assessed the staircase. He knew that for the sake of his joints he should venture forth; get his kneecaps and lower back used to the idea of performing basic tasks. Then again, he had just done a whole show. He bypassed the staircase and took the elevator instead, agitated that a four-second ascent could feel so degrading.

When the doors opened, he padded down the hallway, his loafers sinking into the plush carpet. He checked his Rolex. It was just after one a.m. He entered the master bedroom, glanced once at his wife, who was sprawled diagonally on the mattress, and began undressing. He stripped down to his boxers and thought about the effort needed to manoeuvre Cindy over to her side of the bed. Shifting her dead weight would require more strength than he could muster. Instead, he strolled through the glass tunnel connecting the southern and eastern wings, silently regarding the magnitude of the moon.

In the study, he poured himself a cognac from the bar, and then went to the Batman bookcase, as Cindy called it. If it really had been a bookcase in the Batcave, he'd pull one of the books lining the shelves and the secret passage would open. Alas, his architecture was not so sophisticated. He gripped the edge of the bookcase and pulled. It came free from the wall and silently slid to the side, allowing passage to his thinking room. More stairs, only six this time, but now his feet were moving enthusiastically and he was breathless with excitement.

He also had an erection.

The room was small and windowless, occupied by a large-screen TV and DVD player. His latest DVD was already in the machine, so he turned the TV on and sat back in the leather sofa, sipping his cognac as he peeled off his boxer shorts.

The TV came into focus and the muffled cries of the girls on the screen were like music to his ears. He moaned, the sound airy on his liquored breath. He was waiting for the sequence of screams that began at around the nine-minute mark. That was the best part. After a dozen or so viewings, the visuals bored him. But the sounds those girls made were genuine. There were no exaggerated groans of pleasure, no grunts of glee. Only exquisite suffering. He could close his eyes and listen to their music, re-enacting the event, recalling every sensory detail with vivid clarity: the way their hair felt against his naked thighs, the ridges of their ribcages, the nub of tailbone. His penis jerked as he remembered the way he had introduced each new instrument to the girls, revelling at how their eyes widened with terror. At nine minutes and forty-seven seconds, Glenn Schilling reached orgasm. He had not yet begun to touch himself.

He did not think he would be able to wait until Wednesday for another session.

But at least he would be able to sleep now.

9

'Lena, look at me, honey. Concentrate now. I want to make something very clear to you. Are you following what I'm saying?'

The girl looked up from her dinner of tinned spaghetti. After watching *Saturday Night Splendour* in silence, she had begun talking and hadn't stopped until well after midnight, delivering the details in fragmented mono- logues that drove Francine insane with frustration. Then she'd realised Lena was hungry and that she might be able to think better with some food inside her. So she'd grabbed the spaghetti, heated it in the microwave and given her two pieces of buttered toast to go with it.

'Everything you have just told me is extremely serious. You have to make absolutely sure that what you said is the truth.'

Lena slurped up spaghetti, tomato-sauce freckles dotting her cheeks. 'It is the truth. They take us to his house by the ocean.'

'I believe you,' Francine said. Her wrist throbbed from writing, but it was easier this way. She could make bullet points rather than record the girl's ramblings. She flexed her fingers. 'But if I'm going to take this thing any further, I just… I need to know if you might be unclear about any of it, or maybe if you've exaggerated certain things.'

Lena shook her head and put her fork down. 'What do you mean, take it further?'

'I mean…' Christ, she didn't know what she meant. Pain bored through the centre of her skull. Every nerve in her back felt pinched. 'I mean I will have to figure something out.'

'You can't go to the cops. They already know.'

'I don't think I could take this to the police even if they didn't. This is an extremely serious accusation and you're the only proof I have. So what do I do?'

'I don't know,' Lena shrugged. 'Not my problem.'

'You've just told me that one of the most famous men in America is raping young girls… that my daughter is among his victims… that *you* are one of his victims. But all I have is your word for it. Now I can't go to the cops because, according to you, they're in on this whole thing.'

'They *are.*'

'That's the only part that doesn't make sense to me, Lena. How could the police knowingly let this happen?'

Lena's eyes flicked around, a frog tracing the movements of a fly. 'The police work for them. They come to the house and laugh at us. They *laugh.*'

Francine nodded wearily, then set the pen down. 'All right. I guess we have to leave it there for tonight. You've given me a lot to think about.'

'What are you gonna do?'

'I don't know,' Francine replied, blinking rapidly, the corners of her eyes burning with fatigue. 'I don't have a whole lot of options, do I? Maybe I'll see if I can speak with Glenn Schilling.'

'No, you can't do that,' Lena said shakily. 'You don't understand the trouble you'll bring.'

'Enough, Lena.' Francine held up her hand. 'I don't want to hear any more of what I *can't* do. I've got to do something.'

'You don't know what they're like…'

'Lena, I said enough. I don't want to hear any more protesting. You don't need to get involved in any of this. I'll do it alone.'

'But what about me? What will I do? They'll come and get me when you're gone! They'll take me back!'

'I'm just thinking aloud,' Francine said. 'I'm tired.'

'Francine?' Lena's voice was frail and childlike. 'Don't do it. Don't go after them.'

'What am I supposed to do about Autumn?'

'Even if you got her back… She's not the same little girl you lost.' She blinked and tears plinked onto the counter. 'None of us are.'

Francine stiffened. 'Why don't we call it a wrap? Put your bowl in the sink when you're finished.' She turned and headed to the bedroom without wishing Lena good-night. She didn't get undressed, just flopped down on the mattress. Her thoughts flapped around like bats in a cave, darting aimlessly, never settling.

-

When Francine woke, she knew immediately that some-thing was wrong. She sat up, groggy and confused, frantically looking around her bedroom. She'd left the light on. In many ways it was a familiar feeling: often when she'd gone to bed drunk, she'd wake in the middle of the night convinced that she'd left the stove on or that she hadn't shut her apartment door properly. Of course, it was all just alcohol-induced paranoia, but she still had to get up and check. This time, though, there was cold clarity in her unease: something *had* roused her and it wasn't just in her imagination.

She could hear that the TV was still on in the living room, and her first thought was that maybe a loud sound had jolted her – a scream or an explosion from a movie perhaps. Or maybe Lena had dropped something.

She stepped out into the hallway and walked to the living room. 'Lena?' she called, not too loudly in case the girl was asleep. The living room door was wide open. She poked her head inside. 'Lena?' She wasn't there. Francine walked over and tapped on the bathroom door. Empty. Then it hit her in a flash of ice-cold panic. *She's gone.* She scurried to the front door and saw that it had been left open a crack, a frigid breeze breathing into the apartment. She flung the door wide and stepped out. 'Lena!' she yelled, not caring that her sudden cry would more than likely rouse her neighbours. She hurried to the edge of the balcony and peered down into the black courtyard below, but could see no sign of the girl.

She turned and ran back inside the apartment, slipped into her sneakers, grabbed her keys and headed out into the night, running down the stairwell and emerging into the parking lot. She shouted Lena's name again, louder this time, and heard her own voice come bouncing back to her. She looked at the dumpster, thinking that Lena might be hunkered down with the garbage where she'd hidden her bag, but there was no sign of her.

She got in her car and began driving with the head-lights on full beam. A cat darted out in front of the vehicle and narrowly avoided getting crushed. She kept watch on both sides of the road, thinking that maybe Lena was on foot and trying to thumb a ride. She circled the block, then tried a different route. Where would the girl go at this time of night? And why would she just up and leave like that without any warning?

I should have just dragged her to the police station and forced her to tell them.

No, that wouldn't have done any good at all. The only possible outcome of that scenario would be Lena getting fast-tracked to a padded cell. Francine was sure that the girl would've wigged out and they wouldn't have taken her seriously at all.

So why are you *taking her seriously, Francine?*

Because she was telling the truth and Francine believed her. And now Lena was somewhere out there, alone, running around scared and confused.

Francine cursed and dug her nails into the steering wheel. She'd only spotted a couple of people on the streets so far, and they were both men. Shit, for all she knew, Lena could already be in someone's car on her way out of town.

It was possible that in her anxiety she would head to a more populated part of town, somewhere busy. The huge chipped statue for Johnny's Donuts loomed through the fog, a couple of cars parked in front of it. It was a twenty-four-hour joint, a place for truckers to stop off and get a fix to prevent them from falling asleep at the wheel between deliveries. With it being the only establishment open along the strip, Francine drove towards it. She parked up, got out and rushed through the automatic doors. 'Excuse me,' she said breathlessly to the plump supervisor at the counter, 'but has anyone seen a girl running around near here?'

'A girl?' the supervisor asked, her stomach bulging in her stripy green and white shirt. 'What do you mean?'

'She's a friend of mine… about eighteen years old, blonde, skinny. You seen anyone like that?'

'No, I don't think so,' the supervisor said. 'You can ask them.' She pointed at the two men eating their doughnuts at separate tables.

'Sorry to bother you guys, but either of you seen a girl, about this tall, with straight blonde hair?' Francine called to them.

The men shook their heads.

'What's she done?' one of them asked.

'She hasn't done anything wrong. She was staying with me, and—' A cacophony from outside stole the rest of her sentence: the screeching of tyres, the angry honking of horns, yells and a scream.

Francine hurried out, her head whipping around, trying to locate the source of the drama. Another screech of tyres on tarmac, another frantic scream, someone yelling, 'Call the fucking cops!' It was coming from the other side of Johnny's Donuts. Francine ran down the street and turned the corner. Cars clogged the main road, gathering beneath a bridge. She dashed across the busy street and headed toward the commotion. At least five people were talking on their phones, but the awkward arrangement of the vehicles made it difficult to discern what had happened. She heard someone yell, 'Has anyone got through to an ambulance?' then someone else return, 'What's the name of this street?'

'What's going on?' Francine yelled, still out of range. She saw diamonds of broken glass glittering in the parked cars' headlights. And there was blood, dark red and syrupy, splashed around the tarmac. A few people were crouching over something. As she neared, she saw that the hood of a Ford was crunched in and crinkled, the windscreen completely shattered. Another car, turned diagonally in the road with black skid marks trailing from its tyres, had a deployed airbag but no other visible damage.

Two women were trying to calm a tall man who was leaning against the Ford with his hands over his mouth. He was shaking violently. His face was streaked with blood and embedded with tiny glass chips. The two women didn't seem all that bothered by the cuts, but instead concentrated their efforts on soothing him.

On the other side of the cars, a man stumbled away from the herd and quietly fainted.

The hairs on Francine's arms bristled, her skin breaking out in goose flesh. Her insides felt cold and slippery as she observed the surreal scene before her, trying to make sense of the confusion. She felt completely dislocated; a tourist in someone else's nightmare.

'Squeeze my hand if you can hear me. Can you hear me, sweetheart?'

'Ambulance is on its way.'

'That's it. You're doing really well.'

Francine reached the cars and peered through the bodies that were huddled on the floor. The stink of burnt rubber and the coppery tang of blood made her nostrils flare. She caught a glimpse of the wreckage; a bloody hand being held by a woman in a yellow rain slicker. She tilted her head, her thighs quivering as she continued to walk forward. She saw a shoe sitting by the kerb – a white sneaker with Velcro straps, collecting rain five feet away from the cars.

Her eyes locked on to a piece of bone protruding through faded green sweatpants. It took a few seconds for her mind to calibrate the image and understand that what she was seeing was a shin bone that had broken free of the skin and pierced the fabric. The huddle of Samaritans all seemed to be talking at once, offering support, reinforcing hope. One of them said, 'It's not that bad. The ambulance is going to be here any second. It's not that bad. They'll have you fixed up in no time, okay? It's not that bad.' But it *was* that bad, because even Francine could tell they were speaking to a dead girl.

Lena's mouth hung agape and a perfect halo of blood encircled her shattered skull. In death, her eyes were straight, staring up at the starless sky. Her skin was ashen, as though the colour had been tipped out of the hole in her head, but an expression of total calm had settled on her face.

The frantic ambulance siren distracted Francine and she took the opportunity to step away. She didn't need to see any more. The image of the girl's broken body was embossed in her brain and she would not soon forget it. She staggered, walking drunkenly away from the horror, and used one of the cars to steady herself.

'It's fucked up, isn't it?' said a middle-aged woman with curly brown hair, squinting through cigarette smoke. 'I've never seen anything like it. You want a cigarette?'

'No thanks,' Francine said, turning her back on Lena. Blue light bathed the streets as the ambulance arrived. 'You see it?'

'Oh yeah,' the woman said, her mouth pulling down at the corners. 'I was behind the car she hit. It could've been me.'

'What happened?'

The woman pointed her cigarette towards the bridge. 'She jumped. All I saw was her slam down onto that car there. Boom.' She gestured to the man with the glass in his face, who was now sitting with his back against the car tyre. 'She could've killed him. If she'd hit the roof instead of the hood, she would've crashed straight through, maybe crushed his skull. I don't know what they're doing still talking to her. She's a ghost.'

-

The police arrived shortly after the ambulance and were bullish with their investigation. An officer approached Francine with a notepad, but she shook her head. 'I didn't see anything,' she said before the cop got started. 'I came after.' The cop nodded and moved on to the smoking woman, who was more than happy to reel off her version of events.

'God be with her, that's what I say,' the smoker said. 'Look how fuckin' high up that bridge is.'

Francine thought briefly about giving up what little information she had concerning Lena. But that would invite more questions. Plus it would take her half the night to go through the whole story from the last few days, and by the time she was done with that, she herself might be the one under suspicion. She didn't think they could put her in jail for anything – she was, in her frazzled mind, quite sure that she had done nothing wrong by offering Lena a place to stay. Yet trying to explain why the girl had suddenly taken off in the middle of the night and leapt off a bridge onto the oncoming traffic was something Francine didn't think she'd be able to do.

As naturally as she could, she slipped away from the crowd and started towards the parking lot. Once she was behind the wheel of her car, she realised that she couldn't stop her hands and legs from trembling. She gripped the wheel tightly until her forearms throbbed, clenching her teeth against the surge of emotion that threatened to over-power her. The sight of Lena lying there, crumpled and broken, was just about the saddest, most distressing thing she'd ever seen. It would be harrowing enough to see anyone like that, let alone someone she'd come to know, albeit briefly. Lena had been just a child, maybe one of Autumn's only friends. She'd gone out of her way to seek Francine out, putting herself at what she believed to be genuine risk, all to help Autumn.

Francine screamed and thumped the wheel with both hands.

When her throat gave out and her rage was all but depleted, she turned the key in the ignition. She tried not to think about Lena's doll eyes staring up at the sky, but the resistance only gave the image more weight, animating the scene in her imagination. She pictured Lena bumbling aimlessly along the side of the road, tripping over her own feet, the traffic whizzing by, blowing her hair in her mouth. She imagined Lena clambering over the edge of the bridge and perhaps waiting there a second to admire the view below.

The fall, for however long it lasted, must've felt like freedom.

10

She typed various search combinations into Google but couldn't find anything that directly related to Lena. *How can there be nothing on the internet about this?* she thought. Her bones were sticking out of her fucking clothes. Even if they couldn't identify her, there would still be some kind of report about an anonymous woman plunging onto the traffic, wouldn't there? But not if they were trying to keep this whole thing quiet. Not if they knew exactly who Lena was and were trying to keep her existence a myth.

This led Francine to a new search. She typed in *Lena missing*, and then remembered that that hadn't been her real name. What was it – Cheryl, Charlene, something like that? She sat hunched over the keyboard in thought until the name bobbed to the surface of her memory. She expanded her search to *Cherry child kidnapped*. She skimmed the first page and found an archived article from 2005, printed in the *Hillsboro Scribe*.

The newspaper had used a school photo of Lena to accompany the article. She seemed so different to the young woman that Francine had met. She wore thick glasses that magnified her cross-eyes and was smiling cheekily. She looked *happy*. Christ, Francine couldn't imagine how different she had been as a child, so quick to smile, to laugh. And now she was dead, with no family to mourn her.

I'll mourn you, she thought, her grip tightening around the mouse. Gazing at the photo through the fingerprint-smeared screen, she felt herself welling up again.

That was enough. She was content in knowing that the girl had actually been abducted and hadn't just escaped from some care facility as Will had suggested. Why was she even considering the notion that Lena had been lying when she knew in her gut that it had been the truth all along? Just being cautious, she supposed, and that was a damn good thing. It let her know that she hadn't lost her mind just yet; there was still part of her that considered things such as consequences. And there would be plenty of those for what she had planned. Still, it was important to cross-reference everything. If there was ever a time in her life when she needed to be meticulous, it was now.

She began by trying different strings of words in Google in an attempt to find Glenn Schilling's address. To her utter amazement, there were pages and pages of articles about his various homes, including a mansion in Oakridge and a seafront apartment in Little Peace, a small seaside town with a population of approximately six thousand. She was dismayed to discover that nobody had an exact address, although in the image search there were plenty of photos.

Forbes had run a piece on his Oakridge mansion, detailing the genius of the architecture. He'd apparently built the house from the dirt up, the completion of which had taken almost nine years. Francine assumed the $23 million home would have more than some old geezer manning the electric gate. But then again, maybe not.

Didn't this article just ooze arrogance? Mr Untouchable, Mr Showtime, *The House That Laughter Built*.

She'd made a note of everything relevant to her cause, including the approximate location of both homes and the address of Beachwood Studios, where *Saturday Night Splendour* was broadcast live every weekend.

Glenn Schilling was due a visit. But there was somewhere else she needed to go first.

11

The gun sat in the glove box. Francine couldn't quite recall why she had bought it. It was years ago, when she'd first moved into Morning House and had gotten into the habit of picking up peculiar items that she was sure she would need. During that six- or seven-month period, when in hindsight she could safely say she'd lost her mind, when she was drinking like a goddam fish and couldn't tell which way was up, she had bought the gun and got it registered at the local police station.

Thinking about it now, she'd probably bought it to blow her brains out. Instead, she'd tried her hand down at the shooting range. The first few times she went, she was absolutely useless with the thing. She'd squeeze the trigger with her eyes tightly closed, frightened of the muzzle flash. She'd feel the gun buck wildly in her hands, the recoil climbing her forearms and nesting in her shoulders. After an hour at the range she would be completely drained, her arms and neck aching, but her muscles soon adapted to the stress of those sessions. In a couple of weeks she was even able to hit the paper target a couple of times per clip, though she was no Clint Eastwood.

She parked on the far side of the lot and strolled over to Barnes & Noble. The queue outside the bookstore extended past Starbucks and continued on down the sidewalk. She had expected a trove of dowdy middle-aged single women, the type who bought into all that positive-thinking bullshit, but was surprised when she saw college kids and men in their thirties. She walked to the front of the queue. Nobody gave any sign that they recognised her, and why would they? The only picture of her in his stupid book was a grainy black-and-white photo about an inch tall. She'd had to sign off on the photo and any reference to her name, and was rewarded with a five-thousand-dollar cheque by the publisher. Now, according to the sticker on the new edition, there were over a million copies in print, which she thought might entitle her to a salary review.

'Excuse me,' she said to the woman at the front of the queue, who had her eyebrow and lower lip pierced. Francine knocked on the glass door, harder and harder, until the spotty young bookseller opened it a crack.

'Can I help you?'

'Yes,' Francine began. 'I need you to get a message to Mr Wright.'

'The signing is going to begin in about ten minutes,' the boy said. 'If you join the queue, we'll start letting everyone in soon enough.'

'I know.' She wedged her foot in the door. 'If you could pass on a message to him, I'm sure he'll want to see me.'

'What is it?' the boy huffed.

'Tell him Frankie is outside and needs a really quick word.' *Frankie.* It sounded as foreign to her now as Francine had sounded to her back then. Only Will called her Frankie, up until the divorce at least.

After making love one night, in the drowsy moments before sleep, he had admitted that when they'd first met, he'd thought that was her real name. 'I had no clue it was Francine,' he said, lying on his side with his head propped in his hand. 'You leaned in and said, "I'm Frankie."'

'Oh don't be stupid. Nobody has ever called me Frankie in my life.'

'You did. Maybe you'd had too much eggnog, I don't know.'

She swatted his arm. '*You* were the drunk one. Jesus Christ, you spent about an hour telling me why you thought George Harrison was so cool, why the Beatles were so cool, all because that one goddam song came on. Loser.'

She had been working as an accounting assistant at Dusseldorf International Furniture for less than a year when she met Will at the company Christmas party. He was in press relations: 'You know, making sure our brand identity reaches as wide an audience as possible. I'm telling you, six, seven, maximum eight years' time, everyone is going to be eating dinner at a Dusseldorf table. IKEA is *so* out.'

That night they decided to share a cab, except halfway into the journey he grabbed her and kissed her and they ended back at his apartment.

Ten months later, in Fall, they had Autumn.

–

The bookseller reappeared and unlocked the door. 'All right, come in,' he said, holding it open.

Francine followed the boy through the store and up a flight of stairs. Will sat at a table with his memoir stacked in neat piles and two full-length posters adorning stands on either side of him.

'What are you doing here?' he asked, his expression stony.

'I saw your tour schedule on your website. Thought I'd come and give you some moral support,' she said drily. 'I'm not trying to embarrass you,' she added, hoping that the admission would put him at ease. Apparently it didn't. 'I came here instead of turning up on your doorstep. I thought that would be better.'

'Better for what?'

Francine looked over at another bookseller, who was blatantly eavesdropping. Realising she'd been caught, the girl busied herself away from the table. 'I'm not trying to mess your little thing up here. I know you're working, so I don't want to be trouble.'

'Well you are trouble, Francine. Especially the way you've been behaving lately.' He stood up, towering a full six inches taller than her. 'It's unacceptable.'

'I'm not trying to be a pest.' She held her hands up.

'Then will you tell me what it is you want so I can get on with my work?'

'I want to talk to you after your signing. Just me and you for an hour. There's a coffee shop right next door we could—'

'Absolutely not. No way.'

'What?'

Frown lines carved through his forehead as he scowled. In a low, harsh voice he said, 'I'm not going to sit around in some public place with you so the paparazzi can turn up and snap photos of us together. They've been ringing my phone off the hook because the ten years is coming up, and this is exactly the kind of thing they want.'

'Paparazzi?' She almost laughed. 'All right, fine. I'll follow you somewhere quiet.'

'Francine, listen to me,: it is not going to happen. Whatever crazy thing you have cooked up in your head now, I don't want to be involved, I'm not interested, and that is the end of it.'

The nape of Francine's neck warmed as though sunburned. 'No, that's not the end of it, you son of a bitch. I'm not going to be sent away like some lost dog. You will listen to what I have to say or—'

'Or what? Or *what*, Francine?'

'Or this book signing will get a whole lot more interesting, that's what.'

He shook his head in disgust. 'Have it your way.'

'I didn't want things to have to come to this.'

'I don't even care. Will you do me the courtesy of staying out of sight for the next couple of hours, so I can at least *pretend* to be happy while I sign?'

'I'll be like a ghost,' she said.

12

They found a dingy bar about five miles away from Barnes & Noble and sat in a booth. Will ordered a whiskey and Francine asked for soda water.

Will removed his sweater and undid the first three buttons on his shirt before massaging his neck. He hadn't made eye contact with her since sliding into the booth.

'So where's your creepy little friend?' he asked when the drinks arrived. He held the glass to his forehead like an ice pack.

She waited until the barman was out of earshot before replying. 'She jumped off a bridge.'

'I see.'

'That's not a joke, by the way. She literally jumped off a bridge.'

'I don't care. Why am I here, Francine?'

'Because I thought you might want to know some of the revelations I've learned about our daughter's kidnapping.'

'Revelations… Jesus Christ on a crutch,' he muttered and sipped the whiskey. 'Don't tell me – you went back to a palm reader and she gave you the location where Autumn is buried. Is that it?'

'How can you talk like that? How could you even make a joke so crass?'

'It wasn't a joke,' he shrugged, rattling the ice around the glass. 'I'm simply saying that it wouldn't surprise me if one of these nutcases you've been cavorting with told you that Autumn was buried in the Grand Canyon. Same way it wouldn't surprise me if you went there and tried to look for her.'

'She's still alive, Will. And she's less than a hundred miles from where we're sitting right now.'

'Only a hundred miles, huh?'

'Do you want to hear what I've got to say or not?'

'Why are you even bothering to tell me, Francine? It's obviously some cockamamie theory that doesn't mean anything to anyone.'

'Not this time,' Francine said. 'This is the real deal.'

'Real deal. Got it.'

'What I'm about to tell you is going to sound strange. I still find it hard to believe, but I don't doubt for one second that it's true.'

'Why would you?' he muttered.

'So here goes. One of the men who is directly involved in our daughter's kidnapping – who still has *contact* with her – is...' she paused, swallowed a lump, 'Glenn Schilling.'

Will froze mid-sip. 'Glenn Schilling?'

'There's a whole bunch of them, not just him, but he's the most high-profile, I think. They have these parties in the woods and at his house, and they take the girls there. And they do things with them...'

'Glenn Schilling? From TV? That's who you mean, right?'

'Yes.'

'You're wrong. You're so wrong it's scary.'

'I'm not wrong.'

'Goddam it, you *are*,' he said, exasperated. 'You can't just spout that kind of thing, Francine. The man's an icon.'

'So?'

'So? He's probably raised more money for children's hospitals than anyone in this country.'

'That doesn't mean a fucking thing.'

'Doesn't it?' He cocked his head, his eyes filling with contempt. 'He was kind enough to come to a few of the benefits I threw for Autumn a few years back. I've spoken to the man. He hasn't got a bad bone in his body. He'd give you the shirt off his back if you asked for it. Every time I met him, he'd write me a cheque for ten grand right then and there.'

'Well, there you go,' she snorted, the blood rushing to her face. 'He did that to gloat at you – at us. Ten grand, he probably loses more than that in his pockets when he gets his suits dry-cleaned.' She shook her head, her fingers digging into the tabletop. 'Schilling is in touch with the people that have Autumn, Will. You have to believe me.'

'How do you know this all of a sudden? Who offered you this little pearl of wisdom? Not your cock-eyed loony pal, I hope. For God's sake, this is worse than I thought.' He palmed his head in despair. 'Francine… you can't believe this, can you? I mean, deep down.'

If you're tired, little girl…

'She might've been mixed up, but I think there was something there, Will. I know it; I can *feel* it.'

'The same nut-job that freaked out when I said you should take her to the police, and then jumped off a bridge? Well shit, her words must be worth their weight in gold. What else did she tell you? I hope you got this week's lottery numbers out of her.'

'She said Glenn Schilling is in on this whole thing. He is the key to finding our daughter.'

'Fine. He's the key. Then go and tell all of this to the police if that's what you really believe. Let them look into it.'

She shook her head. 'Can't do that. Lena said the police already know about Glenn. She said they already know about these parties. If I go running to the cops, all that will happen is they'll move Autumn, maybe out of the state. Don't you get it? If they catch wind that I know, then we'll never find her. We've got to go in on this thing alone.'

'*We*, Francine?'

'Yes, *we*. You, me, her parents. We are going to find her together and bring her home. We should look into this, Will. What's the harm in that? Just think about it. I mean, there is something off with Glenn Schilling, isn't there? And the things Lena was saying... look at it like this, if she really was as crazy as we thought, how did she piece this whole story about Autumn together? Right now, Glenn Schilling is the one link we have. We need to follow it up.'

'I can't...' he closed his eyes, 'I can't listen to any more of this insanity. I just can't. I'm leaving.'

He began to slide out of the booth. Francine leaned across the table and clutched his arm. 'What the hell has happened to you, Will? She's our little girl. Don't you care about her any more? You don't love her, is that it? Your own flesh and blood!'

'Take your hand off me, Francine.' He spoke slowly. 'Let me go.'

She released him and leaned back. 'I'm sorry. It's just sometimes it feels like given the choice, you'd be happy to never see Autumn again. And I wonder why, and the only thing I can come up with is that you think her coming back might in some way change what you have now. After all, you weren't a millionaire before she went missing.'

His eyes became black coals. The muscles on either side of his jaw pulsed. 'How fucking dare you?' he hissed, so venomously that Francine thought he was going to reach over and strike her. He'd never been violent with her in the past, never shown so much as an inclination that he might get physical, even during their most tumultuous arguments. But now he was quietly furious, and as he sat there simmering, Francine knew he hated her; she could feel the loathing rolling off him in waves. 'You really are just a horrible, horrible witch. I feel sorry for you, Francine. I honestly do. I hope you get the help you need.'

'It's true, though, isn't it? You've made a whole career off our daughter's disappearance. You make a hell of a lot more money now than you ever did in PR.'

The corners of his lips curled into a mirthless smile. 'So this is what we're really doing, is it? We're going to lay everything out on the table? You know what, I never thought we were going to have this conversation – in fact I really hoped we wouldn't. But if you want to come here with your guilt trips and your accusations, then I think it's about time you heard some home truths. Are you ready?'

She crossed her arms. 'Go ahead.'

'You are the one who let Autumn go off on her own that day. Not me. I've never put the blame on you for that because I knew it wasn't your fault. She should've been under your supervision and she wasn't. That's point number one.' He marked it off on his index finger. 'Point number two, I did everything I could to raise awareness for our daughter. I was the one going on all the TV shows while you were feeling sorry for yourself, too drunk to even show your face. I was the one rallying around the neighbourhood, putting the flyers up, doing everything in my power to get her back. And what did you do? Drink vodka all day then piss our money away on your fucking psychics and TV evangelists. And I still didn't say anything, because I knew you were in hell, I knew you blamed yourself, and you know something, Francine, you should have. Because *you* failed our daughter that day. That's the black and white of it. But it could just as easily have been me that told her to go and get a snack while I looked at shoes.

'In this equation we have you acting like a fucking psychotic, drinking until you blacked out or sobbing into a pillow, being absolutely no help to anyone. And then we have me – someone who tried to raise awareness for our daughter, someone who kept it together so he could talk to the press, the police or any neighbours who wanted to come by and offer a helping hand. Did you ever think that maybe all I wanted to do was get drunk too and just make this whole thing go away? Did you not think that maybe I was in pain?' His voice quavered and he chewed on his bottom lip, his eyes suddenly glistening. 'No, of course you didn't. You probably don't remember any of this anyway. I didn't get any help from you. If there was ever a time when Autumn needed you, it was then, when everything happened, when we could've worked as a team to get her back. It's no good coming to me now, Francine.'

He slammed the rest of his whiskey away then wiped his eyes with the back of his hand. 'So let's move on to point number three.'

'You've said enough,' Francine said, staring at the grooves in the table, tears rolling down her cheeks, nostrils leaking.

'No I haven't. Not by a long shot. Point number three, you are bitter towards me because I managed to channel my pain into something positive. Whether you want to believe it or not, my books have helped people out there, Francine. They could even help you if you bothered to read them. Just look at the signing today. All those people were there to meet me because I'd been a positive influence in their life. You know how many women come up to me who have been abused? You know how many men tell me that my book helped them move on with their lives after their wife left them? And yes, I make a living off it. But you might recall that I had to quit my regular job because I spent the first year doing everything I could to find Autumn. You don't just go back into an office job after something like that. And you begrudge me helping other people, Francine?'

'I... I don't begrudge you anything,' she said petulantly, sniffing up snot.

'Oh yes you do. Come on, we're getting everything out on the table, aren't we? And while we're at it, let's talk about Sheila. You hate the fact that I've moved on because you want everyone to be as miserable as you are. Well, she's my wife now and we're having a baby.'

'I don't want to hear this.' She attempted to exit the booth, but this time it was Will that stopped her.

'Oh no you don't. You don't get to leave yet. You stay right where you are. You're going to hear this once, and never again. You have done nothing over these last ten years except feel sorry for yourself, grasping at straws, putting your faith in nonsense. None of this has anything to do with getting Autumn back, it's always been about you trying to shed the guilt. You don't need a witch doctor or a psychic or some carnival gypsy. You need a therapist. I'm not saying that to make you feel inferior. I'm saying it because I've been in therapy this last decade and it's probably the only thing that stopped me from driving my car into a wall.'

He fell silent and the two of them sat there without speaking for a long time.

'I don't want to have this conversation ever again,' Will said softly. 'I hope you will respect that. And I hope you will take on board what I've said.' He reached into his pocket, peeled off some notes and left them under his empty glass. Then he left.

He had just gotten into his car and put the key in the ignition when Francine emerged from the bar and called to him. 'What is it?' he asked as the window rolled down.

She approached the car and rested one hand on the roof for support. 'I'm sorry, Will. I don't know if I ever said that.'

'You don't have to apologise to me, Francine.'

'You hate me, don't you?'

'No, of course I don't.'

'It's just… sometimes I feel so alone.'

He nodded. 'Sometimes I do too. I think about her every day. And nothing will ever replace her in my heart.'

'Good,' Francine said. 'Then I was wondering if you might want to do me a favour.'

She saw his chest rise and fall. 'What is it?'

'You know some celebrities, right? I mean, I saw your book at the store and there were a lot of big names giving you praise.'

'I don't know them personally. My agent gets the book to them.'

'Do you think your agent might know how I could find Glenn Schilling's address?'

Will shook his head. The window rolled back up. The car drove away.

Francine stood there and watched it leave.

Part Two

13

The darkness was absolute, so black that it was disorientating. A heavy crown of pain sat on her head, and this bothered her far more than the very real iron ring around her neck. The ring, secured to a bolt in the wall, had about an inch of space so that she didn't choke. She was well accustomed to it, knew how to sit so that she could at least find some semblance of comfort and snatch a few measly hours of sleep. But the headache reacted to the slightest movement, sending sparks shooting down her spine.

She sat with her back to the moist stone wall and made a game of feeling the links in the chain, following the curves with her fingers, wondering if there was any weakness in it. Her fingers came to the ring around her neck and she felt the grooves and outline of the screws. Even if she had a saw it would do no good; the teeth would be blunt well before she made so much as a meaningful scratch on the iron.

There was a dripping sound somewhere in the basement but she couldn't work out where it was coming from exactly. Sometimes it sounded loud and sometimes it sounded faint. And sometimes the steady, almost reliable rhythm of the dripping would change – speeding up or slowing down or double-tapping – and she could not quite understand why. She had reached out her hand to the darkness in an effort to capture the droplets in her palm, but even straining against the chain did no good. So instead she licked the wall, her dry, rough tongue running over the bumpy surface. She was thankful of the brackish moisture that sweated on the stone surface, thankful even though it didn't amount to so much as a sip of water. It didn't quench her thirst but it helped to lubricate her mouth, which was as small a mercy as she could ever hope for.

She thought about trying to urinate into her hands for something to drink, but this was not her first time in the basement and it would not likely be her last. She knew that succumbing to filth would land her in far worse trouble when this punishment ended –it *would* end at some point, though she was not sure when. It was the longest amount of time she'd spent confined here, but how long that was exactly she couldn't say. Over a week probably. Maybe two. All she knew was that there was darkness and it went on forever.

She couldn't measure the days by how often the guard came. His visits were sporadic and brief, and he was always silent, manoeuvring through the basement with a flash-light as his guide, casting the beam over their eyes.

On their first night here, Mia had spoken out. She was new, a year or so into her stay, and it was her first trip to the basement. She'd had enough sense to whisper, to ask the others what was going on and why they were being punished, but when only silence answered her, she began raising her voice, outraged at their lack of acknowl-edgement, and when her angry words still received no response, she started to scream. Soon enough the basement door swung open, and a silhouette appeared in the yellow rectangle of light, and then there was the awful sound of Mia being silenced. They hadn't killed her, but that fact only became apparent much later when she started to weep through her broken jaw.

They lived with the sound of each other's chains rattling, the occasional cough and sneeze, and the dry slap of weight being adjusted on the bare floor. Sometimes the ceiling would creak, and if she strained long enough, she thought she could make out the muffled sound of talking above them. But this could very well be her imagination, an auditory hallucination. Driven mad by thirst and sleep deprivation, she had come to almost enjoy these delusions. On one such occasion she had seen the basement light up to reveal that she was not in a basement at all but a park. It was a beautiful sunny day, the sky was a brilliant blue and there were people laughing and smiling all around her. She could even smell the freshly cut grass and marvel at a pair of white butterflies fluttering around one another, the sunlight streaming through their translucent wings. And there was someone over there on the hill, a woman…

Then the darkness slammed down and the mirage shattered, all those lovely details scattering to the farthest corners of her mind.

They all heard the footsteps from outside the basement door, though, and the chains began rattling as the girls sat to attention. They heard the key scratching around the lock, then voices – two men speaking. There was a click, a hum, and a blinding white flash as the sodium lights flickered on. A muted chorus of groans reverberated around the basement as they all clawed at their eyes. Someone jerked against their ring and started coughing.

'Rise and shine, ladies, rise and shine.' It was Joseph's voice, high and jolly.

She looked through her fingers and saw that he was with another man. Someone she'd never seen before. He appeared tall and strong, with a red beard and a bald head.

'Wakey, wakey!' Joseph said. 'Stop squirming around, it isn't that bad.' He clapped his hands together rapidly to get their attention. 'Straighten out, people. You are all going back upstairs into the house, but first I want to introduce you to Abraham. Ladies, are you paying attention?' He put his hands on his hips and waited. 'I said, are you paying attention?'

'Yes,' they all croaked.

'Good, I am glad to hear that. Abraham here is going to be your new keeper, and I want you all to treat him with the same respect and kindness that you showed Lesley, God rest his soul. Now I'm sure all of you are going to help him get into the swing of things while he learns the ropes, and I'm praying to the Almighty that you don't give him any problems. Because, you see,' he patted Abraham on the back and grinned up at him, 'things are going to be slightly different to when Leslie was letting you all go around doing your own thing. Abe here is going to run a tight ship, because he knows how lucky he is to have landed such an important role in our family.

'Now, I'm going to come along and let you off your leashes. I know I don't have to stress this to you fine young ladies, but please don't do anything to embarrass me on Abraham's first day. I might be a soft touch, but he certainly is not. Maybe one or two of you will find that out before the day is over.'

Joseph began unlocking the rings from around the girls' necks. They stood up in turn and swayed on the spot with their eyes closed, massaging their throats. He introduced Abraham to each one as he went along, giving their name and the length of time they had been here.

'And this is Melody,' he said, when he reached Autumn. She knelt before him with her head bowed and let him unhook her. 'She's a veteran here at the camp. She's been here longer than me, even. She's our longest-serving member now. Isn't that right, Mel?' He patted her on the head and an explosion blossomed through her skull.

'Y–e–s,' she rasped.

Joseph reached down, grabbed her gently by the arm and helped her to her feet. She squinted through her lashes and tried to smile but only succeeded in splitting her dry lips afresh.

'We'll get you cleaned up,' he said softly, almost kindly.

'She's a lot older than the rest of them,' Abe observed. His voice was deep and the words came from low in his belly.

'Yes, but she's been a model resident. All the higher-ups really like her and she isn't much trouble at all. Never tried to hotfoot it out, and she's had plenty of opportunities to try when that imbecile Leslie dropped the ball.' He stroked Autumn's shoulder and gave it a reassuring squeeze. 'Plus you might not think it to look at her, but Mel here is one of our best breeders. What are you on now, Mel?'

'Four,' she whispered.

'She just keeps popping them out.' Joseph grinned and moved on to the next girl.

They were led up through the house in single file. Autumn guessed it was early morning as she looked out over the grounds through the barred windows in the corridor. It was raining, and through the leafless branches of the trees on the perimeter of the field she saw smoky white daylight.

Upon entering the shower room, they were made to strip, dropping their sodden gowns where they stood.

'You are all real funky at the minute and I think we can agree that isn't how ladies should smell.' Joseph walked over to a hamper and began removing bottles of shower gel before handing them out to the girls. 'Please be diligent with this because I want you all smelling of roses. No more mucky hair, no more dirty nails. I want you all scrubbed pink – well, that doesn't go for you, Gloria,' he laughed. Gloria was black, twelve years old. She'd been at the house for almost three years. 'Clean, clean, clean, that's the name of today's game.' He clapped his hands. 'Come on, don't be afraid. You've all used these showers before.'

Autumn went to a stall and twisted the taps, flinching as the cold water sprayed her. She tilted her head back and drank, then squeezed shower gel into her hands. She lathered her hair and massaged her scalp with her fingers, scratching the dirt away. Her eyes were achy and dry, so she rubbed them. When she turned to let the shower spray on her back, she looked down the line of girls. One of Mia's eyes was swollen shut, purple and shiny, and the whole side of her jaw was puffy. Too bad for her. That lack of dexterity in her mouth would probably mean she'd be taken out back and put to sleep.

The collective water pooling at their feet was brown from dirt, the remnants of excretion and menstrual blood. Autumn stepped away from it and concentrated on getting clean. While the girls washed, Joseph stood talking to Abe, occasionally pointing at them, supplying trivia.

'All right, let's get you lovely ladies dried off.' He walked to the bench, picked up a stack of scratchy brown towels and began to throw them at the girls. Autumn's fell short and landed in the coppery puddle by her feet. She picked it up – it was already soaked through – and wrapped it around her. 'Chop, chop, chop, this isn't a beauty pageant. We still have the day's chores ahead of you, but first Daddy requires your attendance in the assembly hall. So we are going to go to the dorm, get dressed in our nice new gowns that have been freshly washed and pressed, and smile like this.' He cocked his head and offered a huge plastic grin that seemed to stretch his cheeks all the way back to his ears. Abe did not smile. He glowered at the girls, his prominent brow almost shading his eyes. 'Ah! One other thing I should mention. Daddy is not in the best of moods, so it would be in your best interests to listen carefully and not make so much as a sniffle while he talks. Is that understood? I said, is that understood, ladies?'

'Yes, Joseph,' came the scattered reply.

'Excellent. Well let's skip to it.'

The dorm was exactly how they'd left it. The linen on the bunk beds remained unmade, the pillows lay askew. Barefoot, they hurried across the wooden floor to their respective bunks and stood to attention, waiting for their next command. Two rows down from Autumn, Mia leaned on the metal frame of her bed with her head slumped, holding her wounded jaw with both hands as though trying to keep it from falling off.

Joseph pulled back the door of the closet and fished out a bundle of white dresses, offloading them to Abe. 'They're all the same size, so it doesn't matter who gets what.' As Abe went about his duties, Joseph addressed the girls. 'I want you all ready to go in ten minutes.'

Abe handed out the dresses, pausing here and there to admire a cleavage or a rump. After four children, Autumn's breasts were large and full, and he noticed these immediately, though beyond a cursory glance he seemed uninterested in her.

'What's your name, princess?' he asked Alma, taking a second longer when holding out the dress. Alma was fourteen, but not yet ripe. She was short and petite, with mousy hair and freckles. Occasionally, after a particularly long day of chores or when they were screamed out of bed with only a few hours' sleep, she would break out in acne. Now, after weeks in the basement with no sunlight, her skin was an angry landscape of zits.

'Alma,' she replied.

'Nice to meet you,' he said, his finger stroking her hand before he continued on.

Joseph and Abe stood outside the dorm talking while the girls got ready. Autumn slipped into her dress. On some of the shorter girls it would be a decent length, but on her it fell just above the crease of her ass. The dorm was chilly, her nipples protruding against the fabric, standing out like jellybeans.

'Mia's gonna get it,' Wendy said, ruffling her hair with her towel. 'Look at her face.'

'I see it,' Autumn replied, busying herself with her own appearance. She checked her lips in the steel mirror fastened onto the wall by the bed. Her warped reflection emphasised the severity of the cuts, but even so, it wasn't good. She rummaged around the communal dressing area for the Vaseline, then removed the lid and scooped a chunk out on her finger, applying it to her mouth.

'This is all Lena's fault,' Wendy said. 'I was thinking about it, and that's why they've kept us down there all that time. Don't you agree?'

Autumn casually looked over at the doorway to ensure Joseph and Abe weren't listening or watching. 'Yeah, I do.'

'Maybe she's made it out,' Wendy said, a little too excitedly. She was seventeen years old and had given birth to her third child, a boy, about two months ago. Her stomach was still swollen from the pregnancy and her face hadn't lost its puffiness yet. 'I bet you anything she's made it out.'

'Keep your voice down,' Autumn warned, running a comb through her sopping black hair, which cascaded over her shoulders, dampening the fabric of the dress. 'They must have got her. That's the only reason we were let out.'

'I don't think so. If they didn't catch her after all this time, then she's out.' There was a smile on Wendy's lips. 'Mel, she got away.'

'Don't be so stupid. Lena used to get lost just walking around the house. There's no way she would've made it out of the woods.'

'Maybe she just went in one direction and stuck to it. Kept on going until she found a road or something.'

'No. They caught her. They were keeping us in the basement until they found Leslie's replacement.' Autumn was extra vigilant about whispering Leslie's name, especially after the way Daddy had reacted when they'd all got back to the house and heard the news. He had gone ballistic and had all the girls taken down into the basement. Shortly afterwards there had been gunshots.

'But what if they didn't, Mel? What if she actually got away?'

'Then she got away.' Autumn shrugged. 'Good for her.'

'And if she got away, then—'

'Don't, Wendy. Just stop.'

'But you said it yourself. Lena was crazy as a bag of frogs and thick as two planks, and she made it. If they did manage to catch her then they would've brought her back to the house and strung her up for us to see.'

Autumn found her garland and sat it atop her head. The grounds here were lush with foliage and she often wound buttercups into headdresses or made floral crowns for the others as presents. Her hobby offered her a means of distraction. It had become her trademark of sorts, a trick she'd picked up long ago and one she tried to instil in the others. Go the extra mile – that was the key to longevity in this place. Do what they want you to do and more. It needn't be much, a dab of rosewater here, a smear of glitter there. It stopped you from becoming dull and exhausting your usefulness.

'She's dead, Wendy. She probably wandered around for a while and ended up back at the house. We won't be seeing her again.' Autumn placed her fist in front of her mouth and coughed to rid her throat of the lump that was lodged there.

Wendy reached over to grab her hand. 'Mel, listen, what if—'

'That's enough now, people,' Joseph said, stepping back into the room. 'We don't want to keep Daddy waiting. Let's get going.'

They all hurried across the dorm, their bare feet slapping the hardwood, and were led up the spiral staircase. Joseph, ever the gentleman, held open one of the double doors while Abe herded the girls through.

The carpet in the hallway was the first soft thing Autumn's feet had touched in a long time, and it felt wonderful. She exhaled softly and then gritted her teeth when she had to step off the carpet and enter the assembly hall. It was even colder in there than in the dorm, with a frigid breeze wheezing through the large open space. The girls took their places on the benches facing the stage, and sat with their backs straight and their eyes forward. Behind her, Autumn could hear Mia sucking up the saliva that drooled from the side of her broken mouth. *That's bad, she thought. That's really bad.* She wanted to turn around and tell Mia to stop it, to wipe her stupid mouth and just shut the hell up. She wanted to tell her that unless she got the swelling down and made herself presentable, then she would be going out back.

The twenty-three girls sat in silence. Abe and Joseph stood off to one side by the rear exit, watching the procession solemnly. The guards, most of them new faces, lined the opposite side of the hall, awaiting the arrival of Daddy.

Autumn's eyes rolled to the ceiling. In the plastic casing surrounding the lights she could see the shadows of entombed moths and flies and wondered how they had managed to get inside in the first place. She wanted to yawn but knew not to. Worse, she could feel her eyelids beginning to droop. If she fell asleep while Daddy was talking, she may as well hand him the knife herself. She pinched her wrist as hard as she could, nipping the skin between her ragged fingernails and leaving little crescents in her flesh.

The whine of rusty door hinges echoed through the hall and was followed by footsteps, slow and heavy, from behind the stage's curtain. Horace appeared first, partially concealing Daddy from view as he helped him along, guiding him by the arm. It took a long time for Daddy to reach the armchair that had been left in the centre of the stage, and longer still for Horace to sit him down in it without causing him any distress.

When he was positioned in the chair, Daddy took a few moments to gather his breath, panting open-mouthed from the effort of his journey. At first Autumn couldn't understand why he'd bothered to walk at all – he'd been wheelchair-bound for years, his back so grotesquely hunched that nobody had been sure he *could* walk. And then it dawned on her: he was trying to show that he was still able-bodied, that he could still get around, just in case any of the other daughters tried to test him. *Foolish old man*, she thought. *You need someone to help you on and off the toilet, to mush your food and spoon it to you, to tuck you into bed at night like some little baby, and we're supposed to be awed because you made it across the stage without collapsing like a house of cards?*

But she could tell that his little display *had* awed some of the girls. They were transfixed, their eyes gleaming with wonder, unable to comprehend how a man who was almost two hundred years old could perform such a miraculous task. Two hundred!

-

Had there ever been a time when Autumn believed that? Yes, there had, when she was a little girl and new to the house. And then, one night when she was around thirteen or so, she was taken out of bed by a new guard and led into Joseph's office. He had guided her by the hand, informing her that he thought she was mighty cute, and that she didn't need to be afraid of him. In the office, he had forced her over the table before attempting to sneak her back to bed. The whole thing had lasted less than ten minutes, but in that time the guard had managed to make three very crucial mistakes. The first was that the idiot either forgot or completely disregarded the fact that the house was filled with security cameras. The second mistake was in holding Autumn's face down against the table as he thrust inside her, because it allowed her a look at a very important book that had been left open on Joseph's desk. As her eyes wandered over the text on the pages, she saw the real names and addresses of some of the girls at the house, as well as the schools they attended and their parents' occupations. At the bottom of the right-hand page was the name *Cherry*.

The third mistake the brazen young guard had made was informing Autumn of Daddy's real age. He'd laughed at the suggestion that Daddy was two centuries old. 'Shit, are you really that stupid? Ain't nobody can live that fuckin' long. It's common fuckin' sense,' he'd said, pulling his underpants back up over his dripping flaccid penis. 'You ain't completely dumb, are you? Humans don't live to see a hundred most times, let alone two hundred. What you think he is, a dragon or something? Motherfucker's pushing ninety, if that.'

The next night, Autumn was once again woken from her sleep, but this time it was by the sound of the young guard's protests. A girl called Latoya who used to occupy the top bunk by the barred windows said that they had led the man out onto the lawn in a cage. He was naked, and the men who brought him out were carrying flaming torches.

They poured gasoline over the cage and touched their torches to it. The girls listened, terrified, as the screams escalated into something beyond human agony. Then he stopped screaming entirely, and the only sound to be heard thereafter was the laughter of the other guards.

Autumn had expected Daddy to do the same to her for having seen the book, but he never did. Perhaps the fact that she was pregnant with her first child saved her life; it was the only way she could rationalise it. A girl's firstborn was always of great significance at the house.

–

Now, Daddy's tongue slithered out of his mouth to lick his lips in preparation for speech. 'I expected better from you all,' he began, his neck craned out like a turtle's from its shell. 'While you were all partying and enjoying yourselves, one of our helpers passed away. He had been with this family for over twenty years, long before any of you were born.' His rheumy eyes rolled around in their sockets, his square yellow teeth gnashing between words. 'Do not make the mistake of thinking that Lena's actions won't affect you.' He pointed a shaky finger at his daughters.

'You operate as a whole. If one of you misbehaves, then you are all under punishment. This is the only way I can ensure that you will actively...' he wiped his mouth, 'dissuade any of your sisters from doing something stupid.' The sudden rise of his voice made a few of the girls jump.

He did not speak again for a long time, and Autumn thought he might've fallen asleep. But as Horace began walking towards him, he snapped out of his stupor and continued. 'Lena betrayed each and every one of you. And for what? Leslie took care of all of you, made sure that you had food in your tummies and clothes on your backs, and how did she repay him? By stepping over him in his time of...' he faltered as though losing his train of thought, 'in his time of... need. She left him to die. Don't forget, it is we who have looked after her all these years, we who have given her a better understanding of the world and allowed her to be part of something majestic.' He paused again, his dusty, cluttered mind trying to peck out the next lines of his speech.

'Let me ask each of you a question right now. Do you want to leave? Raise your hand. Go on, don't be shy. If you want to go, then you will have my full pardon. So let's have it. Raise your hand.'

Autumn looked down into her lap, her hands becoming heavy as granite. There wasn't a force on this earth that could've made her raise one of them at that very moment in time. She thought about Mia and Wendy and clasped her hands tightly together, hoping to God neither of them would be foolish enough to take the bait.

'None of you?' His lip curled up. 'Well that surprises me. Because I know full well that some of you are unhappy here. Some of you are dissatisfied with having a place to live, with being surrounded by people who would literally *kill* to protect you! Some of you even plot against me.'

Sweat sprouted on Autumn's forehead and rolled down her face. Her back became moist and she could feel the cotton sticking to it. She bit the inside of her cheek and clasped her hands together tighter in an effort to mask the trembling in her arms. *Wendy, you idiot! You've killed us with your stupid big mouth. How many times have I told you not to speak inside the house, that every room has an ear? You stupid, stupid girl.* She closed her eyes and waited for him to call her name, to illustrate their betrayal.

'If any of you do want to leave, perhaps you should consider something first. I am not holding you here against your will. Each of you is free to go as and when you see fit. But remember this. I have taken you in. You are my daughters. I have taught you love, and with that love there is discipline. I will not have anarchy. I will raise you all to be obedient and decent. Even if it kills me.'

He attempted to stand. Horace rushed to help. When at last he was on his feet, Daddy said, 'My love is like a door that only swings one way. If you are with me, then I will give you the world, as I truly have done. If you are against me and against this house, then you know where that door is. But God help you if you decide to go through it.'

Horace assisted Daddy off the stage. Autumn was soaked with perspiration, her hair sticking to her hot face. She looked over at Wendy and shook her head. Wendy would not meet her eyes.

'Okay, troopers,' Joseph said once Daddy had left the hall. 'We need to get you back in the swing of things. We have a lot of ground to cover before next week. We are expecting visitors and this place has fallen into a shambles while you've been resting in the lower deck.' He never called it the basement, as though the very word were somehow too common to be part of his vocabulary. But in reality, he didn't want them to hear the truth of their situation: that they had been shackled by their necks in a cellar and left to piss and shit and bleed all over themselves. 'We need to clean this house until it is spotless, and then you could all use some time to get yourselves looking decent. We are going to be entertaining a lot of guests next week, and I want you all to sparkle.'

14

The silence that settled over Oakridge at night was not always perfect. The eerie stillness for which the neighbourhood was renowned was often perforated by the click of insects in the neatly preened lawns, the jagged screams of coyotes shuddering through the surrounding valleys. There were no sirens, though, no overexerted engines or squealing of tyres, no drunken arguments or pounding music. Even the volume of the rain seemed to dampen as it fell, careful not to disturb the precious calm, as though some treaty were in place. There was enough space between the mansions that any two neighbours might go weeks or even months without laying eyes on one another. Each property was a gated community: vastly expansive and wildly expensive, built for the elite. Beyond the double-glazed windows and the velvet curtains, the occupants of these fortresses created their own utopias. Behind the reinforced doors, one would observe more drug and alcohol abuse than in your average impoverished project building. This sordid open secret was something that the community of Oakridge understood and coveted.

Cindy Schilling understood the concept possibly better than anyone else in the neighbourhood. At the tender age of seventeen, she had left her home in rural Alabama with her parents' blessing to pursue a career in Hollywood. She told them, quite matter-of-factly, that she was going to be a famous actress and more than likely a millionaire by the time she hit twenty-one. It wasn't difficult to imagine. Having been a local pageant queen as a child and being the most beautiful teenage girl in her town, Cindy was set to take on the world. She knew that when she walked into a building, she was the most attractive person in it. She knew that when she talked to men, they melted. She knew that when she passed other women on the street, they regarded her with a sour mix of jealousy and resentment, and there was almost no other earthly pleasure that brought a smile to her face quite like it.

Armed with three hundred dollars and a portfolio of professional headshots and glossy glamour poses (taken by some guy at the mall who was doing a special one-day deal), Cindy managed to talk herself into a meeting almost as soon as her bus pulled up to the station. Starshine Cross was a prolific independent agency that operated out of an office in downtown LA. Cindy walked boldly into the reception and told the woman working the phones that she had an appointment.

'Who with?' the receptionist asked, unimpressed.

'Oh gosh, I'm so embarrassed but I completely forgot his name.'

'Did you really?' The receptionist was already bored with the spiel, having heard a variation of the hustle a hundred times before: silly young girls with aspirations of making it big without knowing the first damn thing about the business. 'Well, what's *your* name? Let's start there.'

'Cindy Wilcox.'

The receptionist sighed as she went through the diary, resenting having to perform the charade. 'There's no Cindy Wilcox down for an appointment.'

'Well there's obviously been some mistake. I've got a twelve o'clock meeting with…' She paused, drawing on her acting ability to feign memory loss. 'Oh what *was* his name? Was it Michael?'

The receptionist neither confirmed nor denied, her face remaining impassive. While Cindy scrambled for another avenue, a man emerged from the elevator behind them and strolled through the reception. He wore shades, a blazer with a polo shirt beneath, and white slacks. The diamonds encrusted in the face of his watch threw rainbow light around the room. He pushed the shades up onto his head, his eyes rolling up and down over Cindy's body. She smiled at him.

'It might have been him,' she told the receptionist, all the time maintaining eye contact with the man.

'It might've been me what?' he asked, smiling.

'Daniel, this girl says she has an appointment, but she isn't down on the list and doesn't know who her meeting,' behind Cindy's back the receptionist made quotation marks with her fingers, 'is with.'

The man looked at his watch. 'Well I have about an hour before my next appointment. Perhaps you'd like to come through to my office?'

'Yes, I'd like that,' Cindy told him, turning to smile facetiously at the receptionist as she sauntered into the office with her catch.

They skimmed over the pleasantries and Cindy produced her portfolio, taking every opportunity to flash some flesh his way. He flicked through the photos within the plastic wallet, stopping every now and then to admire a certain pose.

'So you're looking for representation, is that it?'

'Yes, very much so. I want to do movie work mainly, but I'm open to TV too.'

'I see. Have you ever acted before, Cindy?'

'I've been in some high-school plays, but nothing professional. You have to start somewhere, right?'

'That's right,' he grinned. 'But unfortunately we only take on experienced clients, actors with a body of work behind them. We sometimes represent unknowns, but that's only on a referral basis.'

'In that case, I'll refer myself to you!' She gave him her best lilting laugh, parading the perfect pearly-white teeth.

He laughed along with her, but it was altogether more reserved now. Cindy persisted, the smile no longer touching her eyes. She launched into a rendition of Robert Duvall's napalm speech from *Apocalypse Now*. Daniel interrupted her.

'I think you're good—' he began, but it was Cindy's turn to interrupt.

'I bet you've never seen a woman do that scene, have you? I just wanted to show you my range, to let you know I can do it all.'

Ignoring her, he continued with his original train of thought. 'I think you're good. But you need to get real-life experience. You need to be going to auditions, getting some seasoning. You might not want to hear that now, but it sets you up for later down the road.'

She sighed. 'Do you want me to suck your dick?'

'Excuse me?'

'Do you want me to put your cock in my mouth? Will that help this awkward little transition?' She stood up and began striding around his desk.

'I think it'd probably be best if you left, actually.'

'Oh shit, did I misread you? You didn't come across as a fag.'

'I'm not gay.' He stood up and opened the door for her. 'You need to leave. Now.'

She laughed and snatched up her bag and folder. 'You'd better take a good long look at me, because a year from now, you'll be crying into your Wheaties wondering why you let the opportunity pass.'

Ignoring the taunt, Daniel said, 'Try one of the smaller agencies. I wish you the best of luck.'

'Faggot.'

Cindy chose not to take Daniel's advice. She began floating around bars, oozing past doormen with suggestive promises. She went to parties, got introduced to cocaine and quickly forgot about acting. There was a far easier way to reach her end goal, once she figured out what her actual ambition was. To be famous was really only a by-product of her one true need – to be rich. And in a town like Hollywood, she didn't need to work to be rich; she just had to fuck someone who was and latch onto him.

By the time she was eighteen, she was savvy enough to understand that the young rich guys were not to be counted on. Sure they gave her plenty of blow and packed more pills than a pharmacist, but they were emotionally detached. They liked to party and fuck, but once that was over, they sent her packing with cab fare in her sweaty palms. There were never any follow-up dinners, or even acknowledgement upon re-encountering her at the hot spots. It took a whole year for her to figure out that partying for the sake of partying was getting her nowhere fast. She was living day to day, stealing from the men who took her home and retreating to a cheap, roach-infested condo on the Eastside.

The day her trajectory changed, she was in the back of a cab on her way over to the Roxy to try her luck with a young guitarist who'd been doing the rounds. Rumour was he was on the verge of signing a gigantic deal with Sony, and Cindy wanted in. The cab passed an auditorium with limousines parked out front and a gaggle of elderly men dressed in tuxedos filing inside. Instinct took over before her brain had quite figured out what she was doing, and Cindy told the cabbie to stop the car before throwing some notes at him.

Getting out of that cab was the best decision she would ever make. Because inside the auditorium was a man named Glenn Schilling, who, in her charming teenage naivety, Cindy didn't recognise. Truth be told, it was only much later, when the romance was in full swing, that she fully grasped the magnitude of her catch.

She married Glenn seven months later in a private ceremony in Puerto Rico. As they sipped champagne at the reception, she leaned in and said, honestly and earnestly, 'Marrying you has made all my dreams come true.' What she failed to tell him was that not only had the marriage made her aim of becoming wildly rich a reality, but that she had managed to do it over a year ahead of schedule.

Now Cindy sat in her calfskin chair by the window smoking a cigarette. She was drooping from the Valium and tequila and had been staring at the sky hoping to see lightning. Every now and then, the clouds would flash and fracture. She liked it when a storm raged, because she wanted a catastrophe. These days her only fantasies were of some world-changing event, the polar caps finally melting, or an earthquake that would rip the continents in half. She wanted the world to turn upside down and for everyone to be fucked: misery and death for all.

But as she waited for that one perfect boom of thunder, something peculiar happened. Beyond the numbing warmth of her stupor, a low twinge of déjà vu registered. She saw a blue car drive past that she was sure she had only seen a few minutes before. It was difficult trusting her mind with anything these days, but she was fairly certain about this. When the car drove past a third time, the tyres creeping along the tarmac, Cindy fought her way to her feet and walked to the other window at the opposite end of the master bedroom. The house tilted and jerked around her, but she ignored it, pulling back the curtain an inch and peering out into the rain-slicked road. The car rolled to a stop a few yards down and the headlights died. Cindy watched the vehicle for a minute, waiting for the driver to get out. When a few more minutes had dragged along, she pressed her palm against the window. 'Something weird is going on out there,' she mumbled. 'A car… just parked across the street down there… drove by… drove by a few times before. I think someone is watching us.'

She waited for a response, and when she received none, she stumbled around to locate Glenn before realising that he was up in his thinking room. She looked out of the window at the car again.

'Maybe we should have George check it out,' she said through heavy lips, forgetting immediately that Glenn was not there to hear her. 'Could be something... don't you think?'

15

The heavyset clerk at the convenience store assured Francine that Triple Xplosion was not only the most brutal caffeinated drink that the store sold, but that she probably wouldn't find anything better that was actually legal. 'Trust me, you drink this, you ain't sleeping for two days. People on crack have a better night's sleep.' Francine bought a six-pack.

Staking out Schilling's place was boring work, but the clerk hadn't been lying. One can of that junk set her nerve endings alight, made the act of staring at the mansion somehow bearable. She had seen the curtain twitch in the upstairs window a couple of times, but with the rain blurring the windscreen it was difficult to get a clear view through her binoculars.

Her lingering doubts snuck up on her during the dull stretches, and she had bitten her thumbs raw contemplating it all. Why couldn't Will have at least considered the possibility that Lena was telling the truth? Was it really that difficult to believe? If it was, why couldn't Francine herself acknowledge it? The more she turned the conundrum over, analysing it from every perspective, the more convinced she became. The fact that Lena's story about Schilling was so far-fetched and obscure somehow only made it more plausible.

Having someone in her corner would've made this so much easier. Even if she could have got Will to admit that there was a possibility, no matter how long the odds were, it would've been enough for her.

The first twenty-four hours passed uneventfully. Every hour or so, Francine saw a silhouette flutter by the curtains. The shape was definitely female: Schilling's wife or a maid. She'd identified the house from the picture she'd seen in *Forbes* and had her assumption confirmed when she drove by the grounds and saw the initials GS embossed in the gates. Now all she had to do was sit tight until Saturday, when he left for his show.

She'd wanted to be close to the house, to get a feel for it, and hopefully to catch a glimpse of the icon himself. She assumed that would make what she had planned easier to do, rather than turning up and going in cold. But when she finally saw him leaving the mansion and pottering around to the garage, she was flooded with doubt. Schilling was just a brittle old man who in any other surroundings could've been on his way to the post office or the supermarket for a loaf of bread. Yet still the sight of him made her heart beat in her throat and drew the moisture out of her lips. Yes, he might appear frail and a far cry from the maverick who slid up and down the stage every Saturday, but he was evil. She had to remember that.

On her third visit to the gas station, the manager approached her to ask why she kept using the bathroom, glancing suspiciously between her and her car parked out front. She rattled off an excuse, but it didn't sound convincing. It was only when she saw herself in the mirror that she realised why the manager was growing increasingly concerned. The lack of sleep, coupled with the shitty diet, had taken its toll. Clusters of red spots flared on her cheekbones. The circles around her eyes were so dark that she looked like a victim of domestic abuse. In only a few short days, the weight had melted from her frame and her head suddenly seemed too large for her spindly neck. The clerks out front probably thought she was a meth addict.

She cleaned herself up beneath the unforgiving bathroom lights and hurried back to Schilling's, keeping a watchful eye out for any other places that she might be able to use as a rest stop now that she'd exhausted the gas station.

She turned the engine off, unwrapped a candy bar and fixed her attention on the windows. When it turned midnight, she jotted down *Day 3. No Sign* in the diary she'd packed. In two days' time, Glenn Schilling would be making his way over to the TV studio to film *Saturday Night Splendour*. And then what? The plan had all seemed so streamlined in her mind: wait for Schilling to leave his mansion, then scale the wall, somehow break in without setting off the security system, and rummage around until she found something that linked back to Autumn.

She knew that if she lingered on the uncertainties, she would just talk herself out of it. Because the more she thought about what she planned to attempt, the more ludicrous it seemed. What if she did somehow manage to break in? And what if, in this perfect scenario, she was able to go through the whole damn place with a fine-tooth comb and still find nothing? Where would she go from there?

'Stop it,' she whispered to herself, forcing the doubt out of her mind. 'Just stop.'

Francine had got out of the car a couple of times to walk past the grounds in an attempt to get an idea of the layout of the house. As far as she could see, there was a CCTV camera posted on each corner of the roof, like gargoyles, and a guard manning the front gate. But if she could get over the wall at the rear of the property, she'd be able to waltz right on over to the back door. Glenn Schilling was a national treasure, and probably had a lot of crazed fans, but Francine was willing to bet good money that none of his groupies had ever gone to the lengths that she was planning on.

The days melted into one seamless stretch of time, a perpetual twilight that enveloped her. Were it not for her trips out of the neighbourhood, she could easily have believed that time was in fact standing still. She had not seen any other cars drive down Glenn Schilling's street, nor had she encountered any dog walkers or neighbours going about their business. There was nothing but the patter of rain against the roof.

In the early hours of Saturday morning, she finished her last can of Triple Xplosion. She had managed a whole week on sentry duty. How could she have been such an imbecile? Why had she just rushed into this thing without any proper planning, without even attempting to consult somebody for advice? *Because there was no time*, she assured herself. No time for common sense either.

An unfamiliar sound roused Francine. She checked the dashboard clock. Hours had passed. A limousine drove past and she hunkered down in her seat. Clearing a line in the condensation on the window, she followed the limo as it drove into the grounds of Schilling's house. She started the ignition and drove up the street, pulled around in a U-turn and idled on the corner so that she could see the vehicle when it re-emerged. She didn't want Schilling to notice her car as he passed. A few minutes later, the limo drove back through the gates, turned left then continued on, never crossing Francine's path.

There was a minute of uncertainty as she pondered her next move. She killed the engine and hurried over to the back wall. It was twice her height, with no obvious ledges for purchase, just smooth stone all the way up. A running jump might do it if she could manage to stretch up and grab hold of the top of the wall, then clamber with her feet.

As she stood sizing up the task, the weight of reality crashed down on her. There was no way she could scale the wall. There had to be another route in. She followed the wall around and came to a cylindrical pillar that marked the corner. She tested her foot on its base and hugged her arms around it. She attempted to shimmy up, but dropped off almost immediately. She tried again, except this time she used the toe of her right sneaker to press inside the crevice where the wall met the pillar. It was gruelling, and the effort it demanded from her arms and legs was immense.

At last she hoisted her right leg up and onto the top of the wall. It felt like her head might burst from the stress, her biceps bunching as she wrestled the pillar, a cold greasiness congealing in her stomach. She was boiling hot and could feel perspiration running down her torso from her armpits. She checked her jacket pocket to ensure she still had the gun, then swung her other leg over and dropped down into a hedge that lined the wall of the backyard. A rod of pain shot up her shins as she landed.

16

The smell of wet grass and exotic flowers filled Francine's nose as she peered up at the darkened windows of the house, the only light coming from the ground floor – an area that she assumed was the kitchen. She trudged out of the bushes and began edging around the grounds. According to the journal she'd been keeping, the maids seemed to come at around seven in the morning and leave at six in the evening, but those were weekday hours. She wasn't sure if they had additional staff at the weekends.

The garden was filled with statues, and as she neared the mansion, a large rectangular swimming pool came into view, lit with underwater spotlights. It was the epitome of excess: an outdoor pool in a city with almost ninety inches of rain a year.

She was panting by the time she reached the steps leading to the conservatory, and considered stopping for a few seconds to recover. A sudden blinding light bathed her and she automatically dived across the wet grass and slid behind the knee-high stone wall. She scrunched her eyes closed waiting for the alarm, but was met with silence. Peeking out, she saw that she'd activated a motion-sensor light.

On all fours, she watched the kitchen for any sign of movement. A minute went by, then another, and when there was still no activity, she got up and darted to the sliding doors that led to the kitchen. She was now in plain sight, and if anyone were to walk into the kitchen or along the hallway beyond it, they would see her clear as day. She twisted the handles, but the doors were locked. She didn't need much more confirmation than that, so she abandoned the doors and rushed around to the side of the house.

The motion-sensor light switched off and she was plunged back into darkness, with only the spotlights from the pool to brighten the way. Her breathing sounded too loud in her ears, but there was nothing she could do about it; she was on the verge of hyperventilating from the adrenalin. With her back to the house, she shimmied against the wall and reached another door. A small green light glowed above a keypad. She didn't dare touch it. Instead, she tested the handles, found this door to be locked too and carried on.

She continued to skirt the mansion around to the front of the property, where she slunk into the shade behind a column. She was standing at the top of the long driveway and could see the circular fountain, the guard at the gates and the street beyond. In front of her was the main entrance to the mansion: two huge double doors. With sweat dribbling down her face thick as cooking oil, she wondered what would happen if she walked over, rang the bell and shoved her gun in the face of whoever answered. Before she could act on the thought, she hurried across the concrete porch and started a sweep around the other side of the mansion.

She was about to glide straight past the garage when she skidded to a halt. It was *open* – only halfway, but that was enough. It was more than a coincidence, surely; it was a godsend. Yet still she hesitated. Everything she'd done up until this point could be explained if she were to be caught and arrested: her fragile state of mind, the approaching anniversary of Autumn's disappearance. Jumping over Schilling's wall and running across his lawn was forgivable. Anything beyond this point was not.

Every impulse in her body screamed at her to stop. Some internal warning system linked to the rational part of her brain flashed on red alert, and she gave herself a moment to back out and fully acknowledge the grievous error she was about to make. Then she looked over her shoulder towards the guard's booth, decided that she was obscured enough to continue, dropped to the ground and scooted under the door on her belly.

Groping blindly, she got to her feet and felt her way across the garage, bumping into a vehicle. As soon as her knees touched the car, she cringed, expecting an alarm to sound. All the moisture in her body was leaking out of her pores, leaving her mouth dry as parchment. Taking baby steps, she moved in the direction she assumed the internal door would be. Her feet kicked a set of stone steps and she reached out, finding a banister and pulling herself up. She stroked the surface of the door at the top, hoping to find the handle; when she did, she held her breath and turned it.

The door opened. Francine didn't immediately emerge into the house, but instead placed her ear against the inch-wide gap and listened out for sound. Nothing. She pushed the door open, and the slow creak of the hinges was like a train screeching to a halt against the silence of the mansion.

She was presented with a long hallway lined with big paintings in elaborately carved frames. Each was lit to reveal the intricacy of the brushstrokes on the canvas. In the centre of the hallway was a security camera, the type they had at the casinos to catch people rigging the machines. Francine ignored it, knowing there was no other way into the house.

The place smelled like a hotel, she thought absently as she wondered which direction to go in. The stairs seemed most logical, and so she ascended, her wet sneakers leaving faint impressions in the carpet. She stopped halfway up, wondering what to do about them, but decided it was unimportant. Unless she was caught outright, Schilling might very well think that the footprints had been left by a careless gardener. After all, she wasn't going to steal anything; if she had wanted to, those paintings would already be off the wall.

At the top of the stairs, she walked past the elevator and tried one of the doors along the hallway. She reached inside the room and flicked on the light to reveal a study with a globe sitting atop the far end of a mahogany table. Displayed on the walls in frames were pressed butterflies and beetles and the skeletons of several large winged creatures that might have been bats. She closed the door and tried another room – a bedroom with a large window facing the front of the grounds. A gigantic aquarium glowed on the far side of the room, the shadows of the fish moving lazily over the walls. This didn't look like the master bedroom, but she allowed herself a minute or so to nose through it. Finding nothing of interest, she moved on.

The next room along the hallway had a large pool table, a bar, and a hexagonal table in the corner with piles of neatly stacked poker chips. There was an old-fashioned jukebox too, but she didn't go near it for fear that it might be motion-sensitive like the lights in the garden and come to life. Satisfied that there was nothing of use to be had here, she backed out and carried on with her search. The next couple of doors were locked, so she moved along until she neared what she assumed to be the master bedroom. The faint, tinny sound of a TV could be heard from within, and knowing that someone was on the other side of the door made Francine's heart pinball in her chest. She reached into the front pouch pocket of her rain jacket and withdrew the gun. The metal felt slippery in her clammy palm and she noticed that the barrel was wavering as her hand trembled. She took a deep breath and pushed open the door.

The TV was curved and paper-thin. The brilliant colours splashed out of the screen and flooded the room in frenetic light. Francine turned and saw a naked woman propped up on the four-poster bed, her eyes gleaming slits. She inhaled sharply and almost raised the gun, but the woman made no move. On the bedside table was an obscenely large wine glass, stained red, surrounded by a cluster of pharmaceutical bottles. Francine stepped closer and saw that the table was also littered with dark green marijuana buds and tobacco from a packet of crumpled cigarettes. Now she could smell the pungent weed smoke clinging to the chiffon curtains that hung from the posts surrounding the bed.

The woman was completely passed out, her chest rising and falling slowly, her lips purple from the wine. Her breast implants jutted unnaturally from her emaciated chest and her sunbed skin looked tight and sore across her torso. Her pubic hair, Francine noticed, was trimmed into a small triangle. A six-foot black-and-white photo hanging on the wall behind the bed depicted Schilling and this woman dressed for an awards ceremony of some sort.

Francine tucked the gun back into her pocket and rifled through a few drawers, finding silk undergarments and a selection of vibrators and dildos. She tried the walk-in closet and began leafing through the jackets that hung on the racks above the outrageous collection of shoes. When she found nothing, she went across to another door in the bedroom and opened it.

She had to let her eyes adjust to the light in order to ensure that what she thought she was seeing was actually there. It was a glass tunnel that stretched on to another part of the house, concealed from the outside by the way it was positioned between the slanting sections of the roof. She remembered seeing a photo of Schilling standing in the tunnel with a pipe in his mouth, gazing up at the dazzling sun through the domed ceiling. An eerie, crawly feeling spread across her, and just before she stepped into the tunnel, she realised she was scared. What she was scared of, she couldn't quite say, only that it felt as though the adrenalin had dissipated and her faculties had returned. For that one second she was completely sane again and understood what a monumentally bad idea this whole thing was. She had broken into the house of one of the most beloved entertainers in the country, and she was armed.

Yes, and let's not forget why *you're armed, Francine. You have that gun because this sick, fucking bastard hurt your baby girl. He knows where she is. That's what kept you awake this whole week, that's what got your crazy fucking ass up and over that wall, that's what got you where you needed to be.* The blurry image of the Polaroid flashed in her mind and she once again lost her reservations.

She had started to walk through the tunnel when a voice stopped her. 'I don't think we need any laundry done at this hour.'

She whirled and saw the woman leaning against the bedroom doorway. She was still naked, her head tilting to the side.

'And if we do, it can wait. There's probably more for you… more for you to do downstairs in the… in one of the other rooms. This is… You shouldn't be up here.'

'Are you okay, Mrs Schilling?' Francine asked. Instinct had taken over and she pretended to be a member of staff.

'Cindy,' the woman breathed. 'I don't like it when you all call me Mrs Schilling.' Her head lolled back and she staggered on the spot. 'Makes me sound… so… fucking old.'

'Sorry, Cindy,' Francine said. 'Why don't we get you back to bed?'

'What… are you doing up… here at this time of night?'

'I'm just making sure everything is okay,' Francine said, studying Cindy's face for any sign of recognition. There was none. The woman was drooling and wiping her mouth with the back of her hand.

'Doing some spring cleaning… is that it?'

'Yes, exactly. Would you like some help getting back to bed, Cindy?'

'I'm not a fucking child… Unless you… Are you trying to tuck me in? Are you some kind of lesbian?'

'No, not at all.'

'My husband doesn't like… the help going across there…' She pointed behind Francine and down the tunnel. 'You're not allowed.'

'Yes I am,' Francine said, coolly. *Because that's exactly where I need to be, isn't it?*

'Nuh-uh.' Cindy shook her head unsteadily. It rolled around on her neck like a spinning plate balanced atop a stick. 'Glenn'll get real mad if he finds you.'

'No he won't,' Francine said, conjuring a saccharine smile. 'His instructions were for me to clean that section of the house. Why don't you go on back to bed?'

Cindy's mouth hung agape as she stumbled towards Francine. In any other setting, she would've looked like one of the crack addicts who patrolled the bus station hassling passengers for spare change. She was mumbling *no, no, no, no* and shaking her head defiantly. 'You're not allowed up there.'

'Let's not argue about this, Cindy,' Francine said without any trace of a smile. She grabbed the woman by the arms, feeling nothing but bone. It was like taking hold of a bundle of sticks. 'You need to get back to bed and let me get on with my work. Come on, I'll take you.'

As she manoeuvred Cindy around with the ease of a mother handling a toddler, the other woman reached out for the door jamb and halted their progress. She looked up at Francine, and now there was a faint spark of recognition in her eyes, like candlelight at the bottom of a dark well.

'You don't work for my husband,' she said, each word suddenly perfectly pronounced as the fog began to clear. 'You don't… What're you doing in our house?'

'I'm a special cleaner. Your husband only hired me today.' Francine forced Cindy backwards and plonked her down on the bed. 'Now go to sleep and let me do my job.'

Even in her lethargy, a small part of Cindy seemed to recognise the threat of violence lurking beyond Francine's words. She reached down for the bed sheet and pulled it up to her neck to cover her nakedness.

'You're not going to give me any trouble, are you?' Francine asked.

Cindy blinked as though she couldn't quite understand the question, and then said, 'You have leaves in your hair.'

'Don't worry about that,' Francine said. She went back over to the drawer with the vibrators in and looked for a pair of handcuffs. Finding none, she removed a pair of stockings and returned to the bed. She dropped the pretence. 'I'm going to tie you up. If you scream or do anything to upset me, I'll come back here and hurt you. Put your arms out.' She began tying Cindy's wrists to the bedpost, knotting the stockings so tightly that the woman's veins bulged. If she was in pain, though, it wasn't registering.

'Can I trust you to be a good girl, Cindy?'

'Yes,' she said. 'We don't keep any money here. There's nothing in that part of the house except my husband's study.'

'Good. Then I shouldn't be too long.'

'Wait!' Cindy lurched up, her fake breasts unmoving. 'I have some jewellery if you want it… diamonds. You can have it all.' She sucked up saliva. 'If you untie me, I'll take you to the safe.'

Francine removed the gun from her jacket and let Cindy's eyes catch the steel. 'Don't give me a reason to hurt you, Cindy, please. If you yell for help, I'm going to put you to sleep.' Ignoring the woman's pleas, she turned back towards the doorway.

The room at the end of the tunnel was spacious and filled wall-to-wall with books. Francine saw an oak desk with a decanter holding amber liquor, and a collection of crystal tumblers. Her mouth dried at the sight of the alcohol, but she resisted the urge. She felt jittery and dislocated. Part of it was the sleep deprivation, but a bigger part of it was the sheer unreality of it all. Her skin bristled with anticipation, and she felt sharp. The danger of her situation had heightened her senses and her mind was completely clear. She looked around the room, considered going up the ladder to the next tier then decided against it. There was a door on the far side of the study, but it was locked.

'You've got secrets here, haven't you?' she said aloud.

She sat down in the leather chair and took a moment to really look at the room. It was a library full of journals and other hardbound books, just like one of the rooms she'd peered into earlier. Why would he need two rooms like this? If Cindy hadn't reacted the way she had, dragging herself down from her high to try and prevent Francine from progressing, then she might have thought nothing of it. However, now she recognised the phoniness of it all: the vast rows of books that all looked alike, the lack of detail in the interior decoration that was so prevalent throughout the rest of the mansion.

She did a slow lap of the study, running her finger along the books, perusing the spines. There were encyclopedias, atlases, medical journals. Nothing jumped out at her, but she was absolutely certain that there was something here. She marched back to the master bedroom and found Cindy gnawing at her restraints like a wild animal snared in a trap, her bumpy spine like a dinosaur's back.

'You trying to run out on me, Cindy?' Francine asked, beginning to enjoy this character she was playing.

'Please… let me go. I won't call the cops. You can take whatever you need…'

'Shut up and listen to me very carefully. I'm going to ask you some questions and I want you to give me honest answers. If I think you're lying, I'll shoot you. Do you understand?'

'I don't know what you want…' Cindy mewled, twisting away.

'Settle down. I want you to tell me what's in the study.'

Cindy's already dilated pupils seemed to expand like puddles of oil. 'Books, my husband's writing stuff…'

'Cindy. Don't play with me.'

'There's nothing down there. It's just the other part of the house.'

'So why doesn't Glenn like people going there?'

'It's where he goes to think.'

'I'll bet it is. Cindy, you're going to tell me what he's hiding in there.'

She shook her head and her eyes darted away. 'Nothing,' she said, slack-jawed. 'It's his study… What're you talking about, *hiding*? He's a goddam fucking celebrity, a—'

'You're lying to me, Cindy. I can always tell when I'm being lied to, and you,' Francine removed the gun from her pocket again so Cindy could see, 'are a bad liar. One more chance. Please, Cindy. Know that I am serious.'

Cindy nodded miserably.

'Good. So I'll ask again. What's he hiding?'

'I... I honestly don't know. If I knew, I would tell you. Please...' Cindy's head dipped defeatedly. Twin runners of snot streamed from her nostrils and collected in the ledge of her collagen-curled upper lip. The pillow behind her head was sopping wet. 'Who are you?'

'Do you really want to know?'

Cindy's eyes became wild with terror.

'I'm the mother of Autumn Cooper-Wright. She was kidnapped almost ten years ago. Your husband knows her. And judging by the look on your face right now, I'd say you probably know exactly what I'm talking about.'

17

'You're crazy. Don't you know they'll lock you up? You'll go to prison for the rest of your life.' Cindy's voice was shrill with panic.

'Who's going to lock me up?' Francine asked, rubbing her thumb over Cindy's clammy forehead. 'Nobody knows I'm here.'

'Glenn will be back soon.'

'Do you think I'm scared of your husband?'

'I don't… I don't…'

'You don't know? All right, I'll tell you. Right now, you hold the key to the rest of your life. This house is full of secrets, isn't it? Well, I'll let you in on a little secret of my own, Cindy. I wasn't sure before, but now I truly think I have lost my mind. And thinking about my daughter, what your husband has probably done to her, it makes me want to put this gun in your mouth and blow your fucking brains all over this bed. I really want to do it, too. Believe me, Cindy. I'm itching to hurt someone.'

Before she had a chance to reply, Cindy urinated in the bed.

–

Francine pushed Cindy down the tunnel with the gun pressed against her back. Cindy, now dressed in a silk nightgown at Francine's insistence, laboured along, her shoulders hunched, her footsteps unsteady. She sobbed as she walked, explaining that she and Schilling were on the verge of divorce, that they should never have married in the first place.

'If I'd known… I would never have got involved in any of this… You don't know what it was like for me.'

Francine resisted the urge to prod her for details. She knew that engaging in any kind of conversation would sidetrack Cindy, and right now she needed her scared and willing to cooperate.

'Here we are,' she said, lowering the gun. 'Show me what it is I'm looking for.'

Cindy turned, the flesh around her bloodshot eyes puffy and crinkled. 'I want to thank you. I really want to tell you how much I appreciate this.'

'Appreciate what?'

'You coming to my rescue.'

'I'm not here to rescue *you*,' Francine said, her voice weighty with disdain.

'Maybe not in that way, but you've given me the chance to be free. I've kept his secrets too long. Much too long.'

'Well now's your chance to unburden yourself. Make sure you do it properly.'

Cindy took a breath. 'Before I show you, I just want to… explain. I'm not like him. You have to believe me. I'm nothing at all like him.'

'I believe you,' Francine said slowly. 'Speed it up.'

Cindy gave another sob, then retreated to the corner wall and grabbed hold of the bookcase. 'I can't do it.'

'Do what?'

'It's behind here,' Cindy said. 'His thinking room.'

Francine walked carefully to the bookcase. The shelves were lined with botanical reference books. 'Behind here?'

'Yes. I swear. Just pull.'

With her left hand, Francine gripped the shelf and tugged. She felt it loosen against the wall. A couple of books fell. She pulled harder, and there was a click as the shelf dislocated entirely. She pushed it to the side, marvelling at the ingenuity of the design, and saw a narrow staircase ascending.

'You first,' she ordered.

There was a noticeable change in air density with the bookcase open. Francine could already feel her guts churning, a feather stroking the nape of her neck. She followed Cindy up into a small dark room. 'Turn the light on,' she said.

'There isn't one. Only the TV.'

'Well turn that on.'

Cindy fumbled around in the dark until the blue glow of a screen brightened the musty space. Seeing how small the room actually was made Francine's chest tighten. Her heart began to pound as claustrophobia crept up on her. On the floor, dozens of shiny discs gleamed in the TV's light. At a glance there might have been close to a hundred, possibly more. She saw the red standby light of the DVD player and reached down and pressed play, then waited for the DVD to load. The screen came to life and revealed the inside of a house. It wasn't Schilling's, though; Francine could tell that even through the cameraman's shaky handiwork.

Naked, mostly bloated men with limp dicks lined the corridor. They were smoking and drinking out of fancy glasses. There was laughter too, tumbling off the paisley walls. The cameraman weaved through the house, coming to a cluttered kitchen where a saggy middle-aged woman with bleached blonde hair was tending to a tray of hors d'oeuvres and cackling at some unheard joke. The cameraman continued the tour and appeared on the threshold of a smoky room that had been stripped of furniture, where a very young, blindfolded girl was standing at the centre of a circle of jovial men. The cameraman yelled something, and the men all smiled at the camera and waved. On the other side of the room, a woman with short hair spoke casually to a very old man as though the lewd act were not happening.

Francine was clutching the gun so hard that the criss-cross grip on the handle bit into the flesh of her palm. She wanted to shoot the TV and then put another bullet in Cindy's head. She fixed her gaze on the floor, but was unable to escape the pitiful moans. 'No more,' she pleaded. 'Stop it.'

'It isn't me, I swear to God. I promise it isn't me. I don't go to these things. You believe me, don't you? I swear.'

'Turn that fucking thing off!'

Cindy scrambled for the DVD player and ejected the disc. 'You have to believe me… it's nothing to do with me. I stay at home… I stay at home…'

Francine bent down and picked up a handful of the DVDs, shoving them into her jacket pocket. The newspapers might like to see them. That was something she could think about later. Right now, she needed to leave. She grabbed a fistful of Cindy's hair and forced her down the stairs. When they were back in the study, she made Cindy close the bookcase so that it was just as she'd found it. Then she motioned with the gun for the other woman to exit.

Back in the foyer of the house, Francine could just about make out the guard at the gate.

'See that guy?' She pointed through the huge window by the front door. 'Call him and tell him to take off.'

Cindy walked to the wall phone and picked up the receiver. 'I don't think this is going to work,' she said.

'Why not?' Francine asked, without taking her eyes off the guard.

'George has worked for Glenn for over thirty years. He'll want to know why I'm sending him home, and even then he won't take my word for it.'

'You're his boss. *Make* him do it.'

'I'm telling you, he won't,' Cindy whined. 'I can phone him and speak to him, but all he'll do is come up to the house and check in on me. You don't want that, do you?'

'Then you'd better think of something to send him packing.' Francine looked over at the antique grandfather clock. 'Is that the right time?'

'Should be.'

'Your old man is off the air in ten minutes. We want to be out of here before he gets back.'

'We?'

'Do you have a sister?' Francine asked.

'Yes. I have two.'

'Names?'

'Kelly-Jo and Loretta.'

'Phone George and say Loretta is at the airport. She's just flown in and doesn't have anyone to pick her up. Tell him that you can't send a cab to get her because…' Francine had to pause for thought. 'Tell him that Glenn should have already cleared this with him. Make out like it was Glenn's mistake.'

Cindy pressed a button on the dial pad and put the conversation on speaker. Francine watched George through a gap in the curtains as Cindy began spinning her tale.

'Well what time is she supposed to land?' George asked with a mixture of annoyance and panic.

'I think her flight touches down at ten. Oh, please tell me you'll be able to get her. I gave her your name and everything, so if I tell her to get a cab, she'll have an anxiety attack. I swear I could just kill Glenn for this.'

'I won't get there for ten,' George replied. 'She might have to hang around.'

'I'd prefer that than for her to get in a cab. I'll phone her as soon as she touches down and let her know you're waiting.'

'What about the gate?'

'Oh, don't worry about that.' Cindy gave an effortlessly lilting laugh. 'I don't mind going out to open it. God, you make me feel so lazy sometimes, George.'

'I don't know about this, Cindy. Are you sure you wouldn't prefer to have a limo pick her up?'

'Oh God no. She hates fuss. Please, George; it would really put my mind at rest if you could do this for me.'

There was a pause. Francine stared at Cindy.

'All right, well I'd better skip to it,' he said grumpily. 'I'm gonna have to put my foot down to get there in time. Let's hope there isn't any traffic.'

Cindy hung up, and Francine watched as George opened the gate and set off down the street to his car.

'What do we do now?' Cindy asked.

'We need to wipe all the security footage on the cameras. Then I'll let you grab your pills. I don't want you going through withdrawal on me.'

'My pills? What're you talking about?'

'The ones next to the bed. You can bring whatever you think you're gonna need.'

'Are you taking me somewhere?'

Francine didn't reply.

18

The trolley was loaded with meals consisting of tinned mackerel, a hunk of bread, an ice-cream scoopful of salty mashed potato, and a freckled banana for dessert. There was a tower of plastic cups, to be filled with tap water from the dented metal jug. It was the same supper every day for the girls in the cells; boring, yes, but a damn sight more nutritious than the crackers and runner beans they used to get. With all the girls that fell sick while they were pregnant, someone suggested that maybe the issue arose from them not getting enough vitamins. Some of them got scurvy; their gums would bleed raw, and the sharp edges of the crackers would scratch them even worse until they had to spit blood after every bite of food.

Autumn opened the wicket and slid the tray of food through the black rectangle until the pale, needy hands came out to receive it. *You don't know how lucky you are*, she thought, remembering the taste of blood in her own mouth, the sores that would erupt on her skin.

She came to Janet's cell, pulled the wicket down and peeked through the rectangle. 'How's the belly?' she whispered.

Janet stepped forward rubbing her stomach. 'Getting big. My back hurts.'

'It's a boy,' Autumn said, pouring her a cup of water and sliding the tray in.

'You think so?'

'Most definitely.' She gave Janet an understanding smile.

'How can you tell?'

Autumn shrugged. 'Just can.'

–

She'd had three boys and one girl herself, or at least that was how she remembered it. It had always been difficult to discern after the birthing process what sex the baby had been, as it was snatched out of her so quickly and whisked away, never to be seen again. In her memory, unreliable as it was given the overwhelming pain and exhaustion of the ordeal, Autumn could remember seeing her three sons for maybe a couple of seconds each as the nurse bundled them into her arms, red and gory. She could remember their high, piping screams and the way they kicked the air. And then they were gone.

She had had her first child at thirteen. It got easier after the first one; she came to recognise and anticipate the pain, and knowing just how bad the labour would be somehow took some of the strength away from the terror. But that first one was scary. She knew exactly what Janet was going through with the back pain; Autumn's first boy had been so big that he'd pushed against her spine and distended her stomach grotesquely, and they'd talked about cutting him out early. In the end, though, he'd fought his way out, and Clarissa, one of the older girls at the time, had made it clear to anyone who would listen that Autumn was going to die trying to deliver him.

But Autumn didn't die. She endured pain beyond comprehension, agony that transcended physical feeling. It went on and on, a seemingly endless tide of suffering. She was strapped to the bed, lorded over by men she knew and some she didn't – any one of whom could have been the child's father – as well as some of the more experienced girls who'd helped with births in the past. In the chair in the corner of the medical room sat Daddy, his black cane across his lap. He was present at every birth, no exceptions. He had given instructions to observers and nurses alike, and then chastised Autumn when she screamed too loudly. 'It doesn't hurt that much, for God's sake,' he said, the contempt dripping from his words. 'Be a woman, will you!'

The men had smiled at her, patting her head as though she were a dog that had just fetched a Frisbee, the excitement shining in their eyes. The other girls went about their work, doing everything they could to ensure that the baby lived; Autumn was obviously a secondary concern. The pain ballooned through her as the baby made its exit plans, reaching an awful crescendo until somebody said, 'There's the head.' At this, one of the men helped Daddy out of his chair and he took centre stage, standing at the foot of the bed with a VIP view. A thin smile appeared at his lips, and even in her ungodly state, Autumn would always remember how he balled his frail, veined fist and punched the air victoriously.

–

'Any more bleeding?' she asked Janet now, checking to make sure the guard at the end of the corridor was still reading.

'Just spots here and there. Is that normal?'

'Sure,' Autumn said, not really knowing if it was or not. She had a feeling that Janet's baby would make it, but she'd been wrong in the past. 'Gotta go, okay?' She reached through and squeezed Janet's hand, then pushed the trolley on to the next cell, the wheels squeaking as it rumbled over the uneven tiles.

When she came to the last cell and opened the wicket, no hands reached out to retrieve the tray. Autumn bent down and peered in. 'Everything okay in there?'

'Hey!' the young guard yelled, looking up from his book. 'What do you think you're doing?'

'Just seeing if India is all right.'

'Well don't bother. Leave the food and move on.'

Autumn chanced another look. 'Sir?'

The guard stood up. He was new, recruited after Leslie's unfortunate passing. Rumour around the dorm was that Daddy wanted to run a tighter ship in the wake of Lena's breakout and had ordered military expertise. This one took his work extremely seriously, it seemed. Ever since he'd started, Autumn hadn't seen him wear anything other than army fatigues. He was always clean-shaven, with shiny boots, an army-issue cap covering his head and partially concealing his eyes. At first, Autumn had thought his blotchy red cheeks were the result of the chill in the air, but upon closer inspection it seemed to be some sort of birthmark.

'What is it?' he growled

'She's coming to the end of her term,' she replied, staring at the circles of light on the toes of his boots. 'I can't see inside her cell, but maybe someone should check on her.'

'Are you trying to give me face, girl?'

She shook her head vehemently. 'No, sir.'

'Then shut your trap and get on out.'

As Autumn started to turn the trolley around, she looked at the black rectangle again. She stopped, and turned back to the guard. 'She could be hurt.'

'What did you say?' he bellowed, marching towards her.

She knew it was a mistake; even as the words left her mouth, she wanted to quickly gobble them back up. She pointed at the meal on the tray – the only meal that hadn't been collected along the row of cells. She had done trolley duty many, many times before over the years and knew the warning signs when something was wrong. Girls had died in those cells because their screams went unanswered. Some of them just bled out. Some would collapse while trying to do light exercise to alleviate the stress on their bodies, and then slip into a coma. Autumn had seen it all. And one of the most obvious indicators was a girl not collecting her tray.

'I can't see inside, but—'

Her sentence was disconnected as the guard grabbed her around the throat and slammed her against the barred window behind her. The pain as his palm pressed against her larynx was not completely foreign; some of the guests liked to choke the girls while they had sex, and then of course there was that awful ring in the basement. But of all the various pains she was intimately acquainted with, having her throat crushed was the hardest one to adjust to. Black spots popped in her eyes and her limbs went rigid.

'You're not to speak to me unless I speak to you first. You're not to ask me any questions. You're not to tell me anything, do you understand me?'

Autumn couldn't nod, couldn't mouth the word 'yes'. She just remained pinned to the wall with her tongue lolling out of her mouth and her eyes scrunched closed. She could feel herself slipping... slipping...

The grip loosened enough to allow her air but no room to wiggle. She coughed.

'You think I'm like that slob you used to have watching over you? No way, girlie, not a fuckin' chance. Things have changed around here. When you're in these halls, I'm the ruler of your existence, the god of your world. You'd better get wise. I *own* you.' As he spat the words into her face, his breath sweetly sour from gum that'd been chewed to death, he began to feel under her dress. His hand cupped her privates and squeezed. 'Down here, I own every part of you, you little cunt.'

'Ca—'

'What?' A thick vein bulged in his head and his face turned red with outrage. 'You trying to backchat me?' The hand that groped between her legs lifted her onto her tiptoes.

'Camera,' she finally managed, and as soon as she said it, the clamp around her neck relented and the soles of her sandals were once again firmly on the ground.

'Dumb fucking bitch. You think that applies to me?' he said, but already his voice was lower, more controlled.

'No, sir, I don't,' she replied, waiting patiently for his hand to drop away. 'I just don't want anyone to get into trouble, that's all.'

Her eyes met his and there was an unspoken under-standing between them. The guard didn't own her or any of the other girls in the cells: Daddy did. The staff were not, in any circumstances whatsoever, to interfere with the girls. There were exceptions to the rule, of course. For example, it was expected that a staff member would discipline a girl who stepped out of line as long as he didn't do anything that might sully her. This was what made the brutal attack on Mia in the basement so alarming, but then again, these were stressful times and Lena's escape meant examples needed to be made.

The guard's radio crackled on his hip, distracting him.

'Davey? We need you out front, right now,' a voice said breathlessly. Outside, the floodlights came on, illu-minating the grounds.

The guard grabbed the radio, held it to his mouth, 'What's the situation?'

'We got a runaway.'

Autumn didn't hear any more. The guard replaced the radio and jogged down the corridor. She saw that he wore a pistol pressed against his lower back, in the band of his trousers. When he was out of sight, she turned and looped her fingers through the cage over the window and looked out on to the field. A couple of the guards were running across the wet grass with German shepherds. The dogs' breath came out in puffs of steam, their tongues lolling. She heard a car engine rev somewhere around the front of the house, accompanied by frantic yelling. She listened harder, and thought that it might be Joseph barking commands.

'What's going on, Mel?' Tulip asked, with her face pressed up against the wicket.

'Someone's made a run for it,' Autumn replied, without diverting her attention from the field. She saw Joseph marching across the grass to brief two other guards before pointing at the trees in the distance. The guards ran off with big rifles that had torches atop the barrel.

'Who is it?' one of the other girls asked.

'I don't know,' Autumn said. 'I can't see.'

'Wendy,' someone said. 'Bet you anything.'

'Please don't let it be Wendy,' Autumn said, so quietly that none of the others heard. 'Oh please, Wendy, please, please, please.'

With their mouths right up against the wickets, the pregnant girls began to throw conversation back and forth.

'They'd better catch her,' someone said. 'I can't go through the basement again.'

'Basement? You better wish it's the basement! They won't put us back down there, not if we didn't learn our lesson the first time round. No, they'll do something worse.'

'Like what?'

Autumn turned around. 'Hey, keep your voices down,' she hissed. 'You guys want to get in trouble too?'

'We already are in trouble! Even if they catch Wendy, they're gonna punish *us*.' Tulip released a long groan that reverberated down the corridor and infected the other girls, who began wailing too.

'Mel, you gotta do something!' It was India, who had now taken her tray into her cell.

'Oh, you want me to do something?' Autumn snapped. 'Why didn't you appear when I had your tray ready? I thought something was wrong with you.'

'What? I was asleep?'

'Asleep, my ass. Didn't you see me getting choked out here for trying to help you? Don't act like you didn't hear it. He nearly broke my fucking neck.'

'You have to do something,' India repeated, completely ignoring Autumn's words. Not a single one of them cared that one of their sisters was out there running for her life. Not one of them could see past her own swollen belly. 'Once they get her, they're gonna put us in the cages.'

'Or the boxes,' Janet added. 'The boxes are worse.'

'Please, Mel, you're the only one that can do something,' India whined, her puffy face filling the rectangle through which the food was passed.

'What do you want me to do, huh?'

'Anything!' Tulip screeched. 'Go talk to Joseph, go talk to what's-his-name... the new guy, Abraham. Straighten it out.'

'Yeah, try and straighten it out,' India added.

Would any of them do the same if the tables were turned? No, of course they wouldn't, but just then they were wild with fear, a bunch of cows in their pens waiting to be slaughtered. Autumn had to remember that she was dealing with heavily pregnant girls here, the oldest of the bunch only sixteen. They were scared out of their wits, and half mad with boredom and sensory deprivation as a result of being locked up for so long. At least in the dorm the girls got to stretch their legs, do their chores, sometimes even stroll on the grass.

'If it's Wendy, they'll catch her,' Autumn pointed out. 'There's nothing anyone can do now.'

'Maybe there's nothing anyone can do for *her* dumb ass, but you might still be able to help *us*,' India said. 'I don't just mean us here in the cells, I mean *all* of us.'

Autumn shook her head, disgusted. Her longevity was her curse here at the house and she bore that cross every time there was a crisis. Throughout the basement punishment the whispers had scuttled to her in the dark like blind mice looking for morsels. *Can't you get us out of this, Mel? What are they going to do with us, Mel? What should we say next time they come down here, Mel?*

She stomped off down the corridor and entered the stairwell. Behind her, someone wished her good luck; sounded like Janet. She could hear the tramping of guards running through the various floors as they filed out of the house and into the grounds. Maybe it would be better if she just waited in the stairwell for things to calm down a bit. If she got in the middle of the traffic, she was more than likely going to get knocked on her ass, or maybe one of them would open fire on her thinking she was Wendy.

And then it occurred to her, an idea that struck her mind like a flash of lightning and illuminated tunnels of thought that had long since darkened. With the commotion that Lena's exit had caused, she was willing to bet that Joseph would send every single one of the guards out after Wendy so as not to have a repeat of the embarrassment. Wendy was very attractive and had wide hips, which made her a valuable asset, but that wasn't the only reason why they couldn't afford to lose her. The primary concern was that Lena's departure had made the others brazen, inspired them to act upon lunatic fantasies of escape. When they caught Wendy – and they would catch her – an example would need to be made; the preggos in the cells were right about that. Perhaps they would put her in a cage and set her alight in front of the rest of the girls to extinguish any ideas they had of getting itchy feet. Or maybe they would cut her tongue out or hack off her ears and make her live out the rest of her miserable life like that. They'd done it before.

Right now, though, none of that mattered. The one thing that did matter was that for the first time in perhaps ever, Autumn had the perfect distraction for her own escape.

She leaned over the banister and peered down the stairwell. She could see the guards rushing out, their radio correspondence echoing off the concrete walls. So far as she'd seen, they were all going north-east through the trees, but she would be stupid to trust that alone. There was a strong chance that they had a lead on Wendy and were organising a campaign to stalk her down, but they could just as easily be running blind.

If Autumn was going to do anything, she would have to slip out of the back through the window in the pantry – a concept she'd cultivated ever since she'd set eyes on the small square aperture as a ten-year-old girl. Nobody would be in the kitchen at this time, and none of the other girls would be out of their irons and wandering the halls. Autumn herself was the only girl on active duty, the only girl in the whole building not being supervised.

She ignored the elevator and instead ran down the stairs, her loose sandals slapping the concrete. When she reached the ground floor, she hesitated, expecting a guard or another member of staff to come crashing through the door. The deer-in-the-headlights routine only lasted a couple of seconds, though, and she went through the door as casually as she could. If she got sprung in the hallway, then she would proclaim that she'd been on dinner duty and was returning because she wasn't sure what was going on. It was a weak excuse, one that she hoped she wouldn't have to use.

She came to the brightly lit reception of the house, where she was visible from all angles through the wall-to-wall windows. She tiptoed to a pillar and put her back against it, her heart punching out of her chest. Just up ahead was the kitchen, but she would need to dart out and expose herself to the full view of the house to reach it. She looked through the window and saw a four-by-four heading into the woods beyond the grounds with a massive spotlight beaming from its roof. *How far out is she?* she wondered. *When could she have possibly made her move? Was she on cooking duty? How much of a head start did she have?* It didn't matter, not now anyway. Either they would catch Wendy or they wouldn't, and neither scenario had any significance for Autumn's plan.

She dashed through to the kitchen, expecting one of the guards to still be there stuffing his face, but she was greeted only by her own distorted reflection in the hanging pots and pans. When she got to the pantry, she heard voices in the foyer where she had been just seconds before. She froze, rooted to the spot, her sanity threatening to unravel under the weight of her fear. She swallowed, listened as the voices grew fainter and fainter still, then looked up at the square pantry window.

She grabbed the largest knife from the block on the counter. The shelving unit in front of the window housed cans of beans, powdered milk, soup and sardines. She used the shelves like a ladder, hoping that the wood was fastened firmly to the wall so that she wouldn't collapse in an avalanche of cans. When she was high enough, she reached out and began to use the knife to unscrew the clasp on the small window. It was rusty but not immovable. She pushed the window with her palm. It didn't budge. God alone knew when it had last been opened. Years ago? Decades, possibly. She grunted and pressed all her weight on it, almost toppling from her perch on the shelves. There was a screech as the wooden frame scraped free of its fixture and a cold blast of air blew into her face.

She wasted no time revelling in her victory, but instead began the awkward process of wriggling out of the window. The space was just wide enough to accommodate her head and shoulders, but it was a tight, almost impossible squeeze. She angled her head and one arm out, then placed her hands on the damp brick wall either side of her and pushed against it. It was as though she was fighting her way out of the house's birth canal, seizing her opportunity to be reborn.

There was no easy way to make the fall onto the grass below, so she simply extended her forearms and hoped that they would take most of the impact. They didn't. She rolled forward and slammed down onto her back, winding herself. She lay there a moment unable to breathe, clutching the knife against her chest with both hands, gasping as though she'd just saved herself from drowning. There was no time to lose, though. Before she'd even got her breath back fully, she groped around in the darkness for her misplaced sandal, slipped it back on, and ran for the fence in front of her, sprinting across the grass, arms and legs pumping. Behind her she could hear an orchestra of chaos: guards yelling, the faint rumble of Jeep engines, baying from the German shepherds. It sounded far away, in the opposite direction, but she didn't once slow down or peek around to check.

The stretch of land that led to the fence was perhaps two hundred metres wide, and she ran every step as though the dogs were at her heels, slavering for her flesh. There was one place along the barrier where the ground dipped down into a furrow. It was inconspicuous enough to go unnoticed by casual observers, but Autumn had lived in the house for years, had earned the trust of the guards and the staff and was allowed from time to time to roam the ground freely. She knew all the weaknesses of the place, the nooks and crannies that provided hiding places if you were small enough.

When she reached the spot, she dropped onto her stomach and snaked her way under, the mud working as a lubricant. Once she was on the other side, she stumbled in among the trees, holding her arms across her face to protect it from brambles and branches.

It wasn't until she was deep in the forest, her lungs burning, that she relented and finally turned. She could see pinpricks of light in the distance, but she could no longer hear anything other than the sound of rain pattering against the trees, and the angry wind. Then, very abruptly, there was another sound. Laughter. It took her a second to realise that it was her own.

She was free.

19

The road before her was a black void, endless and unchanging, like a snippet of footage stuck on a loop. Francine was going to crash the car, she felt that quite strongly, and yet she would rather total the vehicle than stop.

The excitement of the break-in and kidnap and the bittersweet thrill of progress had long since ebbed, as had the effect of the Triple Xplosions, and now exhaustion was stalking her vehemently, coming to collect. In her haste to catch Glenn Schilling unawares, she'd depleted everything she had. Her bones were leaden and clicked at the joints. Her back was a tapestry of pain from the stress of sitting and sleeping in the cramped confines of the car for so long.

She clicked on the radio, hoping that the noise would keep her stimulated and stop her from falling asleep. Along with the monotonous squeal of the windscreen wipers it helped fill the silence but did little for her eyelids, which continued to slide closed. Her head dipped a couple of times and the car veered, but she managed to snap awake and right it before they left the road.

If Cindy realised how close they'd come to an accident, she did well not to show it. Or perhaps she was waiting for an accident, *hoping* for it. She didn't blink, didn't shift her weight in the seat to get comfortable; didn't cough. The only thing she did do was wipe her mouth when she began to dribble. Now that the other woman was coming down, Francine thought she would likely see a very different side to her. But that was good. She wanted Cindy itchy and unbalanced; she would be easier to manipulate that way.

Francine opened the window to allow the cold breeze in. Rain flecked the side of her face. She was running low on fuel and was on the verge of total burnout. Little Peace was still over a hundred and fifty miles away according to the highway signs, so she got off at the next exit in a place called Green Grove, and drove until she found a string of motels.

'This isn't Little Peace,' Cindy said, squinting through the rain-blurred windscreen.

'We're stopping for the night.'

'Oh.'

Francine pulled up in the gravel courtyard and shut the engine off. 'Cindy, look at me. Cindy?'

Cindy turned her head, her mouth agape. It was as though she'd just woken from a deep slumber and her senses hadn't quite returned.

'We're going to walk into that office and get a room for the two of us, and you are going to keep your mouth shut. If I have even the slightest suspicion that you're trying to make eyes at the clerk or do anything to jeopardise me, I'll start shooting. Do you believe me?'

'I'm not… I'm not gonna.'

'You're not gonna what?'

'I'm not gonna do nothing bad, I promise.'

'You better not, Cindy, I swear to God you better not, because up to now I think I've been pretty fair with you.

178

And I'll continue to be fair if you stay straight. So that means when I get this room you don't try any funny stuff. Do we have a deal?'

'Yeah.'

'Good. Come on then.'

Francine gathered her backpack, which now contained several bottles of pills, and stepped out of the car. Cindy was slow in following, buckling against the door as she exited the vehicle. Francine strolled around and grabbed her by the arm.

'What's the matter with you?' she whispered as she propped the woman up and dragged her across the gravel.

'Tired,' Cindy said.

'Well you're going to be sleeping soon, so just come on.'

A bell tinkled as they entered the empty reception of the motel. The smell of alcohol and cigarette smoke clung to the scuffed eggshell-coloured walls. A moment later, a woman appeared wrapped in a moth-eaten woollen cardigan, seemingly irritated at their arrival.

'Need a room for the night,' Francine said, wasting no energy on pleasantries.

'How many?' the woman asked, producing a clipboard with a form.

'One room, one night,' Francine replied.

'Fill this in. It'll be $34.50 for the night plus tax.'

Francine moved Cindy to a faux-leather chair and plonked her down, then returned to the desk and began scribbling through the form.

'What's wrong with her?' the woman asked.

'Too much to drink.' Francine slid the clipboard back before producing her purse from her backpack. 'Take a card?'

'Sure.' The woman reached under the desk, keeping her eyes on Cindy as she brought out the card machine.

Francine made the transaction and the woman handed her a key from the corkboard. 'Number sixteen. Checkout's at eleven, breakfast served from seven thirty until ten. You need a Wi-Fi code?'

'No.' Francine walked over to Cindy, who was slumped in the chair with her eyes closed. 'Come on, up we get.' She grabbed her by the armpits and hoisted her to her feet, then slung an arm around her waist and helped her out of the reception.

Once they were in their room, she clicked the light on, locked the door behind them and guided Cindy over to the bed. Even at a glance in the dingy light, she could tell it was broken in the middle. When Cindy shifted on the mattress, the springs whined. That was good. Francine would be able to hear every movement if Cindy had the bright idea of getting up in the night. The woman's eyes were already closed and her head was sunk deep into the tatty pillows.

'Hey, wake up.' Francine slapped her cheek lightly until her eyes fluttered open. 'One more briefing before you go to sleep.'

'What is it?' Cindy croaked.

'I've locked the door and I have the key on me, so don't bother trying it. I've got your pills too, and I'll be more than happy to prescribe them to you tomorrow when we set off.'

'I'm not gonna do anything,' Cindy whispered. 'I'm here to help you.'

'Good.' Francine thought about turning the light off, but decided against it. She wanted to be able to see at all times. Her body felt heavy as an anvil, but she needed to shower. Taking the backpack with her, she went into the bathroom, leaving the door wide open. She peeled off her stinking clothes and stepped into the tub, her legs trembling as the water hit her. Looking down at her body, she saw ribs protruding. She was in bad shape.

She thought about everything that had transpired over the course of the evening and wondered what Glenn Schilling was doing at this moment. Would he be worried that Cindy was gone? By now he would most likely have checked with George the gate man and discovered the ploy to get him away from the house. He would probably be frantic with worry. Would he go to his thinking room and notice the missing discs? Would he check the security camera footage and notice it had all been wiped? These thoughts brought some semblance of satisfaction. She wanted Schilling confused and enjoyed the idea of him being antsy. Hopefully he would lose plenty of sleep.

She turned the shower off. She could have quite easily spent another hour under the hot water, washing the tension away, but she had to sleep, if only for a little while. She dried herself with the scratchy towel on the rail, then rooted through her backpack for sweatpants and a T-shirt. Once she was dressed, she lay down on the bed next to Cindy.

Now that she was finally in a position to get some sleep, she couldn't seem to stop her mind from whirring. She thought about the journey ahead tomorrow, another long drive before the real work began. Everything had gone her way thus far, and it was only as she replayed the events in her head that she realised how remarkable her luck had been. It had almost been too easy. That thought worried her. Tomorrow she would try and lure Schilling to Little Peace, assuming he wasn't already on his way there now. What if he didn't play ball? What if he called her bluff? She had no plan B if things didn't go well tomorrow, because in truth, she didn't even have a plan A. All she had was a loose set of ideas and best-case scenarios.

She reached into the backpack and found Lena's Polaroid. She spent a long time staring at it before she finally fell asleep.

20

Joseph Eames stood on the lawn with his radio in his sweaty palm, puffing on his ninth cigarette of the evening. He was sucking them down to the filter and his throat was beginning to feel scratchy. It was a cold night but he was hot inside his suit, his armpits and balls slippery with sweat. It had been over two hours now since the alert went out.

Wendy had been mucking out the pigs under the supervision of one of the guards when she'd apparently twisted her ankle in the mud. Lilli, the other girl on slop duty with her, had gasped and trembled violently against the neck ring as she'd told them what had happened. 'The guard told her to get up and she said she couldn't. She said she'd heard her ankle snap and she needed help. Then when he came over she stabbed him in the neck.' She'd expelled her answers in quick bursts, her eyes wild with fear.

'Stabbed him with what?' Joseph had asked as he paced up and down the basement. The girls shouldn't have been out there still doing chores at that time of night, but with the change in security it had taken a little while for them to get into the rhythm of things.

'I think it was a knife, sir.'

'What do you mean, you *think* it was a knife?'

'I didn't really see, sir,' she'd said, easing her fingers into the collar to relieve the pressure on her neck. 'He told me to carry on with my work, so I went over and poured the slop, sir. I just heard a sound, and when I turned around I saw Wendy running away and the guard on the floor.'

In all the years that Joseph had managed the house, very few girls had tried to escape and none of them had ever attempted violence. Now in the space of a month they'd had their first runaway and their first attack on a guard. He knew that he couldn't be blamed for Leslie's untimely heart attack, but there was a very real feeling that the man should have been released from his duties a long time ago. He had been at the house longer than even Joseph had, and he'd known how to handle the girls, but he'd let himself go in recent years. The problem was that finding suitable candidates for the job took a very long time. There were background checks that needed to be made, and everything had to be cleared with the higher-ups. It was easier to let things go on as they had done; if it ain't broke, don't fix it.

Now things were beyond broken. Lena, who was too ugly to serve at the parties but who had remained at the house because she had become something of a fixture, had somehow got the smarts to run. This surprised Joseph for two reasons. Firstly, he hadn't thought any of the girls would attempt to cross Daddy. And secondly, he'd doubted Lena had a coherent thought in her head. She was a slobbering idiot and madder than a March hare, but she *was* good around the house. She never complained, never seemed to get tired, and she helped break the new girls in when they arrived.

Despite the fact that they hadn't managed to pick her up in the woods, Joseph didn't believe for a second that Lena had found her way to the road. An experienced hiker would have trouble traversing the vast expanse of forest. No, in all likelihood she had curled up somewhere and died of exposure.

Regardless of how far she'd made it, the result was the same. The other girls knew that she was gone, and it sparked something inside them. *Or maybe this was all planned.* The rogue thought drifted through his head. *Maybe Lena wasn't as fucking silly as she made herself out to be. Maybe she had enough smarts to pull the wool over all our eyes. Christ, how could he not have foreseen this?*

He'd thought that the crop of new guards, who'd been given instructions to be firm with the girls and keep an eye on them at all times, would make a world of difference. But now look. They'd already let their defences down and one of the guards was dead. Less than a fortnight on duty and that fucking little bitch Wendy had cut his throat. The man had been a war veteran, with two tours in Afghanistan; he had survived a hail of bullets, bombs and missiles only to have his life cut short by a sixteen-year-old girl. It was lunacy, it was unthinkable and it was... scary. The girls were starting to turn, slowly but surely, and this spelled danger for the house.

Joseph saw a Jeep returning with its spotlight turned off. He took one final drag on the cigarette and then flicked the butt into the grass. The Jeep slowed as it reached the edge of the lawn and he walked to the passenger door. 'What's the latest?'

The guard held up a finger, indicating for Joseph to hold on as he listened to his muffled radio. When it silenced, he said, 'They got her.'

'Positive?' Joseph asked.

'It seems so.'

'I don't need "seems so", I need yes or no.'

The guard frowned, and Joseph noticed the web of thin scars running down his chin. 'Yes, they got her.'

'Then where is she?'

'Charley's bringing her in.'

'Alive?'

'I don't know,' the guard shrugged.

'Do you think I'm asking you these questions for my health?' Joseph smacked his own radio against the Jeep door. It had been no good to him; he hadn't been able to decipher a damn word through the blasts of static. 'Find out!'

The guard spoke without averting his eyes from Joseph. 'Charley? Is the girl alive? Over.'

There was a pause before the radio returned an answer. 'She's breathing. Dog locked onto her leg so it's chewed to hamburger meat, but she'll live.'

Joseph snatched the radio out of the scarred guard's hand. 'Get her into the basement. Have her leg dressed so she doesn't bleed out. Can you do that for me, Charley? Over.'

'Affirmative,' Charley replied, and the radio went dead.

Joseph exhaled. The nervous energy had been bubbling for so long, but now the pan was off the stove. He wasn't ready to laugh just yet, but the relief he felt at that particular moment was almost orgasmic. He ran his palm down his face and then wiped his nose on the back of his hand.

'Tell the others that I want all the cars off the lawn and the dogs back in the pens. Let's wind this clusterfuck up as fast as we can.'

He turned and jogged up the steps and into the house. Joseph had been in love with this house from the very first moment he had set foot inside it. He adored the spaciousness, the unashamedly old-fashioned decor that made you feel as though you were stuck in some earlier period of time. When he'd discovered that Daddy – Mr Wydebird – had originally intended the house to be an addition to his Wydebird Lodge hotel chain back in the fifties, his love for the building swelled even more. He was enchanted by the idea that it was part of a hidden history, and proud to serve in a place that very few people had seen. Yet he did not feel that way now as he strode through the reception. The air was still and the silence was cloying. The heels of his shoes clicked as he walked. He entered the elevator and pressed the button for the fourth floor before assessing his appearance in the mirrors. His hair, usually gelled into a neat comb-over with a perfect parting, was tousled and wild. He smoothed it down as best he could, and straightened his red tie. His cheeks were blotchy from the cold and his forehead shone with sweat.

The elevator doors opened and he made the walk to Mr Wydebird's chambers, rapping lightly on the door. He heard heavy, thudding footsteps from inside before Horace answered.

Horace looked one generation removed from Neanderthal man, with a big flat face and a brow so heavy it was difficult to see his eyes. He was not a talkative man, nor had his duties ever required him to be, but his brutish facial expression told Joseph everything he needed to know: *You better have good news.*

Joseph bypassed Horace and strode over to the bed, where Mr Wydebird was propped up on a stack of pillows. The old man looked frail and sickly, with his cheesy skin and his cotton pyjamas and the stink of oils and antibiotics wafting from him. But deep in his bony, furrowed face, his misty eyes glinted with cruel intelligence. He didn't open his mouth, which was curled inward without his dentures, nor did he react as Joseph gently took his hand and kissed it.

'Sir, today has been full of surprises. I wish I could say that they have all been pleasant, but I would be lying. We've had a few scares, but I am delighted to tell you that everything is fine now. It's all back on track. We've apprehended the girl and she is being linked up in the basement as we speak, awaiting your judgement.'

Mr Wydebird's mouth moved as though he were gumming a hard-boiled candy, and his gaze was fixed on the window. 'You're sure everything is all right?' he asked.

'Yes, absolutely, one hundred per cent.' Joseph laughed airily.

'You're a liar,' Mr Wydebird croaked, turning his head slowly like a piece of rusted machinery. 'We are *not* all right.'

'I apologise,' Joseph said, looking at the floor. 'I think perhaps I misunderstood the context of your question.'

'We are far from all right, Joseph. So we have the girl back – that's all very dandy, isn't it? But it doesn't make things all right. Not by a *long shot.*' The old man jerked forward from the pillows, spittle flying from his gums. At the other end of the chamber, Horace began to approach but was waved away. 'Answer me this, Joseph. Is Hendricks all right?'

'Hendricks? I'm, uh… I'm not…'

'You don't know who he is, do you?' Mr Wydebird smacked his thin lips. 'He's the young man whose throat the girl slashed. You hired the fucking man, Joseph, surely you remember his bloody name!'

'Yes, of course I do,' Joseph said, closing his eyes in concentration as he located the ex-soldier's details in his memory. 'Benson Hendricks, inducted through the Chicago branch of the Group, served four years as—'

'I don't need his biography, you stupid boy. He's dead. That is the only detail that matters at this very minute.' Mr Wydebird coughed into his fist, but the coughs evolved into splutters and he was soon fighting for breath. This time he did not shoo Horace away as the man clomped over with a handkerchief to collect the almost neon-yellow phlegm from his master's lips. Horace reached for a sippy cup from beside the bed. Mr Wydebird turned his head away petulantly, but Horace persisted until the straw found its home and the old man took a few sips. Satisfied, he folded the phlegm-filled handkerchief and backed away.

'The man died,' Mr Wydebird said, stabbing his index finger down onto the mattress beside him to punctuate his point. 'The man died and the girl got away. So you've provided the house with not one, but *two* problems. The first was locating the stupid child, and the second is burying this incompetent that you hired. What do you have to say for yourself?'

Joseph shook his head. 'I can't say anything that will make it any better, except that we have the girl back now.'

'Girl. You haven't even told me which one it was that tried to run.'

'Um… Wendy.'

'Are you asking me or telling me?'

'It was Wendy. Definitely Wendy.'

Mr Wydebird chewed this over, his dull eyes rolling slowly in their sockets. 'Very good-looking child. It's a shame she wasn't watched more closely. Perhaps if you had been doing your job correctly in the first…' he stopped, coughed, and sighed, 'the first place, then you would have spotted the signs a lot sooner.'

The room was stifling. They kept it hot because Mr Wydebird didn't like to be cold and couldn't afford to catch a chill. The heat amplified the synthetic smells and made Joseph feel as though someone were blowing a hairdryer on him from a foot away.

'With all due respect, sir,' he began, his neck itching as sweat dripped off the back of his head, 'her actions weren't planned. This all stems back to Lena. The girls have become bold, arrogant almost. I checked the rota, and today was the first day since Lena's disappearance that Wendy has had chores outside. She acted on impulse and she didn't get very far. I think it was actually a very rewarding exercise for the new guards.'

'You think she acted on impulse, do you?' Mr Wydebird asked.

'Yes. Truly I do.'

'Then perhaps I should have Horace crack your head open to see what's going on in there. I am starting to think that the guards are not the only things that need to be upgraded around here.'

Joseph opened his mouth to speak but could only produce a weak whistling sound from deep in his throat. His mouth clicked shut. He tried again. 'I'm sorry, Mr Wydebird. I've been here for a long time but I don't have your wisdom. There are very few that do. I can absolutely assure you, though, that I am watching these girls like a hawk. The guards I've hired are all trained professionals, all specially recruited through the Group. They—'

'Oh do shut up, boy.' Mr Wydebird turned his face away and made a wet sound of disgust. 'You truly make me sick to my stomach, do you know that, Joseph? You are supposed to be the manager here, but I don't think you could manage to piss into the ocean and hit water, let alone run a thriving branch of this organisation. Your complete disregard for discretion is dangerous for all of us. First Leslie, and now this. If you were me, what would you do?'

Sweat stung Joseph's eyes. His stomach began to cramp. 'Mr Wydebird, please…'

'Mr Wydebird, please,' mocked the old man, his reedy voice quavering hideously. 'I'm thinking that maybe it isn't the girls who are the cause of all this grief. You are supposed to lead by example. What exactly is it that you have taught them?'

'I don't know,' Joseph whimpered, tears mingling with the sweat.

'I think tonight we should bury two bodies, poor young Hendricks and "I Don't Know" Joseph. How about that?'

Joseph clasped his hands together and bowed his head. 'Mr Wydebird, you don't need to do this. I can look after the house. I will rectify the problem. This will never, *ever* happen again.'

Mr Wydebird's hand slithered over and seized Joseph's wrist. 'It had better not.' His mouth turned down in a horseshoe grimace, his hooded eyelids rising ever so slightly. 'Because if there is one more problem, Joseph, you will know suffering like no man has ever known it before. Is that clear?'

'Yes, sir,' Joseph said, wiping his nose in the crook of his arm. He got to his feet and cleared his eyes with the heel of his hand. 'What will you have me do with Wendy?'

'Why don't you tell me what you think should be done?'

'I think we should burn her in front of the rest of the girls. We should show them that this won't be tolerated. We should—'

'Full of cruel ideas, aren't you, Joseph?' Mr Wydebird's cheeks puffed out as he coughed. 'You know exactly what to do to punish a child, but not how to prevent that child from misbehaving in the first place. How would you like me to have *you* burned? Perhaps you should consider your answer before you speak, because it was a very real question.'

'I don't want to displease you any more than I already have, sir. Please.'

'Then get out of my fucking sight. I'll send Horace down to the girl when I'm good and ready, but in the meantime, remember this, you are on very thin ice. Now go.'

Joseph nodded. He thought about thanking Mr Wydebird for sparing his life, but decided that the best thing to do would be to leave as quickly as possible. He felt like he was in a sauna and wanted desperately to be away from the room, away from the old man and Horace and those chemical smells. He rushed out, closing the door firmly behind him.

He stopped off at the bathroom on the third floor and soaked his face with cold water before snatching a wad of paper towels from the dispenser. The liquid feeling he'd had in his guts had now set to concrete and he didn't think he'd be able to empty his bowels even if he wanted to. He stood there for a while, holding on to the sink and shaking all over, on the verge of hyperventilation. He thought for a second that he might spin out and collapse in a heap, but his heartbeat eventually steadied to something like normal.

He left the bathroom and took the stairs down to the ground floor, not wanting to be locked within the confines of the elevator. The key thing, he told himself, was that he was still alive and the girl was back where she should be. Surely, if anything, tonight's little episode showed just how resilient he really was: a problem arose, he addressed it and then found a way to solve it.

When he got to the foyer, he went to the cabinet on the far side by the staircase and fixed himself a large measure of Scotch. Sipping the drink, he paced the length of the reception, staring out at the field, rolling the glass across his forehead. The floodlights were still on, but the only reminder of the evening's excursion was the deep gouges in the grass that the Jeeps' tyres had made. He slid the door open, stepped into the cool night air and set off around the outside of the house. Lights were on in the guards' quarters up ahead, and a few of the men were milling around outside, smoking. Joseph could see the disdain on their faces as he approached; the bitter resentment in their body language triggered by the murder of one of their colleagues. He sought out Abraham.

'Has anyone done a head count on the girls?' he asked.

'Not that I know.'

'Why not?'

'Because we weren't told to.'

'You're the head guard, Abraham. I expect you to be a bit more vigilant than this.'

'I follow orders. Our priority was to apprehend Wendy.'

'Yes, but some initiative wouldn't go amiss, for Christ's sake.'

'When Hendricks got cut, I rounded all the girls up and locked them in the dorm.'

'All of them? So you *did* do a head count?'

Abraham didn't speak for a moment. 'I didn't do a head count but I'm sure it was all of them. They were all in the canteen, eating.'

No, not all of them, Joseph thought. His heart stuttered in his chest and a jolt of pure, white-hot panic surged through him.

'You want me to go up and count 'em now?'

'No.' Joseph shook his head, his lips numb as he spoke. 'I'll… I'll do it.'

He turned and raced into the house, running up to the first floor and rattling through his keys until he found the one that would open the girls' dorm. The lights were all on and the girls were lying in their beds… except for two very obvious omissions.

The bunk bed that Wendy shared with Autumn was empty.

Part Three

21

She's out there somewhere, Francine thought as she exited the car, staring at the sprawl of forest on the sloping hills below. Through the dense expanse of trees, she could just about make out a sliver of ocean, could already taste the salt on her lips. She took a big lungful of air and regarded the scary ash-grey clouds. *I'm close now, I can feel it.* She was standing on the precipice of a winding road that spiralled down to sea level. She wondered how many cars had gone careening over the edge and been ripped apart by the jagged rocks. It wouldn't take much: a mistimed turn, a bit too much speed.

She'd stopped to get a good look at the area. The vastness of the forest was to be feared and respected. The weight of the situation suddenly dawned on her. Autumn was somewhere in there. Perhaps Francine would enter the forest and vanish from existence too. After all, nobody knew where she was. Work would find a replacement; Will would sell another book.

'You'll die, you know,' Cindy said from inside the car, as though she'd been screening Francine's thoughts.

'What's that?' Francine asked, getting back inside the vehicle.

'You'll die,' Cindy sneered. 'What did you think was going to happen? You thought you were going to go storming in there with your little gun and demand to see your daughter? They'll laugh at you. Then they'll take turns raping you. Then they'll *really* torture you.'

Francine started the engine and continued her slow descent down the winding road. 'You've perked up.'

'I just want you to know what you're going up against. There's still time to back out of this thing.'

'Why would I want to do that?'

'Because you can't win.'

Francine laughed gently. 'You might be right. But I guess we'll have to see, won't we?'

She came to the residential part of town and cruised along until she located a string of stores peppering one side of the junction. She parked up in front of the mini-mart, turned the ignition off and removed the keys.

'I'm going to be less than one minute inside there. You won't make any fuss, will you?'

'How could I?'

Oh you could if you wanted to. And I think you might just try it when you get a window of opportunity, but this isn't it, honey.

Francine got out and locked Cindy in the car, taking the backpack with her. She didn't want Cindy self-medicating without her permission.

Country music greeted her as she entered the mart. She looked over at the old woman behind the counter, but she didn't seem particularly curious about her new customer. Francine threaded the aisles, finally stopping at the section that stocked home supplies. She was looking for duct tape, but then spotted a packet of plastic cable ties. Perfect. She grabbed microwave waffles and some croissants, then approached the counter.

'Howdy,' the old woman said, as she began tapping prices into the till.

'Hello,' Francine replied, fingering through the trinkets on the impulse-buy rack to the left of the counter. There were Little Peace magnets, postcards and even bottle openers, all of which cost a buck apiece. There was also a road map, the front of which read: *ROUND THESE PARTS, YOU CAN ALWAYS FIND A LITTLE PEACE (population 6,000)*. She added the map to the items, paid and left.

When she returned to the car, she caught Cindy staring sulkily through the fogged window. She got in, chucked all her stuff on the back seat and started the engine.

'Direct me to Glenn's place.'

'I'm feeling low,' Cindy said, resting her head against the window. 'Can I take one of my tablets? Please?'

'You can take whatever you want when we get to the house.'

'You said I could have something when we set off.'

'I don't think I did.'

'Look, I just need something to even me out. I feel like shit.'

'Direct me to Glenn's house quickly then.'

'Oh for fuck's sake! Have you got to be such a fucking bitch *all* the time? I thought you wanted me to help you find your daughter! I'm going to be no fucking good if you have me all strung out and tense, am I?'

'Glenn's house.'

'Maybe I can't think straight.' Cindy folded her arms across her fake boobs. 'Maybe I won't say another word until I'm allowed some medicine. My fucking head is *killing* me.'

Francine sighed. 'I know it's on the seafront. I'm quite sure I'll find it either way. The only difference is how quickly I get there.'

Cindy screeched and slapped the dashboard.

–

Glenn Schilling's property in Little Peace was far more modest than his Oakridge mansion. It was a one-storey building that sat on a cliff overlooking the crashing waves. There were no other houses around, only trees and rocks. Francine stood at the window imagining what the sunset would look like on the horizon, the red-orange sky reflecting in the water.

Behind her, Cindy scuttled over to the wine rack and selected a bottle without prejudice. She grabbed a glass and said to Francine, 'Do you want one?'

Francine checked her wristwatch. It was ten to eleven in the morning. 'What day is it today?'

'Huh?' Cindy screwed her face up.

'I don't know what day it is.'

'Me neither.'

Francine thought about it, remembered that Schilling had been out shooting his show the night before – *Saturday Night Splendour* – and realised it was Sunday.

'No thanks,' she said.

Cindy took the bottle over to the long glass table by the window and began stabbing a corkscrew into the top of it, leaving sprinkles of cork all over the table. Eventually, Francine snatched it out of her hands and took over. She pulled the cork out with a pop; the dark, fruity scent of the wine making her nostrils flare and her mouth flood with saliva. She handed the bottle back to Cindy before she could get too attached.

'Thanks,' Cindy muttered.

'No problem.' Francine pulled up a chair opposite the other woman and looked out of the window at the ocean.

Cindy sucked from the bottle greedily, panting each time she removed her lips. When she was good and ready – and she'd made a sizeable dent in the bottle – she put it down, wiped her mouth and said, 'You don't have a plan, do you?'

'I've got a couple of ideas,' Francine replied without looking away from the view.

'You haven't thought this through. You're going off emotion. It's no good. Common sense should tell you that much.'

Francine leaned across the table and confiscated the wine. 'Then you'd better help me think something up. Because I'm not going to let things go sour on me before I let them go sour on you first. You can count on that, Cindy. Right now, every word that comes out of your mouth should be something to help me find my daughter, because you are literally talking to save your life.'

'You won't kill me. You don't have it in you. I can see that with just one look at you. You're upset, and maybe you deserve to be, but you don't have to throw your life away over this. You've already committed a serious crime and could face a long time in prison, and I really don't want to see that happen to you. I—'

Francine stood up, grabbed the mini-mart bag and removed the cable ties.

'What are you gonna do with those?'

'I'm going to bind your wrists behind your back.'

Cindy looked over at the door, then back at Francine. Francine shook her head.

'You don't have to do that. I'll tell you anything you need to know.'

'I'm not so sure,' Francine said, biting open the packet and walking around behind Cindy's chair. Cindy tried to rise and Francine shoved her back down. 'No, Cindy. You're not going anywhere. So be good and put your hands behind your back.'

'I said you don't have to do that!'

She slapped Cindy as hard as she could on the side of the head, the palm of her hand catching the woman's ear. Cindy's head cracked to the side, the blow almost knocking her off the chair. She screamed and tried to wriggle loose, but Francine was in control, one hand clamped on the back of her neck, holding her in place. She dug her nails into the skin on Cindy's neck until she could feel the knobbly bones of her spine between her fingers.

'Give me your hands!' she demanded. When Cindy refused, Francine hit her again, and again, smacking her across the head with her open palm. 'Don't make me give you something to cry about, Cindy. Give me your fucking hands!'

Snivelling, Cindy submitted and placed her hands behind the chair. Francine bound them using three cable ties – one around each wrist, with another one connecting the two like handcuffs.

'Here is what I understand so far,' she began, but her words were lost beneath the sound of Cindy's sobs. She clapped her hands together, spooking Cindy further. 'Concentrate, Cindy! Look at me. Here is what I understand so far. There is a group of people who kidnap children and take them to a house in the woods that they call the 'big house'. There they use them for sex. They pimp them out and have orgies with men like your husband. Tell me more.'

'I don't know any more,' Cindy said, her mouth moving like a fish out of water, searching for something that might satisfy Francine. 'That's it. That's the top and the bottom of it.'

'Tell me more.'

'It's got nothing to do with me. It's him! It's Glenn. It's his people. I'm nothing. He only married me to keep me on his arm for publicity. A man as famous as him, he can't be without a wife, can he? Everyone would think he's a fag!'

'I think if I were to watch those DVDs through, I might see you on one of them. Am I right, Cindy?'

Cindy's eyes flicked around the room, looking at everything except Francine. Fresh drops of sweat pushed through the pores in her shiny, smooth forehead. Sweat pooled in the hollow of her throat.

'I'm going to watch those DVDs, Cindy, so I'm going to find out either way.'

'He makes me go. I don't do anything to any of the girls, though, I swear to God. You give me a bible and I'll swear on it with my life. Sometimes I have to do things with the other men, but mostly they're there for the girls… the young ones.'

The muscles on the hinge of Francine's jaw bulged as she clenched her teeth. 'You've gone this far, Cindy. You may as well tell me everything.'

'But I'm telling you, I don't know it all! Honestly! Honest to Christ above.' When she said that, Francine heard a twang in her accent, like something from down south.

'Tell me more.'

Cindy's chest heaved as she breathed, her purple-stained tongue wagging. 'What are you going to do with me?'

'I don't know yet. If you're helpful, probably nothing.'

'How can I be helpful? Glenn's the one you need to be asking!' A snot bubble expanded in one nostril and popped. 'He's part of it. Ask him; he'll give you the answers.'

'I *will* ask him. But first I'm asking you. How often do these gatherings take place?'

'It's real random. All different times.'

'The house on that DVD I watched. Where was that?'

'I can't remember.' She looked at Francine, and seeing she was growing dissatisfied, amended her answer. 'It's just a safe house. There's a whole bunch of them all over the place. They switch it up a lot of times.'

'How many times have you used this house we're in now?'

Cindy's eyes widened. 'I'm not sure. I don't think he's ever used this place.'

'The girl who told me about Glenn said that a bunch of girls were brought to his place near the ocean. This is the house she meant. So tell me how many times, and when was the last time?'

'I don't know that he used this place. Did he? That dirty fucking bastard, he promised me he wouldn't do it at one of our houses. He…'

Francine removed the gun from her backpack, stood up and walked over to Cindy. She pressed the barrel into the woman's kneecap and saw beads of sweat break away from Cindy's scalp.

'On the count of three, I'm going to pull this trigger unless I get a straight answer out of you. One…'

'I swear he n–never told me he used this place.' Cindy tilted her head back and sobbed grotesquely. With the amount of Botox she'd had, her forehead didn't even crinkle.

'Does Glenn get to call these people up and order the girls like some kind of takeaway service? How does it work?'

'Member…'

'Speak up.'

'He's a gold member. I can't…'

'He pays these people money, yes?'

Cindy nodded.

'So they must have a location near here if he's getting them delivered. There's miles of forest out there. The house is somewhere in the forest, yes?'

'I think… yes.'

Francine felt her heart leap in her chest, almost painfully. 'Is there any way we can get them to deliver my daughter here without involving Glenn?'

Cindy shook her head, her sopping hair sticking to her milky cheeks. 'He knows their number. I don't speak to them directly. Only him.'

Francine stood up and paced the room pensively. It was only a matter of miles now. The only thing that stood between their reunion was a bunch of trees. And what else?

'You've been to the big house? The one in the woods?'

'Yes.'

'What's the layout? How many girls do they keep there and what kind of security do they have?'

Cindy didn't speak for a beat. Then she groaned again and said, 'Lots of girls and lots of guards.'

'How many guards? Come on, roughly, it doesn't have to be an exact number.'

'I don't—'

'Take a fucking guess, Cindy.'

'Fifteen? Twenty. Something like that.'

'Armed?'

'Of course they're fucking armed.' She mewled like a cat. 'They'll kill you… just fucking… kill you…'

'Does Glenn ever call these people up when there isn't a gathering? Let's say he came down here and ordered a specific girl, would they bring her?'

'I don't know. Probably.' Francine removed her phone.

'You better hope they do.'

22

The cell phone's jagged ringtone pierced the silence. Through the steam of his coffee, Glenn watched it vibrate across the countertop. He did not immediately answer, but rather sat there, hands clasped around his cup, waiting for it to become inanimate again. One of the cleaners, Rosa, popped her head into the kitchen.

'Your phone is ringing, Mr Schilling.'

Without looking away from it he replied, 'Yes, I know.'

'Would you like perhaps for me to answer?' she asked, confused as to why he was letting the phone rattle away. Before he could speak, the phone went silent. 'Never mind. I'm sorry to bother you, Mr Schilling.'

'No bother,' he said, still watching the phone. A couple of seconds later, it rang again. This time it managed to shake its way over to the edge of the counter. He thought about letting it fall and smash on the floor. Before it could, he put on his reading glasses and reached out to grab it. Holding the screen a few inches away from his face, he swiped the screen to answer it.

'Glenn? Glenn, can you hear me?'

'I can hear you,' he said slowly.

'Good. What... um...' She coughed. 'What are you doing?'

'I'm having breakfast,' he said drily.

'Oh, right. What are you having?'

'I'm having coffee,' he sighed. She hadn't picked up on the fact that it had gone four in the afternoon. 'I'm not particularly hungry today for some reason. Can you guess why that might be?'

There was a pause. Her breath came through the speaker in a raspy crackle, as though she were holding her handset too close to her mouth. 'Because I left last night?'

He sipped his coffee. 'That could be it.'

'Yeah…' Another pause. Another cough. 'I had to go suddenly.'

'Yes, I noticed. You sent George on a wild goose chase as well. I'm guessing you have some sort of explanation to offer?'

'I do. I'm at the house in Little Peace.'

Glenn carefully placed the cup down on the counter and gripped the phone tighter. 'What are you doing there?'

'I needed to get away.'

'Did you now?'

'Yeah. I just… I got frightened. I took some pills and I got spooked.'

'Spooked?'

'Yeah. I was thinking about—'

'Don't say anything stupid on the phone, Cindy.' The first note of anger crept into his voice.

'Sorry.' She wheezed, coughed, groaned.

'What's the matter with you? You sound like a sick dog.'

'Too much wine last night.'

'Mmm. I noticed you didn't take any of the cars. So who are you with?'

A pause. 'I'm alone.'

'No you're not.'

'I am,' she croaked before clearing her throat. 'I got a cab.'

'A cab for almost two hundred miles?'

'Yeah. So?'

He stroked his chin where the first dots of stubble were starting to sprout. He took a moment before speaking again.

'Shall I tell Juanita to make dinner for you tonight?'

'No, I don't think so.'

'I see. Well, let me know when you're coming home and I'll have one of them make you something. Goodbye, Cindy.'

'Wait… Glenn, wait. You still there?'

'I'm here.'

'I was thinking you could come down here. To the house.'

'Why would I do that?'

'It might be nice. We could go for a hike, walk along the beach…'

Glenn stood up from the stool. 'Am I on speakerphone right now, Cindy?'

A pause. 'Yes.'

'Why am I on speakerphone?'

'I'm not feeling well. I'm lying on the couch. Glenn? You still there?'

Ignoring her, he said, 'Who are you with, Cindy?'

'Nobody,' she replied flatly.

'Hmm. So you mean to tell me that there is nobody in that house with you right now?'

'Yeah.'

'Then I'm going to send George up to come and get you. I want you back here. If you want to walk on a beach, I'll take you to California.'

'No. I really think you should come here. Please don't let me down, honey cake.'

The line went dead at her end. Glenn held the phone for a moment longer, fidgeting with anger and uncertainty, tapping his finger rhythmically on the screen, thinking.

Honey cake. Joseph's wife made it at every gathering and it tasted godawful, but over the years Glenn and Cindy had used the term as their codeword: 'Keep Friday clear in your diary, we're going to get honey cake.' But what did it mean in this context? Were they holding her for some reason? Were they mad at her for something – or more importantly, were they mad at him? If they were, then there was no need to be this cryptic. If they wanted him, they would scoop him right off the stage of his show on live TV if they had to.

He stood up and walked over to the back door that led to the garden as he considered the phone call. It was quite possible that all the strangeness was nothing more than her drug-induced paranoia. God only knew how many irrational episodes of hers he'd had to tolerate. Sometimes she would believe that there were people on the lawn spying on them with binoculars, or that members of the Group were driving by the house with listening devices to pick up on their conversations. Her latest concern was that there were men entering the house at night and creeping around inspecting things, an idea that obviously stemmed from the way the old place creaked and groaned at night.

The fear had been one element of his wife's life that Glenn couldn't fully control. It had grown worse the more she dabbled with those wretched pills, until it had warped her mind completely. When she was awake she was unsure of reality, and when she was passed out she was dead to the world. In all instances she was a liability, but a necessary accessory to his life. It was her simple-mindedness that had caught his attention in the first place and made her a suitable candidate for the role of his wife. Her willingness to detach her feelings and her complete lack of a moral code – accompanied by what had once been a stunningly beautiful face – had made her a worthy asset. But he'd always known the day would come when she would trip him up. When her drug use increased and rendered her housebound, he had thought it would work to his advantage. She was easier to control this way, less opinionated, less prone to show him up in public. The opiates massaged all her stubbornness away until she was nothing more than flesh on a stick.

But now this.

'What to do, what to do, what to do…' Glenn muttered as he watched a crow swoop down to the poolside and dip its beak in the water.

As he saw it, one of three possible things might've happened. The first was that Cindy was telling the truth and had gone overboard with the pills, had a psychotic episode and fled the house. Getting a cab to drive all the way to Little Peace was indeed excessive, but it fitted the scenario. The second possibility was that she'd been summoned to Little Peace by someone from the Group, though Glenn couldn't understand why. If they wanted to hurt her, they would do it here; there was no need to play a game of cat-and-mouse. He knew he was power-less against them, so this whole ambiguous charade didn't quite fit. The only other thing that he could think might have happened was that Cindy was luring him into some kind of trap. Did she have a lover? Was she attempting to overthrow him, maybe set him up to take a fall and make it look like an accident? She wouldn't be that stupid, though, would she? She might just be.

Glenn thought about calling Joseph, had even located his number in the phone book, but finally decided against it. If this was nothing to do with the Group, his call would raise suspicions and then they would surely investigate. They kept tabs on all their members, of course, but this line of action would warrant further scrutiny, and frankly, he didn't need that kind of pressure, not at his age.

He remained calm as he strolled through the house to the studio and punched in the code to unlock the door. That calmness rippled inside him when he noticed that the monitors were all switched off. They were *never* switched off. He turned them back on, logged into the Mac and attempted to locate the footage from the last twenty-four hours. He couldn't. He phoned Steve, the computer guy.

'Hi, Steve, it's Glenn. How are you?'

'Oh hi, Glenn, I'm good, thanks. You?'

'Smashing, smashing. Listen – would you happen to know why the security monitors were all turned off in the studio? I'm assuming you haven't been here in the last week or so?'

'Uh, no, but Cindy called me late last night talking about the cameras, so it might've been her. Did you check with her?'

'No, not yet. What did she call you about?' Glenn attempted to avoid making the question sound accusatory, but was unable to fully dilute the concern in his voice.

'She, um… she asked me how to wipe the cameras. So I talked her through it.'

'Did she say why?'

'No, I don't think she did.'

Glenn nodded. 'All right, that's great.'

'Is everything okay?'

'Everything is dandy, thanks, Steve. Give my best to your wife, won't you?'

'Sure will, Glenn. You need me to come round and fix it all up?'

'No, that won't be necessary, Steve. You have a nice day.'

Glenn ended the call and strode through the house, passing the various cleaning staff tending to their duties. His chest felt like a clenched fist as he picked up the pace, breaking into a jog. He burst through the door of the master bedroom and continued down the glass tunnel until he reached the study. By this time he was wheezing, and his heart was thumping like a temperamental drum.

As he walked over to the bookcase, the ripple of worry became a rough tide. He slid the door aside and ventured up the narrow stairs. Everything looked just the way he'd left it, yet something niggled at him. There was definitely something amiss, he just couldn't place it right away. Was it the smell? No, he didn't think so. Had Cindy been up here and disturbed something? God, just the thought of her coming into his private place made him want to smash her skull to pieces. He bent down and pressed the eject button on the DVD player.

There was no disc inside.

He began to cough involuntarily. His head swam with confusion. It was then that he noticed that his collection of DVDs looked smaller, though he couldn't be sure if he was imagining it. Damn it, he knew he should have taken better care of them. It would hardly have taken an effort to buy cases and organise them in some sort of coherent order.

He went back downstairs and slid the bookcase closed, then called Cindy. She didn't answer. When it went through to voicemail he said, 'I would like you to call me back as soon as humanly possible, please. Thank you.'

He stood there in the study watching the phone in his palm, waiting for it to flash to life. After five minutes or so, he tried again. This time it went straight to voicemail.

He began to laugh. This was by far the most interesting thing she'd ever done in all the years she'd been married to him. It was also the angriest he'd ever been with her, and that too was new. He never really managed to get beyond disinterested annoyance, and now he was *seething*. All he knew for certain at that moment was that if she didn't have a good explanation for this foolery, he would kill her.

23

The distant sound of voices roused her. Autumn peered out from her hiding place beneath the knot of tree roots. The space was just large enough to keep her concealed from view and had sheltered her from the rain during the night. She hadn't expected to sleep. She had run through the forest aimlessly, tripping and sliding on wet bark, scraping her skin on foliage, stubbing her toes on mossy rocks, and had almost broken her ankle half a dozen times. It was only when her body began to rebel and each exhalation felt like her lungs would burst that she slowed to a walk. She was limping through the darkness, feeling her way blindly with only the full moon to offer light. In the pale glow, she spotted the bolthole, wandered over and crawled inside. Her body began to recognise the cold again, and she shivered, rubbing her arms for warmth. She scooped leaves over herself to form some damp insulation, which kept the chill at bay until sleep took her.

She wasn't sure how long she'd been out for. She lay there rigid, eyes peeled. She knew the search party couldn't have brought the Jeeps this deep into the forest. One thing she had remembered to do was deviate from the natural path that led to the main road, choosing to clamber over hills and along trenches instead, navigating felled logs that would prevent a car's progress. It was the only way she could put herself on some sort of even ground with them, making sure they would have to track her on foot. She'd had maybe an hour's head start, and she'd used the time well.

One of the many problems she'd woken up with, she now knew, was that she'd strayed too far from the path and was unsure of which direction she'd come. The only indication was the sound of the guards, but even that was difficult to determine, the way their voices bounced off the trees and ricocheted around her. They had the dogs with them too, and each time one of them bayed, Autumn flinched.

She waited and listened, never taking her eyes off the arrangement of trees directly in her line of sight. She noticed her breath escaping her mouth in little clouds, and to prevent it, she began breathing through her nose instead. Her teeth chattered, but she couldn't seem to do anything about that.

The voices became louder, and she was soon able to identify words and decipher snippets of dialogue. The barking seemed sporadic enough, which she supposed was a good thing. The guards certainly didn't seem alarmed at how vocal the dogs were; in fact quite the opposite. She heard one of them tell a dog to shut the fuck up; the dog barked back by way of reply and laughter followed.

'I feel like we're close now, boys,' one man said, as their bodies carved out silhouettes in the mist. Five of them were combing the area, coming directly towards her. Autumn began to pee involuntarily, and the warm urine was soothing against her cold legs.

They stopped at the foot of an incline that would lead them directly to her. Each one held a rifle. Suddenly the dog began bucking against its leash.

'I said shut your noise, you stupid fucking mutt!' the guard yelled, and his words travelled all the way up to Autumn. He sounded tired and bored.

When the dog didn't obey the command, one of the other guards said, 'She might've picked something up.'

'Yeah, probably another fucking woodchuck.'

Autumn could see the dog's eyes staring up at her as though it could see her, yet the men surrounding the animal did not follow its gaze.

'You wanna let her off the leash just in case?'

'I'm not going after her if she decides she don't wanna come back when I call her.'

'Hector, don't be a fuckin' asshole. The dog might've picked up the scent.'

'Fine, I'll let her go. But look here: all around where we've been walking there are twigs and branches and shit covering up holes like a bunch of sand traps. If she falls into one and fucks her leg up, I'm putting a bullet through her head and one of you motherfuckers can explain to Joseph why we came back short one dog.'

The other guards laughed. Hector removed his cap, wiped his brow, then spat on the floor. 'She's seen a woodchuck. I'm not in the mood for it.'

The dog tugged against the leash, desperate to hunt.

'That's why we brought the dogs, idiot. I'd rather come back short one dog and with the girl,' one of the men said. 'Y'all keep laughing and joking, but it's our fucking asses if we don't find this little bitch.'

'She ain't this way, I'm telling you,' said another; Autumn thought he was called Danny. He turned and pointed east. 'If she's anywhere, she's by the road. Ain't no way she made it this deep through the night. Too fucking dark. If she's clever, she'll have stuck to the road. Only thing likely to happen if we keep on this direction is we'll get ourselves lost, and that will be a whole lot fuckin' worse than a dead dog. We already look like a bunch of assholes as it is.'

Once again the dog released a harsh series of barks and growled ferociously.

'Whoa, listen to that,' one of the guards said. 'She's spotted something for sure. Let her go, Hector.'

'You gonna fetch her back?'

'I wasn't asking you, I was telling you, motherfucker. Let her go.'

The other guards laughed, but Hector didn't move. When the dog rattled another series of violent barks, he subsided and released it. The German shepherd flew up the hill. A scream rocketed into Autumn's throat but she managed to keep it locked in her mouth. The animal was less than thirty feet away, close enough for her to make out the thick webs of saliva dangling from its black gums. Its muscles stood out through its shaggy fur, and as it ran, Autumn could clearly define the guttural rhythm of its breathing. She braced herself, curling her fingers around the knife handle.

The dog was almost on her when it abruptly changed direction and darted off, snapping its jaws, completely ignoring Autumn. She listened as its barks and snarls receded into the distance.

'Aw, Christ, where's she going?' Hector asked, then put his fingers to his mouth and whistled. The sound pierced the forest and reverberated through the trees.

'After a squirrel, it looks like,' another of the guards said, unable to keep the amusement out of his voice. 'She's gonna come back with supper for us.'

'Christ, we'll be camping out here if we don't get a lead on this little bitch soon.'

'I told you she ain't this way,' Danny said. 'We're wasting our time out here. They'll pick her up on the path. Come on, anyone wanna bet on it?'

They continued arguing among themselves, staring off up the hill in the direction that the dog had gone. Autumn held her breath, certain that one of them would eventually pan over and see her pale face peering out. She couldn't be sure whether the gnarled tree roots concealed her completely.

'You're going after that damn dog,' Hector said, pushing a smaller guard.

Autumn's throat closed as though a hand was throttling her. She squeezed the knife handle until the muscles bunched in her arm and shoulder and the plastic grip burned her palm.

They came within ten feet of her, squabbling as they ascended the hill. She saw their drained faces and could smell their sweat and the bitter coffee on their breath. The last thing she heard before their voices faded away completely was something about the radios losing their signal, and how they should head back to the path.

It was a very long time before she found the courage to slither out of her hiding place. She flinched as the birds squawked loudly above her, and became deeply unsettled by the beating of their wings as they commuted between trees. Her skin was itchy all over and she kept thinking that ants were marching across her flesh, crawling in her ears. Every now and then she would shake her hair to rid her scalp of some imagined spider or centipede she was sure had tangled itself in there. Her nails were black with grime and she was barefoot, though she couldn't recall when or where she had lost her sandals.

She began to jog through the forest, her soiled white dress billowing behind her. The soles of her feet had become accustomed to the pain, but the impact of her movements played havoc with her knees. Worst of all was her headache. At first she was unsure why her temples throbbed and her brain felt as though it were inflating against the roof of her skull. She thought maybe she'd bumped her head somewhere along the way but couldn't remember doing so. Then she realised that she was thirsty. She'd lost pints of sweat during the night and had peed out what little water she had in her system. When she reached the stream, she would get on all fours and lap the water up like a thirsty dog; she just had to find it first.

The deeper she ventured into the forest, the heavier the doubt weighed in her mind. She had to continually remind herself that Lena had not only escaped from the house – avoiding the other guards *and* the dogs – but that she must have made it all the way out of the forest too. The only way to do that, as both of them knew, was to follow the stream. You would have to be a complete lunatic to chance taking the path, where the cars could easily pick you up. And Lena might've been many things, but stupid wasn't one of them.

Lena had been like a big sister to Autumn, a mentor who'd shown her the ropes upon her arrival at the house. From the start, Autumn had sensed that something was not quite right with the other girl, but as she spent more time with her, she also began to realise that Lena was a damn sight smarter than she let on. It was Lena who'd told her about the stream, about how if you followed it for long enough, it would take you right near the highway.

Despite Lena's attempts to rally some sort of escape committee, none of them took her seriously enough to act upon it. The only proof she had that her plan would work was her claim that several years before, a guest who had come to pick her up in his car had driven out along the highway, and she had glimpsed water through the trees when he allowed her to remove her blindfold. It was the same stream, she claimed, that she found when she'd been granted permission to forage for berries and flowers for the festival, all under Les's watchful eye, of course. Nobody could prove or disprove her theory, so it was far easier to shrug it off as folly. And even if they could have proved that it was accurate, what real difference would that have made? None of them had the guts to attempt a breakout. None apart from Lena, that was.

For a while, Autumn entertained the idea that Lena would have tried to raise the alarm somehow, despite knowing that she wouldn't be taken seriously. There was no way she could go to the cops, though, and with that in mind, what alternative did she have? She could try shacking up with some lonely man who might be naive enough to entertain her story, but would she be able to get him to act upon it? And what had Autumn been expecting anyway – a band of vigilantes to turn up and have a shootout with the guards at the house, before rescuing the girls and returning them to their rightful owners? No, that was absurd. If Lena had made it to the road and managed to hitch a ride somewhere, then she would have used that hidden sense of hers and disappeared forever.

Autumn came to a clearing and immediately felt exposed. She spun around, scanning her surroundings, wondering how best to proceed. If she pushed on further, there was every chance she'd come across water, but then again, there was every chance it would be more trees, more hills, maybe even bears. She thought she'd seen deer prancing in the distance, but when she'd attempted to track the fleeting shapes, they'd vanished into the foliage. How far did the forest go on for? Would she be able to keep walking in the same direction and get to the edge of it? Not a chance. Even when they were driven out, it took them over an hour, and they were always blindfolded.

She did a three-sixty and surveyed the land, scouting for options. She didn't feel completely confident in carrying on the way she'd been heading, especially since she couldn't so much as hear a trickle of water. Everything looked the same no matter which direction she turned: trees, twigs, logs, mist. The frigid air bit into her skin and she hugged herself for warmth. It was as though the whole forest had shifted around in an attempt to confuse her. But that was silly and she knew it; it was her mind playing tricks on her, some optical illusion of nature.

She closed her eyes and rewound her memory in an attempt to see where she'd gone wrong. She was probably too deep in the forest to turn back to the house now even if she wanted to, and yet she wasn't sure she would last another night out here. She was already sneezing and coughing from deep in her chest, her nose running uncontrollably.

Her mind wandered back to Wendy. She tried to imagine the girl outrunning the guards in the night, fighting her way out of the forest and onto the main road. In her mind, she saw Wendy bursting through the bushes and into the path of an oncoming car, which would stop just before hitting her. The driver – a kindly old woman – would usher Wendy into the car and drive her to her home; maybe the old lady had lost a daughter many years before, and as such she would be fiercely protective of Wendy. She'd take her in, feed her hot soup and warm bread, give her clean clothes and a bed. The two of them would heal each other, filling the gaps in their lives.

The fantasy distracted Autumn from her fear that she was lost. She should never have left the house. Now the best she could hope for was that she would curl up and die of hypothermia in the night, but even that seemed unlikely. Knowing her luck, she would probably last a week, thirsty, hungry and bitterly cold. She would die just the way she had lived: miserable and full of pain.

'No,' she said, wiping snot away with the back of her hand. 'It's all under control.'

She walked a bit further and noticed – or *thought* she noticed – that the trees were thickening and growing taller. Was that a good sign, that the trees were at least different? She didn't know. The only thing she did know was that her tongue had seemingly doubled in size from thirst, and she was beginning to feel dizzy. She came to a moss-covered tree that had bowed with age and reached up for a branch, pulling it down and lapping at the droplets of rainwater on the leaves. It wasn't enough, but the moisture was good for her mouth. It was ridiculous how much of a difference a few drops of rain made. She almost began to believe that she wasn't doomed after all.

There *was* a way out, and Lena had found it.

All she needed to do now was stumble upon some berries and she might just be able to pull this thing off. The cold still presented an obvious problem, but if she could find some source of food, and maybe an impression in the ground deep enough to collect rain to drink, then that was a damn good start.

She would walk until the blisters in her feet popped. She would look for some other place to tuck herself away at night, and she would find a way to keep warm. She didn't know how to make fire, but she probably wouldn't have been able to even if she did, given how wet everything was. 'Fuck fire,' she said, forcing herself to believe that the thought of flickering flames held no attraction for her. She had her knife at least, which meant if she saw a rabbit she could snatch it up and kill it.

She saw a large boulder in the distance and made that her target. She would stop there for a break, inspect her feet, see if there was anything that could be done about this cold. All the while she kept her eyes open for anything that she might be able to use as clothing. More than the hunger, the thirst and her various aches and pains, it was the cold that really tortured her. She thought her teeth might break in her gums they were chattering so hard.

She reached the boulder and sat down, bringing her knees up into her chest and hugging them tightly. She blew breath onto her arms and then tucked her mouth into her dress to blow on her chest. It offered very little warmth; it was like holding a lighter flame next to an open freezer. Her eyelids were growing heavy and she briefly contemplated looking for another place to hole up for a nap, but she quickly fought the urge. She hadn't covered enough ground today, and the more time she spent in this forest, the closer she came to death.

The soles of her feet were a horror show. She took one look at them and could not bring herself to do so again. Black blood blisters pulsed on the ball and heel, and the spaces between her toes were stained red, yet she could not feel any pain. Her feet were like two blocks of ice, completely numb from the ankle down.

She bent her head and sighed as fireworks popped in her skull. Every part of her body was heavy, and now that she was sitting down, she didn't think she could bring herself to rise again. Would it be possible to just lie down and go to sleep? Maybe then death would take her easily and she would no longer have to burden herself with the need to survive.

There was a dull thud, and it took her a second to realise that it was the knife slipping from her grasp. Quietly, she began to cry, the emotion running out of her like blood from an open wound.

When she had cried out all the tears that her body could afford, she rubbed her eyes with the heels of her hands. There would be no happy ending to this story. She picked up the knife again and held it against her wrist. One good slice would do it, and then it would be over quickly. One of the girls had demonstrated this back in the kitchen many years before, as they'd been making stew for the day's lunch.

It was only as she lay down and prepared to die that Autumn heard the faint trickle of water.

24

'He's not an idiot, you know.'

'No. He's a child molester and a rapist.'

'He'll be on his way down here with backup. He'll take you out in two seconds flat, lady. This whole thing will have been for nothing.' Cindy's face was ghoulishly grey. She'd aged ten years in the last two hours.

'That's what you want though, isn't it? You want me out of the equation so you can go back to your mansion and your drugs and your disgusting fucking parties.' Francine had checked the gun every few minutes, throwing alternating glances out of the window and at the door, half expecting someone to come crashing through at any second.

'No. You've freed me from all that. I was never like him. Never. But I didn't have a choice, you understand that, don't you? I didn't have a say in the matter. I just had to do as he said,' Cindy croaked, each word a laborious exercise. 'Just do as I was told.'

'You torture children,' Francine said, staring down at the woman. There was no emotion in her face.

'He does it all. Him and his friends. You don't think he's passed me around to people for his amusement? You don't think I'm as much of a victim as those girls?'

'No, I don't.'

The clouds looked like great steel mother ships looming over the ocean. Below them the waves crashed against the jagged rocks and sprayed foam into the air. The daylight was fading fast. It would be totally dark within the hour. Francine didn't like that, but she had no choice.

'He's friends with the police and the judges,' Cindy said, panting. 'Even if I were to go to the cops, nothing would happen. They'd string me up for it.'

'Why are you telling me all this now?'

Cindy sucked air, her head swivelling. 'I don't want to go to hell.'

The laughter took even Francine by surprise, but once she'd started, she couldn't stop. She bent over and rested her hands on her knees, tears rolling down her cheeks.

'Go ahead and laugh. But it's something you should think about too. Especially with what you're planning to do.'

Francine stopped laughing and her face turned to stone again. 'I've been in hell for ten years. There's nothing anyone can throw at me to make my life any worse than it is.'

'Then let me *really* help you,' Cindy pleaded weakly. 'Anything you need me to do, I'll do it.'

'I don't need anything else from you, so shut it.'

'But you don't know Glenn like I know him.'

'What kind of car does he drive?' Francine squinted at the vehicle barrelling along the winding road far below.

'He's got lots of cars.'

Francine bent down and put her lips close to Cindy's ear. 'From here on, you're not to make a single sound. If you breathe too loud, I'll put some wrinkles in that face of yours that no doctor will be able to smooth out. Be a good girl, or you'll be going to hell a lot sooner than you thought. Nod if you believe me.'

Cindy nodded.

Shadows consumed the living room. Now that the darkness had truly arrived, Francine decided that she liked it. It wouldn't be a hindrance to her at all. She walked over to the corner of the living room, where she would be hidden when the door opened and Glenn walked in. She checked her gun was fully loaded again, cocked it and braced herself.

–

Francine heard the tyres kicking up pebbles as the car came round the bend. The engine, which had only been a purr to begin with, died. She trained the gun on the door. Her arms were steady and the gun didn't waver. Her ears strained against the silence, trying to discern who had arrived.

The doorbell rang, chiming through the silent house. Cindy jerked and shifted in the chair, exhaling heavily through her nostrils. The bell rang again and a tiny moan stirred in her throat. Francine snapped her head to the side and cracked her neck, then flexed and curled her fingers more tightly around the gun grip.

'Cindy? Are you home?' It was Glenn. His voice was a lot less jubilant than it was on TV. Now he just sounded like a cantankerous old man. Francine heard a key scratch at the lock, and then the whistle of wind as the front door opened. She closed her eyes and concentrated. She heard feet stepping into the house, the click as a light was switched on. 'Cindy?' She tried to pinpoint the footsteps in an attempt to guess how many people had come in. She opened her eyes and saw a yellow glow seeping in under the door. She inhaled deeply as the handle began turning.

'Cindy, are you in here?'

In response, Cindy gasped. Glenn turned the living room light on.

The sudden luminescence of the lights bouncing off the white walls made Francine squint. She saw the back of Glenn's head, his pink scalp showing through the thinning white hair.

'Jesus, Cindy. What's going on?'

Cindy's eyes widened to saucers, her dilated pupils shooting to the space behind the door where Francine was standing. Schilling began to turn. In his peripheral vision he saw Francine's shape and instinctively jolted away from her, raising his hands.

'You're in charge,' he said casually, using his showbiz voice.

'Don't go near her. Go over there.' Francine pointed to the sofa with the barrel of her gun. 'Sit.'

'Is it money you're after?' Glenn asked, slowly lowering his arms. 'I keep none at this address. But there are plenty of valuable things. Even the crockery is worth thousands. It's yours. I'll help you carry it out. I can always buy more. No big deal.'

Francine grabbed the TV remote and turned it on. She pressed 'play' on a separate remote and the screen came to life. It showed a room in the same house as the first video. Glenn was standing over a girl who was chained face down on a bed. He was hammering her buttocks with a meat tenderiser. The girl's screams were muffled by a ball gag, but the sheer frantic terror she felt resonated through the room. The camera zoomed in on her bloody, savaged cheeks, then changed its drunken focus to Glenn's flaccid penis. Glenn was speaking in the video but the music was too loud and it was impossible to make out what was being said. But the sentiment came through. He was laughing, enjoying himself.

He tilted his head to watch the TV. There was not one twitch of fear in his face; instead, he regarded the screen as though it were a piece of art at a museum. He sighed and said, 'You'll have to forgive me. I took my glasses off and left them in the car. I'm not very good without them.'

Francine snatched Cindy's cell phone off the table and threw it to him. 'I want you to call them.'

'Call who?'

'Whoever those girls belong to. Call them up and say you want a girl by the name of Melody delivered here.'

'I see.'

'Do it.'

'I'm afraid I can't.' He turned on the sofa to face her. 'There's just no way.'

Francine had anticipated this. She placed the gun against Cindy's head. A great gust of breath tumbled out of the woman's mouth and she wheezed, sucking in oxygen. 'Glenn! Do as she says! She's fucking crazy.'

'Oh I don't think she is,' Glenn said smoothly, defiantly. 'I think she's rational. I think we can definitely work something out, but this particular request is simply off the table.'

'Call them. Last chance.'

'I don't think I'll be doing that,' Glenn said.

On the TV, the cameraman swept across to Cindy, who stood naked in the corner of the torture room holding a cocktail in her hand. When she saw the camera on her, she smiled and waved, even did a little drunken jig. She was giggling, her white teeth standing out in the candlelit bedroom, while just off to her right Glenn was hammering some small, anonymous girl as though beating a hunk of beef.

Francine looked down into Cindy's face. Cindy's lips worked silently, trying to find the right words. The only thing she came up with was, '*Please.*'

She switched her focus to Glenn and made sure that he was looking directly into her eyes. He shrugged, glanced across at the TV, then back. 'Whatever you do from this moment on will simply bring you misery. You could kill me, which I think you plan on doing, but then you'd be arrested and spend the rest of your life in prison.'

'You're going to pick up that phone and you're going to call your people. You are going to ask for a girl called Melody to be brought here. You're going to *insist* on it.'

Glenn began to laugh. It wasn't mocking, but rather as though he found the notion genuinely funny. 'No, that won't work. Do I have your permission to fix a drink? I'm very tired from the trip over here, and all this excitement has drained me somewhat.'

Now it was Francine's turn to laugh. 'Do you really think I won't kill you?'

He stroked his chin. 'I think you will kill me either way.' He seemed to contemplate this before adding, 'So right now, the way I see it, I'm dead no matter what I do.'

'Have it your way.' She stood up and held the gun to his head.

'Wait, wait, wait!' He put his hands up, cringing away. 'All right, all right. Let's just hold on a second and work this out, shall we?'

'There's nothing to work out. You make the call.'

'Fine, I'll make the call, as long as you understand what will happen once I do. I want you to fully grasp the ramifications, because you obviously have no idea what you're dealing with here.'

'I'm going to count to three...'

'Okay, you don't need to threaten me any more, for God's sake.'

'Put the phone on speaker,' Francine ordered, as Glenn tapped the number in. The dial tone droned for a few seconds before it was answered.

'Joseph? How are you, old boy?'

'Sorry, who is this?' Joseph returned sharply.

'It's Glenn, Glenn Schilling.'

'Glenn, I'm a little busy at the moment, so you'll have to make it quick.'

'Sure thing. I'm up at the house in Little Peace and was wondering if there was any chance at all that I might be able to make an order.'

There was a beat of silence. 'Your next scheduled gathering isn't until next week.'

'Yes, I know. I was hoping that on this occasion you might be able to make an exception. My wife and I are bored and thought we could have something to play with for a couple of days.'

'Glenn, now is really not a good time for this call. You know the agenda.'

'I know. I thought it was a long shot. Would it make a difference if I were to pay double, just for one girl, of course?'

'No, I don't think so.'

'So there's absolutely no way I can have a girl sent here? Not even if I pay triple?'

Another beat of silence. Joseph exhaled, sounding irritated. 'I'm low on staff today. No deliveries are going to be made until your next gathering. Look, I have to go.'

The line went dead. Glenn looked up at Francine and shrugged. 'I tried.'

'Fine. If they won't bring her here, then you're going to have to take me there.'

Glenn opened his mouth to object.

'Don't tell me you don't know where the house is either, because your bitch wife already told me you do.'

He looked over at Cindy with an expression of disgust. 'Fine. Fine, fine, fine.'

Francine grabbed her bag and waved him towards the door, ignoring a pathetic 'Please!' from Cindy as they left. Outside, she watched him totter over to the passenger side of the car.

'You're driving,' she said.

'But I can't,' he said, blinking at her.

'You can, and you will.'

He looked down at the road winding around the cliff. 'I really don't think that's a good idea. My eyesight is terrible. It was still light out when I made my way over, but there's no way I can get the car down this road in the dark.'

'You're lying.'

'I'm not, I promise you. Why don't you tie me up? I can direct you. I'm sure you're a much more capable driver than me, even for a woman.' He cracked a smile, then shook his head. 'I apologise. I make inappropriate jokes when I'm nervous.'

Francine watched him get into the passenger side, then went around to the driver's seat. She felt in her bag and removed the cable ties. She very nearly put the gun on the dashboard to tie his wrists but thought better of it. He might look nothing more than a frail old man, but she was sure he would find the strength from somewhere if an opportunity presented itself.

'Give me your hands,' she said, then awkwardly bound them with the ties.

'Ooh, that's a little tight.'

She ignored him, holding his wrists to the interior door handle and looping another cable tie around that.

She started the engine and set off down the narrow road that wound round the cliff. She had the full beams on, the light carving a path through the darkness. It was a treacherous descent, the car forced to take up the majority of the road, and she was thankful that she had not made Glenn drive.

When she reached the bottom, she asked him which way to go.

'Carry on in this direction and you'll make it to the junction joining the highway. From there you'll want to take a left.'

She followed his instructions. 'How far away are we?'

He thought for a moment. 'Difficult to say really. You'll want to go down the freeway until we come to a turning called Stack's Point – it shouldn't take much longer than an hour to get there. After that, the journey is a bit trickier, but I'd say we'll reach the grounds in under two hours.'

Francine's pulse began racing. She would be reunited with her daughter in two hours. There was nothing that could derail her now. She pressed her foot harder on the gas, the needle pushing over 100, the night whizzing by in a blur.

With her mind wandering, she forced herself to concentrate on her driving. It was easy to indulge in thoughts of a reunion, but if she were to clip a pothole or skid on these wet roads and blow a tyre out, this whole thing could come to a screeching halt. So far, everything had worked out for her. It was easy to equate her success with something as trivial as luck, but she thought maybe it was a little more than that. She was reclaiming what was rightfully hers. She was owed justice. At that moment, she felt invincible, as though no force on the planet could step in her way. God himself could chuck a lightning bolt out of the sky and she would take it and laugh back up at him.

She was going to get her baby back.

25

It had been over twenty-four hours since she'd made her escape, and Autumn was beginning to hallucinate. She was running a high temperature – she could no longer even feel the cold –and was considerably sleep-deprived. Her head was fuzzy and painful with every slight movement; her skull like a package containing something fragile that had broken.

She inched up the hill to get a better view, clambering along using the trees for support, squinting to focus her eyes. She *had* to be hallucinating; there was no other explanation for it. What she saw forced her to her knees. She held her aching head in her hands and began to rock back and forth.

She had somehow navigated back to the house.

No, it couldn't be. She clawed at the mud. She didn't even realise that she was chanting, babbling incoherently, the world slowly sliding away from her.

The sickness had taken her; that was all it was. She looked out through her matted hair; could see the convoy of cars and the guards walking around. 'It's not real. Not real. No, none of this is real. No, no, no, no, no. Just rest. Please just let me rest a second. Please God, will you just let me rest?'

She scrunched her eyes closed and tried to remember how she had got here. Just before sunset, when she'd discovered the stream, she had been presented with a dilemma. Did she follow the flow of the water or go against it? There was no way to know for sure, but she had assumed that if she followed the flow, it would lead somewhere. But perhaps her perception had been skewed.

Mad with thirst, the first thing she had done was gulp down mouthfuls of the bitter, swampy water. After that, she had struck gold again and discovered a wild tangle of blackberries that, although sour, gave her just enough of what she needed to put one foot in front of the other. An hour later, however, her stomach was twisted in knots and she'd had to squat and empty her bowels. She hoped the berries weren't poisonous.

Now she shuffled over to a tree at the crest of the hill, pulled her knees into her chest and watched the house. Through her fever, the scene unravelled like a hazy home movie, some distant fragment of a dream that lost its lucidity the more she chased it.

'Shh, it's okay,' she told herself, rocking with her eyes closed. 'Everything's okay now.' She tasted blood, thought she was imagining it and then saw the red droplets dotting her knee. Her fingers reached up to her mouth and she discovered that she'd clamped her lip between her teeth. 'Please God, please hear me. Please… help me, God.'

She snapped out of her stupor at the sound of a car engine drifting through the forest behind her. She jerked her head around, feeling the broken glass shift in her skull, but couldn't see any oncoming lights. It was entirely likely that she'd imagined the noise, especially if she truly was hallucinating this whole episode. But now reality was pawing at her with cold, clammy hands, stripping away this convenient fantasy she'd built as a defence mechanism. No, she wasn't hallucinating. She had followed the stream in the wrong direction, linked back up to the path and trekked straight to the one place she'd fought to escape from.

There was no God. She was sure of that now.

'I'm so stupid. I'm so fucking stupid!' As she pounded her head with clenched fists, she caught sight of headlights in the distance. Not only had she looped all the way round back to the house, but she was directly in the path of any cars coming through the forest.

But she was not ready to give up just yet.

–

'Do you mind if I ask you a question?' Glenn said, clearing his throat.

'Yes,' Francine replied. 'I do mind.'

'Given the circumstances, I'm not very eager to argue with you, but I think it might be prudent to find out what it is you have planned.'

Francine wasn't listening; all her attention was dedicated to looking out for the sign that would take them off the road.

'I'm assuming your daughter is at the house. What did you say her name was? Meg?' When Francine still didn't reply, he continued unprompted. 'It doesn't make a whole lot of difference either way, I suppose. You plan to take her back, don't you?'

'I *am* going to take her back. There's no two ways about it.'

'Well, I wouldn't go that far, but your ambition is at least admirable, albeit completely and utterly insane. You won't get within walking distance of the compound. They have guards and dogs and guns. The only thing you will achieve is ensuring us a grisly death. They'll apprehend and torture us and then feed us to the pigs. I've seen them do it before.' He laughed mirthlessly. 'That would be a merciful way to go, given our options.'

'You deserve it,' Francine said. 'You deserve worse.'

'Do I? Well, perhaps you're right.'

'You've raped and tortured children, you sick fucking bastard. You'll get what you're owed. Take my word for it.'

Glenn inhaled, gathering his thoughts. 'We're both guilty of different deeds, that is true. But if we're going to judge one another, we should get all our grievances out in the open.'

'Shut the fuck up.'

'Or what? You'll pull over and shoot me? Go ahead,' he said, the words dipped in amusement. 'I would welcome a quick death. Believe me when I tell you it's a lot less than I can expect once you drive up to the house.'

'You're a boring old man,' Francine said, shaking her head.

'I can't deny that, I suppose.' He struggled to twist around in the seat so that he could face her. 'Celebrities *are* boring. We're a bunch of pampered, unhappy, self-important fools. That's why we sometimes look for other things to help make life that bit more exciting.'

'Is that how you see it, Glenn? You really don't have a conscience at all, do you? You're just a sick twisted fuck.'

'Oh, spare me the Mother Teresa routine, would you? I can't bear to listen to your agonised diatribe, dramatic though it may be.'

'You really are a monster, aren't you?'

'Yes, yes, a monster, a sick, twisted fuck, a boring old man, all of the above. Keep the insults coming if it makes you feel any better.' He gave a dismissive tut. 'You can't possibly fathom my world. How could you? What do you do for a living anyway? Are you a cleaner? Work in a supermarket, something like that? I make more money than I could ever spend. I've slept with the most beautiful women in the world. I can afford anything there is to buy. And you know something? It's tedious. None of it means anything.' He inspected his manicured fingernails. 'I don't believe there is a God, young lady. I think that when you die, that's it, the show's over. My philosophy is to try and find as much fun as I can while I'm still here. That's all I do, my dear. There is nothing personal in it.'

Francine took her eyes off the road and glared at him. 'I hope you're right about the torture. That's the only thing that's helping at the moment, knowing that you will leave this world screaming and terrified.'

He sighed. 'Quite the piece of work, aren't you? And I must say, as insane as you clearly are, it strikes me as somewhat odd that you could be so... hypocritical. Here you are acting like some avenging angel out to rescue your daughter when it was you who put her in this position in the first place.'

Francine's nails dug into the rubber of the steering wheel.

'How did they take her? Weren't you watching? You can't come crying about it now, when the damage has already been done.'

The weathered sign for Stack's Point was partially shrouded by tree branches, but she spotted it just in time for the turning. She pulled off the highway and down the solid darkness of the featureless road. The car began to bounce and rumble as the terrain changed beneath the tyres.

'You should first make peace with the fact that you were a terrible parent,' Glenn continued. 'Perhaps if you had kept a better watch on your daughter, you could've saved yourself years of torment. Still, we live and learn, don't we? I don't suppose you will make the same mistake again. Do you have other children?'

'You're trying to throw me off. It's not working.'

'Throw you off? Didn't I just tell you two minutes ago to shoot me? I couldn't care less, my dear. I'm tied up. I've made no attempt to escape. What does it matter to me?'

Francine swerved and almost pulled the car off the trail and down a hill. She wrestled the wheel, straightened out and continued to creep along. 'Where am I going?'

'Stick to the path, that's all.'

'How deep in do we need to go?'

'It'll be a little while yet. Should give you plenty of time to think.'

'Think about what?'

'About turning back.' He sighed again and shook his head. 'You don't really want to do this, I can tell. You're acting out of some misguided sense of pride. You think that if you make a stand now, it will be all right, that it will count for something. This is all to help you sleep at night, isn't it? But you don't want to die.'

'I don't care about dying. I just want to get my daughter out.'

'Easy to say. But I suppose we'll find out soon enough.'

-

The pleas became more desperate with each passing hour. Joseph had paced the mansion all day, chain-smoking and necking brandy, listening to the hiss and warble of the radio. The girls had remained locked in their dorm, and now there were whimpers to use the bathroom; they knew that if they dared to soil their quarters, there would be penalties. Some cried for food and offered their services for a glass of water. Joseph ignored them all. He was stuck in a helpless pattern, waddling over to the guards' quarters to enquire about updates before doing another head count on the remaining girls. Each time he did, he expected one of the sheep to have gone astray. It would be just his luck, the way things had panned out; if one more thing went awry, he would die of stress.

Rubbing the feeling back into his face, he made his way over to the guards' quarters for the second time that hour. He pushed the door open and saw three guards sitting on their cots while Abraham loomed at the far end of the room, staring out of the window.

'Anything?' Abraham called.

'I should be asking you that,' Joseph spat. 'And what's this?' He swept his arm to indicate the three guards on their beds. 'Do you want me to tuck you in? Read you a bedtime story?' He clapped his hands erratically, the sound jarring in the silence of the large room. 'Get out there and find her! This is turning into an absolute mockery! Do you know what will happen to you if this girl is not found? Do you understand the ramifications?'

'Hey, easy,' Abraham said, strolling down the aisle towards him. His eyes were red-rimmed and bloodshot. 'I'm resting my men. We're going out in units. While one pack hunts, the other pack rests.'

'Rest? I haven't slept in almost two days and you want to talk to me about rest?'

'Easy,' Abraham repeated in a low voice. 'We'll find her. But you need to let me do things my way.'

'Your way hasn't produced any results. That's the problem!' Joseph exploded, spittle flying.

Abraham wiped saliva from his face. 'Then what do you suggest?'

'Let's get something straight, Abraham. I'm not here to *suggest* anything. I'm here to tell you what to do, is that clear? And right now, I'm telling you to get out there and find her. All of you.'

'We need at least one person to stay behind for correspondence.'

'Correspondence? Don't make me laugh. I've got a radio, see? I can correspond with you just fine.'

Abraham scratched his red beard with his fingertips and said wearily, 'If that's an order...'

'It is. And here's another, get her home soon or consider yourselves enemies of the Group.'

Abraham turned away from Joseph and spoke to his men unenthusiastically. 'Okay, you heard him. Let's hustle.'

Slowly, the other guards rose from the beds and assembled their packs and guns. Abraham stopped at the door.

'You do realise that by sending us out you're leaving this place naked?'

'Oh, don't tell me – a girl could go missing, is that what you're implying? No, that only seems to happen under your supervision.'

Abraham shrugged, then led his men out of the dorm and into the misty night.

–

Autumn continued to watch the house. It was all lit up, which gave her a good view of the silhouettes that walked past the windows and across the lawn. Even at this distance she recognised Joseph's saunter and the way he constantly patted his hair down only to have the wind blow it into a haystack a second later. He looked anxious and stressed, and this almost brought the ghost of a smile to her lips. Whenever she blinked, she saw orbs of light and colourful patterns dancing inside her eyelids. She thought that she could hear a radio playing not too far away, but when she tried to concentrate on the sound, it disappeared.

Movement on the lawn distracted her. She squinted and saw the full beams of a Jeep light up, and heard the excessive roar of the engine. Then the vehicle was barrelling across the grass, stopping briefly so that the electronic gate could open before continuing on its way. It jerked from side to side as it climbed the hill and began curling around the path, the headlights washing over the section of land where Autumn was crouched. Suddenly it fishtailed and began sliding sideways. There was a loud screech as the tyres locked, and yelling from inside the vehicle. It was less than thirty feet away from her hiding place.

'Jesus Christ, what now?' Abraham growled. 'What's the problem?'

'I think we're stuck,' Davey said. 'But I saw her. I saw her.' He got out of the Jeep with his rifle slung over his shoulder and charged towards the trees. Abraham caught up with him on the other side of the vehicle and stopped his progress with a palm on his chest.

'What're you doing, Davey?'

'The girl!' he screamed. 'Come on, she's right over there.'

'We've had twenty people comb this area already. If she was here, the dogs would've sniffed her out.'

'I know what I saw.' He grabbed Abraham's wrist and attempted to swipe it away. Abraham used his palm to shove him against the Jeep.

'Don't act like an asshole now, Davey. Don't let what the creep said scare you. You're stronger than this and I need you thinking straight. We're all tired and we all want to find her.'

'Then come with me before she gets loose again!' Davey sidestepped Abraham and started to run into the forest, using the penlight on the barrel of his rifle as a guide.

'Davey!' Abraham yelled after him. 'Don't you dare start shooting in there! Get the fuck back here now!'

'She's this way!' he called, his voice jagged as he ran.

'You wanna follow him?' Dane asked, getting out of the back of the Jeep. He spat a gob of chewing tobacco onto the gravel path and wiped his mouth with the back of his hand.

'He's seen a deer,' Abraham replied. 'I'll have to straighten him out when he gets back. Come on, you drive.'

Dane made his way around to the front of the vehicle and got into the driver's seat while Abraham reluctantly returned to the passenger side, slamming the door behind him. Dane put the Jeep in drive and pressed on the gas, but the Jeep didn't move. The right-hand side was lodged in a deep fissure, and there was a low grinding sound as the tyres fought against the mud.

'Don't tell me we're stuck, Dane,' Abraham said, closing his eyes and pinching the bridge of his nose. 'I don't need to hear that right now.'

Without answering, Dane got out and assessed the situation. 'We're sunk in the mud. I think we need a push is all.'

'I don't fucking believe this!' Abraham once again exited the Jeep and slammed the door behind him. 'We haven't been gone five minutes and we're already stuck.'

'It's awful out here. Too wet,' Dane said, using his foot to scoop earth away from the rear tyre.

'Wet my ass. I'm gonna kill Davey when I find him.'

-

The window of opportunity had opened, but only a crack. It took a nanosecond of contemplation on Autumn's part on whether to capitalise. The guard, Davey, had jogged in her direction with his rifle, his breath visible in the beam of light from the barrel. She didn't think he could see her, as he had made no attempt to fire a shot or warn her not to move. And she could tell by the expression on his face that he was still searching and had not yet pinpointed what he was looking for.

Concealed from sight behind a wide tree trunk, she crouched on one knee, holding her position as the guard negotiated the muddy slope. In his haste, he went too fast, lost his footing and was suddenly tumbling, sliding down the hill on his stomach. His rifle swung around on the strap and lay across his back as he sprawled face down in the mud. Autumn sprang out from behind the tree and dashed towards him, jumping on top of him and pinning him down, then grabbing a fistful of his hair, pulling his head back and plunging the blade of her knife into his neck. He struggled and bucked beneath her weight, but this only caused her to saw away more forcefully. She felt his warm blood wash over her cold hands, and the sharp, metallic smell of it filled her nostrils.

He gargled and tried to scream, but nothing but steam left his mouth. His limbs flapped frantically as he wrestled with death. Autumn's heartbeat accelerated. She felt strong again. She thought about Lena, Wendy, the pregnant girls in the cells, and began to saw so vigorously that the muscles in her arm seized up. She'd dreamed of this moment with astounding clarity. If there was one thing she had wanted more than to escape the house, it was to hurt one of them. She'd never thought in her wildest daydreams that she would have the courage to do it, though. But now that she had, she knew it was the right thing to do. The *only* thing to do.

When he stopped moving, Autumn claimed his rifle.

–

Francine slammed on the brakes and felt the back of the car pull away. She fought with the wheel to prevent the vehicle from spinning out of control or tipping over into the ditch. Her hand snaked out and twisted the dial to shut off the headlights.

'Subtle,' Glenn said. 'I'm sure they didn't see a thing.'

A few hundred yards up ahead, a Jeep was parked sideways across the path. She could see shapes moving in front of the headlights and then continuing around to the rear.

'Who is that?' she whispered, as though her voice might travel out and sail on down to the Jeep.

'How should I know? I can't see a thing.'

'Where's the house? You said it wasn't much further.'

'It isn't. We're quite near, in fact. At least I think we are. It's difficult to tell in the dark.'

'Are you playing games with me, old man?'

'Games? No, why would I play games with you?'

'Then where is it?'

'Right over that hill. I think.'

She stared out at the Jeep in silence. Then she leaned over, popped the cigarette lighter out and held it to the plastic cable tie that bound Glenn's wrists to the door handle.

'Ouch, what're you doing? You're burning me! Stop!'

The lighter melted the plastic easily. Francine got out of the car, walked around to Glenn's door and snatched him up by his shirt collar. Ignoring his protests, she pulled him out of the car and pushed his frail body towards the trunk.

'What're you doing?'

She popped the trunk, clamped a hand over the back of his neck and forced him inside. He tumbled in, all arms

248

and legs, whacking his head. 'No, please, you can't! I'm claustrophobic. I promise you, I'll have a heart attack. Just wait a second, will you?' He sounded close to tears.

Francine ignored him, bundling his spindly limbs within the confines of the trunk. He began to yell, so she smashed the gun roughly into his face – she couldn't really see where she was aiming but was hoping to get his mouth. She felt the blow connect and heard him mewl like a sick dog, then he seemed to fold in on himself.

'I'll die if you leave me in here,' he said weakly.

She removed a handful of the DVDs, stuffed them into her jacket pocket, and tossed her backpack into the trunk after him and slammed the lid closed. Then she got back behind the wheel, put the car in drive and began creeping towards the Jeep in the distance. She drove at a snail's pace. She needed time for the scenery to unfold before her and reveal itself. If Glenn was telling the truth, then the house was just beyond the Jeep. But if that was the case, the men by the Jeep must be guards. They were the enemy.

There was no good way to go about it. She could try and snowplough them out of the way and barrel on down to the house, risking a hail of bullets, and then – providing she survived all that – scramble through the house looking for her daughter.

No, she had to stop thinking with this goddamn lottery-ticket state of mind: that she was lucky to still be alive. But the fact was that so far she'd done everything on impulse, letting her instincts take over. If she actually tried to rationalise what she was doing and paused to think things through, she was frightened that she would find a way to talk herself out of it or lose momentum.

Her palms began to feel wet against the wheel and she wiped them on her clothes. She slipped the gun back into the front pouch of her jacket. It wasn't very sophisticated, but she could grab it quickly if she needed to. She figured she could make the action look natural if one of the men wanted to see some ID.

As she inched along the path, she was soon close enough to make out two men by the Jeep. They'd broken down, or at least that was what it looked like. They were also wearing guns. They still appeared not to have seen her car – they were too busy fussing over the rear of the Jeep. Francine watched them for a moment, chewing the skin away from the corners of her fingers, then began to reverse slowly away, pulling the car off the path and rolling it into the foliage, where it would hopefully be hidden from sight. She opened the door and stepped out. She could hear Glenn pounding away inside the trunk, begging for his freedom. The men by the Jeep would never hear him at this distance, though, so she made no effort to shut him up.

She took the gun out and flicked the safety off before putting it back in her pocket. Then she began to trudge towards the men, her teeth rattling in her mouth, her feet sliding in the mud. Lightning zigzagged across the sky and the rain began to pour down, drenching her.

26

As she got closer to the men, Francine started to pick up on their conversation. One of them agreed to get behind the steering wheel while the other went to give the Jeep a push. They were stuck in the mud, apparently. The aggressive revving of the engine shuddered through the forest, the sudden clamour setting her nerves on edge. The hard work was already done, the difficult choices made. There was no going back now, she realised. It was all or nothing. Find Autumn or die trying.

She was twenty feet away and they still hadn't heard her approach. Their initial plan had failed and now the driver had got out and joined the other man at the rear of the Jeep, combining their efforts to try and free the vehicle from the mud.

'Excuse me,' Francine called, tripping over her feet, weaving along the path. 'H-help, please. Please…'

The two men went for their guns and trained them on the dim shape staggering towards them. 'Who's that?' one of them demanded.

'Please… I've been… You have to help me…' Francine whined.

'Who are you?'

'I've been attacked… You have to help me… Please don't shoot…' She stepped into the puddle of light from the Jeep's full beams and stood there, reeling on the spot, squinting against the light. 'You have to…' As carefully and authentically as she could manage, she dropped to one knee. *Let them see you're not a threat.* 'Are you the army?' she asked, putting a palm up to shield her eyes.

'What're you doing out here?' one of the men demanded, stepping out from the cover of the vehicle, still training his rifle on her. 'Answer me!'

'We broke down and a m-man…'

'What man?'

'A crazy man attacked my husband. I think he's dead. *Please…*' She dragged the word out and made a sobbing sound, bowing her head so they wouldn't notice the absence of tears. *I don't have any tears left for you fuckers. Not even fake ones.*

'You shouldn't be out here,' the man with the red beard told her.

'Abe, this ain't right,' the other man said. 'What do you wanna do about it?'

'It ain't nothing to do with us,' Abe said, gesturing at Francine. 'This isn't our objective.'

'You're the army, aren't you? You have to help me. Call the police. I'm begging you,' Francine croaked.

'What the fuck is going on?' the other man said. 'I don't like this, Abe.'

'Dane, get Davey on the radio now and tell him to get back here.'

Dane held the radio up to his mouth. 'Davey, do you copy? Davey, you out there? Over.' There was a hiss, followed by silence. Francine filled the silence with an exaggerated moan and sniffle. 'Davey? Can you hear me? We need you back at the Jeep right away. Over.'

'Give me that fucking thing.' Abe snatched the radio and growled, 'Davey, I'm not fucking playing games with you. If you're not back here in the next five minutes then I'm gonna stop looking for the girl and come after *you*, and when I find you I'll put a bullet in your fucking head myself. Over.' He slammed the radio into Dane's chest.

'You aren't the army?' Francine asked. What girl were they looking for? Were they still patrolling for Lena? They couldn't be. 'Please don't hurt me.'

'Maybe he's gone too far. He probably doesn't have any signal,' Dane suggested.

Abe looked into the pitch-black forest then returned his attention to Francine. 'What's your name?'

'Francine,' she said.

'Francine, you're on private property. Do you realise that you're trespassing?'

'We… we got lost… I'm so sorry…'

Abe analysed her sceptically, rolling his massive shoulders. His hands coiled around the grip of the rifle. 'There ain't nothing out here for miles and miles. How'd you find this place?'

'Lost…' Francine said. 'My husband took a wrong turn. He thought it would be a…' She covered her mouth and began spluttering for effect.

'We'd better take her in,' Abe said quietly to the other man.

'Take her in for what?'

'To stop her getting in the way of things here, for one. Go and check her out.'

Dane huffed. 'What about Davey?'

'What about him? Do as you're told and let me worry about that fucking moron.'

253

Dane hawked up phlegm and spat it into the mud. With one arm on his gun, the other swinging by his side, he walked over to Francine. His body was shielding her from Abe's line of fire and also blocking her from his sight. As he bent down and reached out to grab her, she pulled her own gun and squeezed the trigger in one rapid movement.

For a few brief seconds she could not see past the muzzle flash, but she knew she had missed – that somehow, miraculously, she had missed Dane at point-blank range, though she had sent him diving off the path. An erratic clap of gunfire came back at her, but she had leapt to her feet before their battle senses returned, and taken off into the trees. She could hear their voices behind her.

'Fucking bitch has a gun!'

'Are you hit? Did she get you?'

'No,' Dane yelled. 'Who the fuck is she?'

'I don't know,' Abe said.

'What the fuck is going on here?'

The lethargy left her body and she dashed through the trees, moving like a woman twenty years younger, all those tedious, gruelling hours of incline sprints on the treadmill paying her back with interest. Her legs were strong and she could run for miles at this pace – leaping, climbing, rolling, it made no difference; she was primed for this very moment. She could hear them pursuing her, shooting aimlessly into the darkness. The bullets peeled past her and ate away at the surrounding trees. She cut left, scouted the forest for their locations. She could only make out one of them, so she aimed and fired, letting off three shots without much hope of them landing. A rat-atat-tat came back at her, the bullets zipping past. She ran on, keeping low, looking for a spot to take cover. There was a felled tree trunk not too far away, so she bolted to it and sprawled on her stomach, lying as still as possible, her gun aiming into the blackness. She listened out for the noise of their movement, could hear their bodies brushing through branches, the chug of their breathing. They were fat and out of shape compared to her. That would work against them.

She saw one of them – Dane, was it? – and fixed her sights on him. He slowed to a trot, then realised he was exposed and in the open and hunkered down on his haunches, creeping with his rifle like a trained marine. Francine kept her gun on him, but she knew that if she shot and missed, she was a sitting duck. He'd spray the log and chop her to bits.

'You see her anywhere, Abe?' Dane yelled, and as he spoke, Francine saw the breath puff out of his mouth. She waited for Abe's reply, hoping it would give her some sense of his position. 'Abe? You got a lock on her?'

He continued to creep towards the log, his head whipping birdlike in every direction. Francine eased herself up slightly and prepared to shoot.

'Abe? You hear me?'

'I hear you,' Abe said, and his voice was coming from directly behind her.

She felt something prod the back of her skull.

'Don't move. Drop the hardware.'

Francine cringed. Dane spotted her and jogged forward with his rifle trained on her.

'I said drop it!' Abe said, jabbing the barrel of his rifle harder into her scalp, jerking her head forward.

The pit of her stomach fell away. She contemplated her options, wondering if it was worth shooting Dane for the sake of it, just to take *him* down at the very least. She knew that it was futile, though. Before she could even touch the trigger, her brain matter would be sticking to the trees like sap. She dropped the gun.

Something cracked her on the head. Her teeth slammed together, clipping her tongue, and her mouth filled with blood. Within a couple of seconds, she was out cold.

27

Autumn often fantasised about her mother. Even up until recently, there were nights when she would wake up completely and utterly convinced that her mom was standing by her bunk, soothing her with a lullaby. When she was younger, and naive to the ways of the house, she'd imagined that her mom was trying to rescue her. Other times she would imagine her speaking to her, asking questions about how she felt, and Autumn would answer them aloud. But then she grew older, became wise and hardened by the touch of men, and came to realise that her sense of her mother was manufactured purely to comfort her. Perhaps it was her psyche's way of protecting her from irretrievable madness.

Even now, having slaughtered a guard like a pig and with the stink of his blood all over her hands, Autumn believed that she still clung to her rational mind. And yet she couldn't account for what she had just witnessed. To call it a hallucination would be to betray her inner self, that quiet, echoing place where lies were not allowed. Because after everything she'd done in the last couple of days, all the hardships she'd faced, all the psychological tricks she'd relied on to keep her mind from slipping down into that viper pit of madness, she truly believed she had just heard her mother's voice.

She stood in the forest, unable to move, forgetting to breathe until the air hitched in her lungs. The rifle became an anchor in her hands, but it was the only thing keeping her tethered to the spot; otherwise a cold gust of wind might've blown her away.

She had watched the entire exchange crouched by the body of the man she'd killed. When she'd first seen the woman on the path, she couldn't quite decipher what was happening, so with the two guards by the Jeep distracted, she had inched closer. The sound of the woman's voice had been like a bucket of freezing-cold water splashing her in the face. All the years spent locked away in the big house had dulled the image of her mother's face, but when she heard her voice, she could picture her perfectly. Memories pummelled her brain, intimate little pieces of footage that she hadn't thought of in years.

If you're tired, little girl, close your eyes and…

But then the woman had pulled a gun and started shooting, before rushing into the trees.

A strong feeling of recognition shivered through Autumn. She had just witnessed her mother attempt to murder those two guards. As she scrambled to piece together the strange episode in her mind, she began to cry, though whether they were tears of joy, sadness or anger, she couldn't be sure. The melange of emotions muddled her senses, and she didn't know what to think, what to feel. She wanted so badly to believe that the woman was her mother, for she'd looked and sounded the part. But if she was wrong, she didn't think she would be able to cope with it. And now a new emotion crept into the mix: fear. Oh, she'd explored the depths of fear so many times before that it was like an old friend to her now, and yet this was something new, another layer she hadn't known existed.

She waited for the noise of her thoughts to quieten, and made a decision.

That big guard, Abe, had thumped the woman over the head with the butt of his rifle and knocked the fight right out of her. Then they'd picked her up and dragged her away, back through the gate and towards the house. If her mom was still alive, Autumn knew exactly where they were going to take her.

With the rifle slung over her back, she headed towards the fence that encircled the grounds. They might have left the front gate unlocked and unmanned, but she was not yet crazy enough to walk through it, rifle or no rifle. Instead she took the scenic route and went through the trees, replaying the scene in her head. It had to be her mom. That was the only thing that made any sense.

She followed the fence around until she came to the dip that would allow her to slip beneath it. She scooted under and re-emerged into the grounds, retracing her steps from earlier. It almost made her laugh: she had returned to the one place they would never think to look for her. That didn't matter, though, because now she was looking for *them*.

She marched across the lawn with strength in her legs for the first time in days. It might've been the gun that lent her strength, or it might've been the sight of her mother; she wasn't sure. Ultimately it made no difference. Everything ended tonight, one way or another.

She approached the guards' dorm from the rear, sneaking up to the back window and tiptoeing to see inside. The place was empty. A sound made her jump and she fell to the ground clutching the rifle. With her back to the dorm, she listened carefully and realised it was the noise of a radio left on one of the beds. She got back to her feet and, staying hidden in the shadows just outside the floodlights' radius, made her way towards the back door of the main house. It was wide open.

The house was completely silent, except for the squelch of her muddy feet sticking to the kitchen floor, and the low hum of the large refrigerator. Her footprints would be a dead giveaway, but there wasn't a great deal she could do about that, so she made no attempt to cover them up. She walked slowly, methodically, the rifle aimed out in front of her ready to go off at the first thing that moved.

She relished the softness of the carpet beneath her feet, the comfort of being inside in the warmth without the rain spitting down on her face. The silence rang in her ears. She was unable to fully adjust to the idea of not having the wind growling through her head. She ventured down the hallway and came to the stone steps that descended to the basement. Before she went down them, she stopped and listened keenly. She thought she heard the clink of chains, but she could have easily imagined it. There were definitely no voices and so she began the descent, one step at a time...

And stopped. There *was* a noise, but not from the basement; from *outside* the house. She craned her neck to see out through the reinforced sliding glass doors, and spotted the two guards standing with Joseph on the porch.

'Explain it to me properly, will you?' Joseph yelled, his voice high and shaky, riddled with hysteria.

'You need to calm down,' Abe told him. 'I can't talk to you when you're acting like this.'

Joseph's jet-black hair was hanging limply down his pale face. 'Just tell me, will you?'

'Maybe we should talk inside,' Abe suggested.

'What's wrong with right here? Who fucking cares?'

'The man upstairs might care,' Abe said, and waited for his words to register.

Joseph's arms flew up in the air and he slumped against the window. 'Fine. Fine, have it your way. I forgot that you're the boss now, not me.'

'Neither of us is the boss,' Abe corrected, pointing upwards. '*He* is. So shall we go inside, or do you want to stay out here and cry some more?'

Without answering, Joseph whirled and charged into the reception area. Autumn ducked down, but was still able to see them from where she was crouched on the stairs.

'The woman jumped us in the road. She had a gun. She just started shooting,' Dane said before Abe pressed a large hand on his arm, cutting him short.

'We don't know who she is,' Abe said. 'We checked her for ID, she had none. We've got her locked in the basement now with a collar on. She ain't going nowhere.'

Joseph covered his face with his hands and shook his head. Without removing them, he said, 'And the girl? I suppose there's no word on her, is there?'

'We were dealing with this woman,' Abe said.

'Who gives a flying fuck about the woman?' Joseph shouted, grabbing two fistfuls of his own hair. Autumn wanted to laugh. 'You should've just put a bullet in her and left her in the road, then carried on with your job. Mr

Wydebird doesn't care about the woman, he cares about the girl! What do I have to do to stress the importance of this?'

'I understand the importance perfectly,' Abe said calmly. 'Me and Dane will get back out there now and continue the search.'

'No, just stop, just stop a minute! We need to talk to the woman in the basement,' Joseph said, wiping his eyes. He started down the hallway, then stopped suddenly. 'You,' he pointed at Dane, 'get out there and carry on. This doesn't take both of you. Go on!'

Dane turned away like a chastised dog and exited the house.

'I have over a dozen of you looking for one girl.' Joseph shook his head in disgust. 'You're supposed to be trained men. What exactly are you trained in? It sounds like this woman ran you ragged, the same way those little girls have done. Do you have no honour?' He was slurring his words, tripping over his tongue. When Abe didn't reply, he said, 'You men are supposed to be able to comb the woods. You've been on tours overseas. And yet you've shown me nothing – NOTHING!'

After a moment's silence, Abe said, 'Are you finished?'

'God, you really are just a big lump, aren't you? Come on, take me to the woman!'

The rifle started to quiver in Autumn's hands as the footsteps grew louder. Her lungs tightened as she fought to control her breathing. The two men appeared at the top of the stone steps, and stopped when they saw the figure standing in the shadows.

'Stay where you are—' Abe began, but Autumn had already pulled the trigger. The gun's barrel jerked up as the bullets sprayed out, tattooing the guard across his stomach and chest. He dropped his weapon and clutched his belly as blood splashed out of him and he collapsed to the ground.

The side of Joseph's face was awash with blood. He reached up to touch his cheek, then looked at his crimson palm in terror, his mouth working soundlessly. As his faculties started to return, he clumsily attempted to scramble up the stairs.

'Don't move,' Autumn said, and her words were enough to stop him in his tracks. He could not seem to look at her, though. His eyes were drawn to Abe's belly, at the way the overhead lights gleamed in the pile of innards, transfixed by the thin wisp of steam rising from the gore.

'M-M- Melody...'

'Don't speak.'

'Yes, you're the boss,' he surrendered, keeping his hands high so she could see them at all times.

'Get down here and open the basement door.'

Gripping the banister, Joseph obeyed the order, his legs trembling as though he'd never used them before. 'Yes, you're quite right. Please don't shoot, Melody. I have a wife. I have two sons. Remember I told you about them? Jack and Ben. Remember?'

'Open the door.'

He brushed past her, the keys jangling in his hand. It took him a while to get his fingers to work and pick out the key that would open the door. It scratched around the lock before he was able to slide it home. The hinges creaked as the door opened.

'Get the light,' Autumn said. Joseph went inside and located the switch, and the basement illuminated in sections.

–

The light hit Francine's eyes and she scrunched them closed. An elevator of pain rode its way up her spine and stopped at the top floor.

Then she saw Autumn and there was no pain. There was no sound. There was nothing in the entire world except the two of them. She tried to get to her feet but was yanked painfully back down to the cold, hard concrete. Pain seared her neck and she began to cough, uncontrollably.

'Get that collar off her!' Autumn screamed. 'Do it!'

Joseph scurried over to undo the ring around Francine's neck. Francine's bloodshot eyes locked on to Autumn, but Autumn remained by the stairs. There was a *click*, and then Francine was free.

'Is it you?' Autumn said finally. 'Tell me if it's you!' she pleaded.

Massaging her neck, Francine stood up and barged past Joseph, walking towards Autumn. Her daughter was not the little girl she remembered, and yet she was – and the contradiction was dizzying. The memories echoed through her mind: Autumn on Christmas morning, tearing open her presents; Autumn in the garden, crouched down on the grass and marvelling at a worm; Autumn in the school playground, laughing with her friends; Autumn in the mall, moaning because Francine was taking too long in the shoe shop and complaining because she wanted to buy a doughnut…

'Stay where you are! Don't come any closer.' Autumn was crying, her face beetroot with the effort. But Francine did not stop walking. She reached out to her daughter and pulled her close, then wrapped her arms around her and squeezed her, kissing her head. She did not speak, just stood there holding her, enveloping herself in her smell, her touch, her warmth. She was in a dream. Touching Autumn made her feel whole again, and just like that, the last ten years of agony were swept away. She had not thought she would ever be happier than the moment of Autumn's birth, but she was wrong. This was more than happiness; it was beyond ecstasy. There were no words for what she felt.

Eventually she broke away, holding her daughter at arm's length.

'Give Momma the gun,' she croaked, so low that Autumn could barely hear her. 'It's nearly finished now, honey. Give me the gun.'

Drool hung from Autumn's quivering lips as she nodded and removed the rifle strap, handing Francine the weapon.

'Good girl,' Francine said, trying to keep her voice firm, trying not to lose her composure. 'We'll hug and kiss and cuddle and cry when we're out of here. But there's a few more things we need to do first.'

'What… Mom…'

'Just stay strong for a little while longer, Autumn,' She leaned forward and kissed her daughter on the forehead, then turned to Joseph, who stood huddled in the corner of the stinking, dripping basement, shaking like a terrified puppy.

'One chance to live,' Francine began. Her focus burned into the man so fiercely that she very nearly missed the other girl chained up on the opposite side of the basement. 'Unlock that girl.'

'Wendy...' Autumn whispered and jogged over to assist Joseph in releasing her. Francine supervised, with the rifle trained on Joseph's head and her finger caressing the trigger. When he unlocked the ring from around Wendy's throat, the girl flopped backwards as though boneless. Autumn felt her neck for a pulse, then turned and slapped Joseph as hard as she could across his face. The clap reverberated through the basement.

'Is she alive, honey?'

'Just.'

'All right. Help her breathe if you can. Try and bring her around.' Just then, Francine thought about Lena, poor damaged Lena, and a fresh wave of hatred rolled through her. 'You, stand up,' she said through gritted teeth to Joseph. He got to his feet, his hands in the air. 'How many men are out there in the forest?'

'About a d-d-dozen.'

'That sound right to you, Autumn?'

'Yeah,' Autumn said, without diverting her attention from resuscitating Wendy.

'Is this man the one in charge?' Francine asked.

'No. Daddy's in charge. He's on the top floor,' Autumn said, looking up from blowing air into Wendy's mouth. Wendy stirred, coughed, but remained motionless.

Daddy? 'So what does this man here know?'

'I know how to get you out of the forest,' Joseph offered. 'I can... I can call the men off you, send them on a wild goose chase.'

'We need one of the cars,' Autumn said over her shoulder.

'Give me the keys to one of the cars. Make it snappy,' Francine said.

He stumbled over, hand in pocket, and produced a set of car keys. 'Black BMW. It's the only BMW there. Please… I can help you out. Just let me live. I have a wife… two sons… please.'

Francine snatched the keys from him. 'Autumn?'

Autumn had her hands under Wendy's armpits, trying to sit her up. 'Yeah?'

'Do I need anything else from him?'

'His book,' she said, meeting Joseph's eyes when he looked over at her in surprise. 'His big book of names. But we don't need him for that. I know where it is.'

Francine nodded. 'Is there anything else?'

Autumn said, 'No.'

'Good. Cover your ears.'

28

They carried Wendy out of the basement with her arms slung around their shoulders. The girl couldn't have weighed more than a hundred and ten pounds, but it was all dead weight. She was semi-conscious, eyes open to slits, feet dragging on the floor. At the top of the stairs they lowered her into a sitting position and leaned her against the wall.

'They're all out there looking for me,' Autumn said, stopping herself from adding 'Mom' just at the last second. She didn't want to shatter the illusion, as though the word would end this whole perfect dream.

'There's nothing we can do about that just yet,' Francine said. 'There are others here at the house, right? Other girls like you?'

Autumn nodded.

'Where are they?'

'They're probably locked up in the dorm. I thought they would be in the basement, but I guess they're not, so they have to be upstairs.'

'Then here's what I want you to do. Go up there and unlock their door and tell them what's happening here. We won't be able to take all of them, but if they go in groups, they might be able to find their way out. Tell them to just get into the woods and stay hidden, and when you and me are out of here, I'll send help to come and get them. Think you can do that for me, sweetie?'

'Yes.' Autumn nodded. 'What about Wendy?'

'She'll come with us, but right now we have to leave her here.'

'Where are you going?'

'Top floor.'

'No.' Autumn's hand reached out and clung to Francine's jacket sleeve. 'Let's just get out while there's time.'

Francine cupped her daughter's face in her hands. The feeling of looking at her daughter, this teenage girl she did not know, was like an out-of-body experience.

'We *will* get out of here. I'm telling you to be strong. You just have to hold on.'

'How can you say that? You can't guarantee that we'll be okay.'

'You have to trust me, Autumn. I won't let you down again. Look at me. We are getting out of here and we are never looking back. God as my witness.'

Autumn blinked away tears and nodded.

'Go and let the other girls out. I have one more thing I have to take care of. Don't hang around, okay? Just do what you have to do and meet me back here. But if you see anyone coming, take off and wait by the car. You got it?'

'Yeah,' Autumn said breathlessly.

'Good.' Francine kissed her firmly on the head and walked away.

-

There was no longer any caution in the way she moved. Autumn ran like a startled antelope, bolting through the corridors. The ground melted away beneath her as she sprinted. She passed the barred windows down the second-floor hallway and cast a quick glance outside. There was nobody on the lawn. She made it to Joseph's office; that vague memory of the guard stuffing himself inside her flittered to her mind as she tried different keys in the lock. She snapped the light on and stood there in the silent room with only the sound of her own thunderous heartbeat for company. It was to the side of the desk: a large leather-bound tome. She opened it up to make sure it was the right one, her grubby hands flipping through the pages, and was finally satisfied. Then she snatched the book up, cradled it against her bosom, and hurried out of the office.

-

Francine took the steps two at a time, following the staircase up to the very top floor. She knew immediately that *Daddy* would be waiting behind the double doors at the end of the corridor, and her stomach did a quick somersault.

The doors opened without a creak and revealed a large room that appeared strangely clinical. An ancient-looking man lay in bed, cocooned in sheets and blankets, a small lamp on the table to his left providing the only light. Francine approached the foot of the bed. The old man's eyes fluttered open and his toothless mouth made wet smacking sounds as his tongue slithered out to lubricate his lips. The skin on his waxy, liver-spotted face furrowed until it looked like his whole skull might fold in on itself.

'Who's that?' he said, his voice like boots crunching on gravel.

Francine stared into his eyes, breathing through clenched teeth. Her shoulders were heaving as she tried to contain the venom bubbling within her. 'My name,' she began, but the venom was too toxic. It corroded her energy, making even speech difficult. 'My name is Francine Cooper. I am the mother of Autumn Cooper-Wright. You know her as Melody.' She spoke clearly and loudly, wanting the words to register the first time, as she did not think she could bring herself to repeat them.

The old man blinked, then said, 'What do you want here?'

'You have stolen my life. You ripped my heart out of my chest. And now I have come to return the favour.' She aimed the gun at the man and watched him. He made no attempt to barter, nor to squirm away. Instead, his ugly little face pulled into a sneer.

'Mel is a good girl. Firm, fertile. She's done well.'

Shooting him would be too merciful. She unhooked the strap from around her neck and threw the gun on the floor. Then she marched over to the old man, wrapped her hands around his thin, brittle throat and squeezed. She felt his oesophagus pulse against her palms, could feel the column of bone in his neck. He couldn't seem to get his arms out of the covers as she strangled him, so he just lay there, his face going from jaundiced to red as the blood vessels burst.

She didn't hear the man behind her. She didn't acknowledge his presence even when he hit her around the head. It was only when he clawed her face and physically wrenched her away from Daddy that she realised she was being attacked. He leaned back and put all his weight behind his next punch. It smashed into her forehead and rocked her skull, and she collapsed to the ground. He stepped over her prone body and approached the bed.

'Can you hear me, Mr Wydebird? It's Horace. Are you okay?' He bent over and Francine could hear him blowing into the old man's mouth. 'What have you done?' he snarled between bouts of breath. 'What have you *done*?'

The rifle was on the floor at the foot of the bed. She reached out for it but saw three hands in her vision, all of them moving in different directions. She shook her head to clear the cobwebs, but that only shifted the pain to other regions of her brain. She tried to get to her knees but couldn't make her legs cooperate. Spiderlike, her fingers crawled towards the barrel.

'Come on, breathe,' Horace pleaded. Upon seeing that his attempts to revive the old man were futile, his hand went to snatch up the phone receiver, but in his haste, he knocked the whole thing to the floor. He bent down, clumsy in his panic, and snatched the phone and the cord up in his arms, bundling it like a baby. He set it back down on the bedside table and stabbed at the buttons with his finger. He was about to dial the last digit when a salvo of bullets tore his skull to pieces.

–

The girls were already at the door, scratching to be let out like a roomful of dogs. Autumn hushed them while she found the right key, telling them to be silent and not say a single word. When she got the door open, she pushed them all back into the room and shut the door behind her.

'We need to go to the bathroom!' Elaine said in a burst of emotion.

Not one of them thought to ask her where she'd been, or why she was so filthy. *Look out for number one, that's the name of the game, isn't it?* No, it wasn't. And maybe that was why Autumn had made it this far, because she did care for the others, she was good for this evil place. 'All of you just shut up for two minutes!' she yelled. 'I need you to listen.'

The girls lapsed into silence, though some of them continued to dance on the spot, eager for the toilet.

'I don't have time to explain this and I won't have time to say it again. All the guards are out in the woods right now. The doors to the house are open. If any of you want to get out of this place, then you have to go right now.' The girls began mumbling and barging in with questions. 'Shut up, just listen to me! You won't all make it if you go as one big group, but if you split up and go in different directions then you might be okay. Do you understand what I'm saying to you?' They stared at her blankly. 'Look, I don't know how much time you have, but I'm leaving right now. I can't take any of you with me, but I'm going to send for help. Just like Lena did.'

'Bullshit!' one of them screamed. 'You're trying to trick us.'

'I'm not,' Autumn almost whined, lacking the strength to add conviction to her words. 'Why would I need to trick you? Look, stay or go, I can't help you any more than that.' As she turned to leave, she heard them muttering and conversing, but she didn't hear the shuffle of feet. She turned around and saw them still huddled in the room. 'Come on, you guys! You can't stay here. Please don't stay here.'

'We're frightened,' little Alma said, her big eyes welling with tears. 'Please don't leave us, Mel.'

'I can't…' Autumn shook her head, hoping she could keep from crying. 'I can't stay. And neither can any of you. Be brave. Come on. Please be brave.'

'We should wait here for the guards,' someone said, and the conversation flapped from talk of escape to the trouble they would all get into if the guards saw the door open and they weren't in bed. 'Maybe we can run to the toilet and get back before they notice any of us left,' another girl said, and right then, Autumn knew it was useless.

She ran down the corridor and made her way back to the ground floor. She was sure the guards would be waiting for her like some horrendous surprise party. She took the last stretch cautiously but swiftly. The house was silent. She peered around the corner and saw Wendy still leaning against the wall, her head lolling to the side. Autumn dashed out and ran to her friend's side, skidding across the floor and skinning her knees.

'Mel… I'm hurt bad, Melly,' Wendy whispered. One of her pupils was black and the size of a penny. 'I think I'm dying.'

'No you're not. You're not dying. But when you're better, I might have to kill you for all the trouble you've put me through.'

'Trouble?'

Autumn shook her head. 'I'm just teasing. You didn't cause me any trouble. In fact, you might've saved me.'

'Where am I, Mel? I can't see.'

'We're at the house.'

'Oh God. It hurts, Mel. I'm hurting all over.'

'It's okay,' Autumn soothed. 'We're hitting the road. Any minute now.' She set the book aside, slumped down on the floor next to Wendy and cradled the girl's head in her arms. There was little else she could do except wait. The longest night of her life was coming to an end. As she stared through the window in front of them, she felt the rhythm of Wendy's breathing slow down until eventually it stopped altogether. She bit down on her lower lip. 'Wendy? You still with me?'

There was no reply. Autumn stroked the girl's hair away from her face. 'I'm sorry,' she whispered into Wendy's blood-crusted ear. She kissed her lightly on the cheek. 'I'm so sorry.'

Autumn wept for her friend. When she wiped her eyes, she saw her mother standing at the end of the corridor watching, her forehead smeared with blood.

'It's time to go,' Francine said.

29

The body of the black BMW gleamed in the spotlights. As they got into the car, Francine said absently, 'Here, you're in charge of this.' She handed Autumn the rifle before adding, 'Put your seat belt on.' She settled behind the wheel. 'Am I right in thinking there's only the one entrance? That one up there.' She pointed at the gate deep in the distance.

'Yes,' Autumn said, clutching the big book of names to her chest.

'Do you know the woods?'

'No,' she admitted. 'I got turned around in them trying to find my way out.'

'But there's a dirt road that takes you right here,' Francine said, putting the key in the ignition. The engine purred to life. 'I came down it. Didn't you try and follow it out?'

'Of course not. That path is the only way in or out of these woods, so it's exactly the way they would've expected me to go.'

Francine still hadn't put the car into drive. She sat upright, her sweaty hands coiling and uncoiling around the wheel. Blood ran down the side of her face. 'We might see them out there in the woods. If that happens, we may need to ditch this thing and get out on foot. But we have a weapon at least. We'll just have to take our chances.'

Carefully she pulled out of the parking space and guided the car across the lawn without turning the headlights on. No one was waiting at the gate, nor did she see the lights of any other vehicles. It was almost too perfect, and the realisation made her throat close to a pinprick. It felt like she was sucking in air through a straw. She was sweating profusely and was having trouble with her vision – her left eye was swollen almost completely closed and the rain blurred the windscreen. In the forest she would have no choice but to use the full beams, advertising her location.

'Did you manage to get any of the other girls out?'

'I unlocked the door, but they didn't want to go.'

'None of them?'

'No… Wait!' Autumn spun around in her seat, the rifle barrel clinking against the window. 'Stop the car.'

'What's the problem?'

'I didn't get the pregnant girls.'

'What?' Francine drove through the open gate into the forest. 'What are you talking about?'

'We have to go back! Stop the fucking car!'

'I can't stop the car, Autumn. What's the problem? Spell it out to me.'

'I forgot about the pregnant girls on the third floor. They're in cells. Some of them are ready to drop. We have to turn back.'

Francine thought about it but made no effort to slow the car. The house was already a glint in the rear-view mirror.

'I'm sorry, Autumn, but we can't. We just can't do it.'

Autumn hammered her fists on the dashboard and began knocking her head against the window. 'Damn it! Fucking bullshit! Stop this fucking car!'

'Hey, calm down.' Francine reached one hand across to try and prevent her daughter doing any more harm to herself, her other hand guiding the wheel. Autumn's sudden outburst had raised goose flesh on her cheeks.

'It's all my fault! They're going to die and it's all because of me!'

Now Francine stopped the car.

'Look at me, Autumn.' Her hands went out to grab hold of Autumn's shoulders, but she immediately thought better of it. The girl would probably not appreciate any physical contact just then. 'Autumn. Focus for a second and look at me. None of this is your fault. Nothing that has happened in that house is down to you, do you understand me?'

'I could've helped them. I could've...' Autumn broke off and shook her head. She sighed and sank into the car seat. 'I don't know what I could've done.'

'If they're pregnant, then there's not a whole lot you can do. We wouldn't have had the space to take them all, would we?' When Autumn didn't speak, Francine continued. 'Look, once we get out of here I'll call the police and tell them—'

'Just stop it,' Autumn said, shaking her head. 'Stop talking and drive. Police won't do shit. A car won't even get dispatched.'

Francine turned her lights on and drove. 'I'm sorry,' she said quietly.

'So am I.'

Ten minutes later, Francine passed the car she'd arrived in – saw it parked just off the side of the road. She thought about Glenn Schilling and whether he had suffocated yet. Probably not. But it was doubtful anyone would get to him soon, and even if they did, it didn't make a bit of difference to Francine. She supposed she would find out one way or another; it'd be all over the TV once something definitive happened. But by that time she planned to be long gone; just the two of them, somewhere far, far away.

Hawaii, perhaps.

'How did you find me?' Autumn said, her head resting against the window. 'It was Lena, wasn't it?'

'Yes.'

Autumn laughed mirthlessly. 'That silly girl. Where is she now?'

Francine paused. 'She's dead.'

'What happened?' Autumn asked without a hint of surprise in her voice.

'I think she jumped off a bridge. I don't know really know why.'

Autumn's throat clicked. 'Lights,' she said, and pointed through the windscreen.

Francine quickly turned her headlights off, though she knew it would be too late. She veered off the path and let the BMW roll down the embankment, narrowly missing a copse of trees. All the while she kept her eyes on the vehicle in the distance as it sped along the path in the direction of the house. The BMW came to a halt and she switched the ignition off and allowed the engine to lapse into silence. Both mother and daughter watched silently as the Jeep rumbled down the path, giving no indication that it had noticed the other vehicle.

They waited a couple of minutes to make sure the Jeep was completely gone, and then Francine started the engine up again and rejoined the path. This time, knowing that the men in the Jeep were bound to discover bodies at the house, she threw caution to the wind and put her foot down. They bounced around the car as it sped along over the uneven terrain.

'It's going to run out, you know,' Autumn said.

Francine looked at the gas gauge. 'We have over half a tank. That'll get us far enough.'

'I meant our luck.'

'It isn't luck,' Francine replied. 'Me finding you has nothing to do with luck or God or anything else. I never once gave up on you. I never stopped believing even when everybody else did.'

'Did Dad?'

'I don't speak for your father,' Francine said. 'Autumn, I want to tell you something. I know you've been through hell all these years, but I've been going through it with you. Some days I felt like… I felt like I was close to you, like I was right there with you. Maybe that's a bond a mother has with a daughter, but I think it's maybe more than that. What I want to say is…' She laughed. 'I've thought about this moment every day since you were taken from me, going over every single thing I would say to you, and now—'

There was a heavy crunch. Francine and Autumn lurched forward. The BMW jerked and fishtailed as Francine struggled to right its course. Light drowned the inside of the car, coming from the Jeep that had rammed them. Autumn screamed and the sound almost perforated Francine's eardrum.

'It's them! It's them! Get us out of here! Get us—'

The Jeep rammed them again and Autumn was thrown forward against the constraint of the seat belt. Francine briefly let go of the wheel and the car slipped away from her. She quickly snatched it back and fought to gain control of the car, but the back end of the BMW was tugging to the right. She pulled the steering wheel in the opposite direction and there was a loud screech from the underside of the car.

'Mom! What do I do?' Autumn yelled, unbuckling herself.

Francine looked up at the rear-view mirror but the Jeep had its full beams on in an attempt to dazzle them. The BMW was still winding in an S, and even with the feather-light power steering, she still couldn't seem to rein the damn thing in.

'Shall I shoot?' Autumn yelled.

'No!' Francine snapped, just as the rear window shattered. A blizzard of broken glass showered them and there was a cacophonous stutter of gunfire. It took Francine a second or two to realise that it wasn't Autumn who'd fired the shots, but the men in the Jeep.

Autumn was hunkered down on the floor, her stomach pressed against the passenger seat. 'Mom! Are you hit?'

Francine didn't know. Her whole body was numb and yet she was still driving for their lives, sticking to the path, doing her very best to throw the Jeep off. 'Just stay down! Stay—'

Another brief clap of gunfire chopped through the car. Francine could feel the bullets biting into the bodywork and zipping past her head, finding their mark in the wind-screen, which somehow maintained its integrity despite being frosted with cracks.

We're gonna die after all, she thought, driving blindly now. At any second they were bound to collide with a tree or veer off the path.

Autumn scooted up and used the butt of the rifle to punch out the shattered windscreen. With vents at both ends of the car now, the cold air charged through the vehicle like a speeding train. The Jeep gave the BMW another little nudge, but Francine had anticipated it and managed to increase the distance between the vehicles just in time.

'Go, go, go, go!' Autumn cheered manically as Francine zoomed away, the engine roaring like a mighty beast. The Jeep moved better on the terrain and did well to keep up, but there was still a sizeable gap between them.

'Let them have it!' Francine shouted.

Without replying, Autumn aimed the rifle as best she could, but the movement of the car threw her balance off and the barrel wobbled as she tried to line the Jeep up in her sights. The vehicle was close enough to the BMW that she could see the guards' eyes widen with surprise as she pulled the trigger. In that split second before the rifle erupted, Autumn and the men in the Jeep shared a moment of telepathy. Collectively, they knew she would not miss at this distance. You could have given the rifle to a blind man and every bullet would've punched home on a target as big as this.

She screamed as the gunfire sprayed indiscriminately across the Jeep's windshield. She did not let go of the trigger until the gun made a rapid clicking sound. The volume of the gunfire in the confines of the car turned Francine's ears to water.

Almost immediately, the light faded from the inside of the BMW. Francine checked her mirror and saw the Jeep rolling off the path like a drunk staggering home. Only one headlight still shone. The vehicle gently bumped a tree and came to a complete stop.

In the distance behind them, the faint sound of a car horn wailed.

30

Soon after they joined the highway, the car began to sputter.

'We have to get off the road,' Francine said, and took the next exit. She didn't feel great about turning off only a handful of miles from Stack's Point, but the BMW was chewed to bits. While they'd been on the highway, the car had been dragging, and she suspected one of the rear wheels was shot out. When she pulled over on a side street and inspected it, her suspicions were confirmed. She and Autumn stood staring at the car beneath the glow of a solitary street light, the sound of the highway whispering far behind them. Bullet holes tattooed the bodywork. It looked like the car Bonnie and Clyde had been killed in.

'What do you want to do?' Autumn asked.

'The car's finished. We'll leave it here,' Francine said, and reached through the window to begin rubbing the prints off the steering wheel. Then it occurred to her how pointless the endeavour was and stopped. She thought about taking the rifle with them, but it was out of ammo. They weren't exactly going to look inconspicuous walking around in the state they were in, but they were going to look even less so carrying an assault rifle. 'Screw it,' she said. 'Let's get out of here.'

They walked side by side down the silent street, like they were the last two people left on earth. It wouldn't have bothered Francine very much if that was, in fact, the case. She reached out and took Autumn's hand. 'Hold Momma's hand,' she mumbled. Blood was pouring out of a gash above her right eye. She wasn't sure what had caused it, but she thought she might've banged her head when the Jeep rammed them. Either that or the flying glass had sliced her. With her free hand, she wiped the blood away.

Then she collapsed.

'Mom!' Autumn's voice echoed down the street. She dropped and crouched by her mother's side.

'It's okay, sweetie. I'm tired. I just need to get my bearings, all right?'

'Let me go for help.'

'No!' Francine pleaded, and a galaxy of stars popped in her vision. With the last bit of energy she had, she cupped Autumn's face and stroked her thumb against her cheek. 'No, don't leave me. You can't leave my side. No more. You're not... you're not...'

A black curtain fell, and Francine was no longer lying on the cold, wet ground, but floating on the surface of a warm pool, light as a lily pad. She flittered in and out of consciousness, the ache in her skull like a thunderstorm.

When she came to, she realised she was deaf. She could see Autumn talking to her but couldn't hear a word she was saying. She tried to say, 'Just wait a second, honey,' but she couldn't hear her own voice either. She tried to sit up, and felt the entire street jerk away from her. Her equilibrium was off and the starless black sky became a swirling vortex. Her skull was overcrowded with a thousand angry complaints, and each time a new throb of pain registered somewhere, the lights began to dim. Was she dying? Perhaps if she were to let the lights go out completely, then yes, maybe she would die.

She rolled away from Autumn and leaned on one arm. Thick red blood was falling from her face and onto the concrete beneath her. She struggled to get to all fours. She felt Autumn's arm around her waist, then felt herself being hoisted up. As she rose, her feet melted into the ground and she completely lost her sense of weight and balance. Had she been shot and not even known it? The only other thing that seemed out of place on her body was the strange numb twinge that strummed along her spine. *Paralysed*, she thought. *I got hit in the spine and now the shock has worn off and I'm paralysed.* But that didn't seem quite right either, because with Autumn's help, she was walking, albeit slowly and awkwardly.

'Can you hear me, Autumn? Because I can't hear you,' she mumbled.

'I can hear you, Mom,' Autumn said, struggling with her mother's weight.

'I don't know if you can hear me… but I think I might be dying.'

'You're not dying, Mom. You're just really hurt.'

Speaking over her, Francine said, 'I don't know if I can go on. This is where my luck runs out, I think.'

Autumn ignored her mother's words and instead continued to usher her down the street towards the glowing sign of the Lucky 13 diner. It didn't look too far away, but under the circumstances it might as well have been on the moon. If they could make it to the diner, there might be the slimmest of chances that they could get washed up, maybe have somebody tend to their wounds without calling an ambulance or alerting the police. How they were supposed to do this, Autumn wasn't exactly sure. Judging by their reflections in the windows of the parked cars lining the street, the occupants of the Lucky 13 would take one look at them and dial 911 straight away.

'Hold on a sec,' she said and rested her mother up against the door of a Chevy. Autumn was dripping with sweat and shaking terribly. She wasn't exactly sure how long her legs would hold her up given that she was undernourished and dehydrated. But she had to find the strength from somewhere, and now, at the very least, they could afford to take their foot off the gas just a little bit.

'I'm okay,' Francine said, resting her palms on the hood of the Chevy. 'It's all right now.' She reached out and touched Autumn's face, as though to reassure herself that it was real. 'I got a bit jumbled up there for a second. Everything went all,' she twirled her finger near her temple, 'funny. I think it's just the wiring is a bit loose, but it seems to be all right now.'

'Can you hear me?'

'A little bit. You sound like you're talking to me from very far away.' Francine laughed, and Autumn saw that her teeth were stained with blood. 'It's just shock. I'll be right as rain in a few seconds.'

'Were you shot? Where does it hurt?'

'It's all in my face and head. That's why I'm messed up. Can't think straight. Took a couple of knocks tonight.'

Autumn nodded. Even through the blood streaming into her vision, Francine saw something terrible in her daughter's eyes. They had taken on a fierce, animalistic quality.

'We need to get back on the freeway,' Autumn said. 'The sooner the better.'

'I agree, sweetheart. Hundred per cent.'

'I can't drive, though, and I don't think you're in any state to.'

'We don't have much of a choice.'

'You can't see properly. I'm going to get us a chauffeur.'

'You're going to have to explain... I can't...'

'There's a diner just up ahead. I'll wait for someone to come out and go to their car, and then,' she removed the kitchen knife from the cotton belt tied around her summer dress, 'I'll get them to come with us.'

'It isn't...' Francine used the parked car for support, palming her way over to the kerb and slowly sitting down. 'It won't work.'

'Nothing we've done tonight should've worked. But it has. This is a piece of cake compared to all that.'

'I don't want you to leave me,' Francine said. 'You might not come back.'

'I'll come back. But I need to do this now, Mom. It'll start getting light soon.'

Francine nodded. 'Wait, look, I can come with you...' She tried to stand up, but came crashing straight back down.

'Just stay still,' Autumn hissed. 'Don't be so stupid. Sit there and stay still. I'll be back soon, I promise.'

'Honey... please... Just be careful...'

'Here.' Autumn leaned down and put the big book of names next to her. 'Guard this with your life.'

And with that, she turned and began walking towards the Lucky 13.

The yellow sun sits in the blue sky and smiles down at them. They're at a picnic table in a park on a hot summer day, shaded by a magnificent oak tree. The gentle breeze sings with the sound of children giggling and is perfumed by a concoction of wonderfully scented flowers.

Will places the hamper on the table and begins unpacking the food from inside. There are roast beef sandwiches with mayo and mustard, a big bowl of leafy salad, a container full of plump strawberries and a tub of cream to accompany them. He removes pre-grilled corn on the cob wrapped in foil, a bunch of glistening dark red grapes bursting with juice, huge, healthy apples, and finally a bowl of potato salad. Oh no, there is more. He takes out a bottle of champagne that has still somehow maintained its coolness, and three crystal flutes to pour it into.

'Okay, here we go,' he says, undoing the foil around the neck of the bottle before thumbing the cork out. With a pop and a plume of foam the champagne dribbles over his fingers, and all three of them squeal with delight. He takes his time pouring the champagne into the glasses while Francine and Autumn begin assembling the plates of food.

Will doesn't make a toast as he hands them each a glass, but they do say 'Cheers!' and savour the first mouthful. Francine says she can't believe the champagne is still cold, the same way she can't believe that the roast beef sandwiches are still hot. She takes a bite of one of the sandwiches, and after a second to let the flavours pass over her taste buds, she knows that it is quite simply the best thing she has ever tasted. They all eat, taking a bit of this and a bit of that, putting the food away in no discernible order. Will bites into a hard-boiled egg, then plucks off a couple of grapes and munches them contentedly. Autumn crunches into a crisp shiny apple and the juice runs down her chin. She laughs, wipes it away and smiles at Francine.

They sit and eat and watch another family across the field. The family – a mom, a dad, three young children and a Labrador – are kicking a soccer ball around; it seems to be a game of kids versus adults. There are no goals and no seemingly obvious point to the game, but the children are breathless and sweaty and laughing like loons and the parents are just as happy, encouraging the kids then gloating playfully when they manage to steal the ball from them. The laughter collects in an unusual but delightful series of notes, like a person attempting to play a harp for the first time.

Francine is the first to spot the dark clouds gathering on the horizon, looming gloomily above the hill. Slowly but surely they begin to broaden, infecting the otherwise perfect blue sky. The family with the soccer ball notice it and their game comes to an abrupt halt. 'Looks like it's going to rain,' the dad says and picks up the ball. The kids groan with disappointment as their father explains that they will have to continue the game another day, but for now it's best to get going before the storm hits.

'Typical,' Francine says, wiping her mouth with a napkin. 'This was almost a perfect day.'

Will nods. Then he smiles, 'But who said any of this was real in the first place?'

She frowns, momentarily confused by the comment. She's about to ask for clarification, but Autumn interrupts her.

'Mom, are you all right? Can you hear me?'

The heavens grumble, and now the whole sky is charcoal grey and blinking with lightning. Francine holds her hand out to test for rain, as though the downpour might somehow miraculously miss their patch and they can continue with the day.

Her palm becomes wet.

'Mom, can you...'

-

'... hear me?'

The rain smattered against the window next to her. She was moving. She opened her eye – the one that wasn't completely puffed closed – and saw that she was cooped up beside Autumn in the front seat of a van.

'Say something if you can hear me, Mom,' Autumn said. She was sitting next to a fat man in dungarees who was driving the van. He glanced over at Francine then back to the road in front of him. Francine's good eye roamed over to Autumn's hand. She had the knife pressed against his ribs.

'I can hear you,' Francine croaked. She sat up and saw that it was daytime. The sky was white and they were back on the highway.

'Where am I telling this man to drive to?' Autumn asked.

'Sycamore,' Francine said. She allowed what was left of her senses to return and then said to the man, 'Excuse me, sir. What's your name?' Her voice was croaky.

'Fred,' the man replied, his jowls wobbling in rhythm with the vibrations of the van.

'Fred, I see you've already met my daughter here. I'm glad she hasn't hurt you, because from first appearances anyway, you seem like a nice man.' She stopped, clutched her booming head and carried on. 'I'm sure you probably hate us for inconveniencing your evening. I'm sorry that you feel that way, because whether you mean to be or not, you're the first friendly face my daughter and I have seen all night. I have to apologise on behalf of both of us for the knife – it is completely necessary. But I also know you're an innocent man just trying to do his job, so I'll tell you how things are going to run from here on out.' She paused; the effort of speaking was like a sledgehammer against the interior of her skull. 'When we hit Sycamore, you're going to pull over and park up at Clucky's, and then you're going to get out of the van. We are going to take the van and borrow it.'

Fred shook his head, his face flushed with rage.

'My daughter will hurt you if you try anything stupid, make no mistake about it. But if you cooperate, here is my promise to you: if you leave me a contact number, I will call you in a few days' time and let you know where you can find your van. You'll probably want to tell the police that you were robbed. But if you don't try and pull anything on us, you'll have the van back by the end of the week.'

'You gonna phone my boss too? You gonna stop him from firing me? Huh? I got a wife and kid at home. What am I supposed to tell them when I can't pay the fuckin' rent?'

'If they fire you because you were robbed, you can sue them for unfair dismissal,' Francine said, and wondered how exactly she'd acquired that knowledge. Perhaps she'd seen it on *Judge Judy*, or maybe she'd just made it up.

'Yeah, right. You're putting me out of work, you know that? You're taking the food out of my baby's mouth. You're—'

'We're not having a debate about this, Fred,' Francine snapped. The pain roared in her skull and she cringed against it. 'You're going to do exactly as I say or you're not going to go home at all. Do we understand each other?' When he didn't reply, she repeated, 'Fred, do we understand each other?'

Through clenched teeth, he said, 'Yes.'

'Good. Just do as you're told and you'll have us out of your hair in no time.'

Francine looked at Autumn, but she was staring out of the windscreen, beguiled by the world ahead of her. Her eyes flashed with excitement as she drank in each tree, each passing car, the array of street lights. She was drunk on freedom.

Francine reached down and clasped her daughter's other hand and watched the world with her.

-

They turned off at the exit for Sycamore. The Clucky's logo wasn't lit up, but there was already a queue of cars for the breakfast drive-thru. Fred stopped the van just before the entrance of the parking lot and left the motor idling.

'So what am I supposed to do?' he asked.

'Get out and ask someone in there if you can use the phone. Call the police, I guess,' Francine said.

'What's all this about?' Fred shook his head. 'Ain't nobody gonna believe that I got stuck up by a little girl with a knife and a crazy woman.'

'They will,' Francine said with a sigh. 'Maybe not right away, but in time they will.'

'So I'm free to go?'

'Free as a bird,' Francine said. He opened the door and jumped down, his face blotchy and worried. 'Fly away now, Fred.'

She watched him waddle off before getting out of the van and making her way around to the driver's seat. Autumn shifted over to the passenger side.

'Are you okay to drive?'

'I'm fine.'

'Where are we going now?'

'Home. We aren't too far from my apartment, but it's a bit of a drive yet. We're going to park this thing up in a back road a couple of blocks away from my place and walk the rest of the way.'

Francine started slowly and cautiously, getting used to the weight of the vehicle and her limited sight. She could just about see through one eye, but the vision was misty. She rejoined the highway and stuck to the far right lane. She kept her speed steady and did not try to overtake any other vehicles. There was no need for unnecessary risks. It would be a mighty fine shame to have gone through everything they had only to lose it all in an auto wreck.

'So what are we gonna do, Mom?'

'The first thing is to go home and rest. I think both of us have earned that much.'

'Are we gonna get in trouble?'

'I think we have a lot going for us right now, and a bit of a head start, but we need to be really smart. See how things play out.' Francine was silent for a long time, breathing raggedly through her mouth. Her tongue was coated in the taste of her own blood. 'When I spoke to Lena, she told me that she was the one who helped lure you away that day.'

'She didn't have a choice. She's the only reason I survived out there as long as I did.' Autumn's voice cracked. 'But she isn't the reason I was taken.'

'What do you mean?'

Autumn clutched the big book of names to her side. 'I mean we were both unlucky.'

Francine thought she understood what her daughter meant but didn't press her. There was a lot the two of them needed to talk about, a whole junkyard of questions that needed to be sifted through. But that would come later. For the time being, they were alive and together. And that was good enough for her.

'You know we're going to have to run, don't you?' Autumn said. 'They won't let something like this drop.'

Francine almost laughed in spite of her injuries. 'Lena did warn me. She wanted to go to Hawaii.' She choked on the last part of the sentence, feeling a rush of gratitude for Lena. 'Maybe that wouldn't be such a bad idea. She hasn't steered me wrong so far. I don't have a lot of money, but your father does. He can get us set up somewhere.'

'You're not together any more?'

'No. He has a new wife, and they're expecting a child.'

'Really? I guess my return might take some of the shine off that.'

Francine shrugged. 'He'll be over the moon to see you. I'm sure of it.'

'And then we head off into the sunset.' Autumn laughed, but there was nothing behind it. 'There's one other thing I think we need to factor into our plans, Mom.'

'Oh yeah? What's that?'

'I'm pregnant.'

31

Nothing could have prepared Francine for the waves of emotion that crashed over her upon their return to the apartment. It was like time was overlapping on itself. There were instances when she saw the little girl she'd lost at the mall, and then there were flashes of complete ambiguity where she didn't recognise this young woman at all. Autumn was at once both her daughter and a complete stranger, and the conflict this caused was staggering. Francine knew it would be a very long time before she got used to it. Still, the complicated clash of happiness and regret that throbbed inside her could never outweigh the exhilaration. Not in a million years, because there, sitting across from her at the kitchen counter, was her daughter. They were no longer rushing, no longer fighting or frantic with fear; they just stared at one another, admiring, examining. Beneath the inescapable cold lights of the kitchen, Francine relished every freckle and line on Autumn's face. But it was her eyes that drew her in, the large black pupils that shone like polished onyx. In those eyes, Francine could see her own reflection, and the sensation sent tremors down her back.

She poured herself a large measure of vodka and drank it down in silence. After a couple more refills, she ran Autumn a bath. Autumn removed her clothes and, with her mother's help, stepped into the tub. The water blackened instantly. Francine took a sponge and gently began to rub the girl's back, clearing away the dirt and grime, revealing the pink and purple welts. Autumn sat with her knees pulled into her chest as her mother poured water over her scalp, untangling the clotted curls, combing out the kinks with her fingers.

'Are you hurt anywhere, baby?' Francine asked, barely able to hold back the tears. What kind of a question was that? She'd been hurt all over, tortured for years. Where did Francine get the nerve to ask this child about pain?

Autumn shook her head. In her own time, she stood up, reached for a towel and wrapped it around her waist, then stepped out of the tub. She drained the murky bathwater and began running the hot water again. 'You're hurt, though,' she said gravely. 'Your face is a mess.' She picked up the sponge from the side of the tub, dabbed it in the running water and gently swabbed her mother's brow. 'You're bleeding. And I think your nose is broken.'

'I'll live,' Francine said, and smiled. Speaking made her face throb.

'You need a doctor,' Autumn said, twisting the tap to shut off the hot water. 'And your head is cut all up here.' She delicately touched the tender skin just above Francine's eyebrow. 'Get in the tub.'

Francine slowly undressed, wincing as she performed the task. She stepped into the bath, collected some water in her hands and splashed her face. It stung ferociously.

'Don't,' Autumn said. 'Let me get that glass out. Where do you keep your tweezers?'

Francine pointed at the medicine cabinet. Autumn located the tweezers and pulled out a bottle of aspirin, then had another quick search for Band-Aids. When she'd found them, she laid the items out on the sink and sat on the edge of the tub. 'Tilt your face up to me,' she said, and Francine obeyed.

Autumn went to work. Francine did not move. In truth, the pain no longer registered. Autumn carefully stuck Band-Aids over the cuts to seal them, then gently touched the line of Francine's jaw, feeling for displacement.

'I can't tell if it's broken,' she said. 'I'd say your nose definitely is. You need to get to a hospital.'

'I just need some rest is all.'

Autumn said no more. Instead, she helped her mother rise from the tub and bundled a towel around her. They went to the bedroom and dried off.

'Go in the wardrobe and find something to wear. My long T-shirts are in the bottom drawer there,' Francine said, removing the towel and drying her hair with it. Each motion she made over her scalp sent echoes of dull pain through her head. She picked up a T-shirt and a pair of sweatpants, slipped into them, then climbed into bed. Autumn got in and curled up against her.

'Are we gonna be okay?' she whispered.

'Yes.'

'Are you sure?'

Francine paused, thinking of how best to construct her answer. The truth was that no, she wasn't sure, but she had a pretty good feeling they could get through this if they stuck together and played it smart. She opened her mouth to say as much, but Autumn was already asleep, snoring gently into Francine's neck. Francine kissed her on the forehead and breathed in the smell of her.

'Thank you, God,' she whispered. 'Thank you so much.'

She closed her eyes.

–

At 10.37 the following morning, Marsha Grains received an internal call from reception. She had been in the middle of crafting an email to an agent regarding an official offer for her client's first baby photos. Her manicured fingernails clicked at the keys as quickly as the raindrops that pelted the pavement outside the office. The shrill drone of the internal ringtone was a sound that Marsha no longer even noticed amidst the cacophony of the manic press room. The ringing died; she looked at the phone once, and then her eyes flicked back to her screen.

'Marsha?'

She unglued her eyes from the email and turned to Sharon, the receptionist, who was standing tentatively next to her desk with a notepad in one chubby hand and a pen in the other. Her face was slack with apprehension.

'What is it, Sharon?' Marsha asked, continuing to type.

'I'm really sorry to bother you, Marsha. I um… I tried to call you, but…'

'Yes, yes, spit it out. What's up?'

'I have a lady on hold who says she needs to speak with you urgently.' Sharon exhaled the sentence seamlessly, not daring to falter for a second.

'Where's she from?'

'From?'

'What company?'

'Oh, she isn't with one.'

'What's her name?'

A twitch of anxiety pulled Sharon's mouth down at the corners. 'She wouldn't say.'

Marsha spun in her chair to face the receptionist. 'Well, did she say what it's about?'

'Yes.' Sharon nodded eagerly and dictated from her pad: '"It's a matter of great importance, life and death, the biggest story of the year."'

'What story?' Marsha asked, irritated.

'She wouldn't say.'

Marsha linked her fingers and cracked her knuckles. 'Give her my email.'

'I… I tried that already but she said it was no good. She said she had to speak to you directly.'

Marsha felt her temper rising. She hated interrupting her emails to take calls; it completely threw off her rhythm and pace, but now that seemed to be well and truly gone and Sharon was still casting a shadow over her.

'All right, put her through.' She fluttered a hand at the receptionist to shoo her away.

The phone rang and Marsha snatched the receiver out of the cradle. 'Got it.' She waited for Sharon to fumble with the phone on her end. When it clicked, she said, 'Hello, this is Marsha Grains.'

The sound of a woman clearing her throat, and traffic in the background. 'Hello, Marsha. Do you have a pen to hand?'

'Yes. Who is this, please?'

The woman ignored the question. 'Glenn Schilling's wife has been abducted and Glenn himself might be dead.'

'What? Who is this?'

'He owns an apartment in Little Peace. His wife should still be there. Now do you have that pen?'

Befuddled, Marsha's brain seemed to stutter. 'Yeah, yeah, I have a pen.'

'Write this down. If you take the Magenta Highway towards Oldcole, there's a turning called Stack's Point. It's not marked on the road signs. It's an old dirt road that leads to what I assume is private property. Have you written that down?'

'Stack's Point, Magenta. What is—'

'Just listen, please. Take the dirt road leading from Stack's Point and you'll find one of Schilling's cars, or you should do if they haven't moved it. He'll be in the trunk. In the trunk with him will be a backpack with some DVDs. I'm sending a sample of one of the DVDs to your office for your attention. It will show Schilling and other men abusing children. Are you with me so far, Miss Grains?'

'Uh… yeah, I'm with you. That's a very serious alle-gation. How do you know all this?' she asked, pressing the palm of her hand against her free ear to block out the office babble.

'That's not important.'

'Look, can we meet up and discuss this, face to face?'

'That won't be necessary. All you have to do is go to Stack's Point. But be quick. I've already called the *Scribe* and the *Daily News*, so they have a head start. Of course, you won't take any of this seriously until you receive the DVD. When you get it, watch it to confirm what I've said. Then you should sell it to Fox News or CNN if you want to make a real splash.'

'Okay, so when will—'

The line went dead.

Epilogue

The Christmas tree was much too big for the front room. It looked ridiculous, especially the way the tip of the tree curled against the ceiling and the chunky, glittery gold star hung down onto the branches below. Will had made this exact point at the market, but Sheila insisted. 'It'll be so majestic,' she said, and continued to hammer him to death with the adjective until he relented. Now, glowing with multicoloured lights – not all white like he wanted – the tree looked anything but majestic: it looked tacky and garish. The baubles were different sizes and styles and were strewn about randomly, and the tree limbs dripped shiny tinsel. Will hated everything about the tree, the same way he'd grown to hate everything about Christmas. 'But you can't be a Grinch *this* year,' Sheila said. 'This year has to be special. A time for new beginnings.'

Sure, Will thought. *Because I can just turn it off and on like that. It's so goddam simple, isn't it?*

Ultimately, though, he knew she was right. To be anything other than jovial, especially considering their new blessing, would make him a fucking asshole. On Christmas Day he would take five minutes to himself, pour out a large measure of whiskey and swallow it down while thinking about his elder daughter, and then he would return to the festivities. At night he would say a prayer for her, perhaps even shed a tear or two.

They sat on the sofa staring up at the TV above the blazing fireplace. They were watching *Guys and Dolls*. An odd choice of movie for Christmas Eve, Will thought, but that was what was on and they were going to watch it, apparently. There were comedy specials on the other channels, or *Scrooged* with Bill Murray – Christ, he loved the hell out of that movie – but they were stuck watching Brando in the least Christmassy movie he could think of.

'I need a refill,' Sheila said, peeling away from Will. Immediately he felt about ten degrees cooler without her clinging to his chest like a leech.

'Should you be drinking so much?' Will asked, knowing that she had plenty of formula in the cupboard and bottles of expressed breast milk filling the fridge. He'd made a joke earlier about putting a splash of rum in the milk for the baby to help her sleep, and Sheila had admonished him as if he were serious. Perhaps it was his tone. He was more than aware of how grouchy he was being. He'd done a lot of media recently and squeezed in as many gigs as he possibly could. Christmas was good for business.

'I'm going to have one more,' she said, pouring a large glass of sherry. 'Did you want one or not?'

'Could you grab me a beer?'

'Beer?' She stood with her hands on her hips. 'Come on, Will. It's Christmas. You can drink beer any time of the year.'

'I can drink sherry any time of the year too, but I happen to hate the stuff and I've already had one fucking glass of it. I'd like a beer, please.'

She huffed. 'What about some mulled wine?'

'I guess I'll get the beer myself.' He stood up and she stepped in his way, her palms pressed against his woollen sweater.

'No, sit. I'm sorry. Let me get it, please. I want to get you a beer.' She smiled at him hopefully. He turned away and sat back down.

When she returned to the sofa with a bottle of ale, Will wondered if she'd done it on purpose. There were more than two dozen bottles of Budweiser in the fridge, and three bottles of ale left over from when her dopey brother had come around at Thanksgiving. Will had tried to get Peter to take the things home with him, but he'd refused, as though he were doing Will a favour.

'I'd better check on Summer,' he said, setting the bottle of ale on the table next to him.

'She's fine,' Sheila said quickly, her face childishly anxious. 'Look, the monitors are on. If she needs us, she'll call.'

Ugh, he couldn't take much more. *She'll call us*. That was Sheila's saccharine phrasing for a gargle on the baby monitor, like Summer were trying to phone them and let them know something was up.

'I know she's fine, but I just want to check. I thought I heard a thud earlier. Just gonna make sure nothing has fallen over.' Like that other idiotic oversized tree Sheila had wanted for outside the bathroom, so that every time he needed a piss in the night he pricked himself with pine needles.

He started up the staircase. When he reached the nursery, he saw through the open door that the star projector was on. He was sure it had been off when he'd last been up here, but maybe Sheila had fiddled with it. Why she would do that when the child was already asleep, he didn't know, but he'd long since given up trying to understand why she did anything these days. 'Don't be such a grouch! It's my baby brain.' Baby brain. Another wonderful term for her being a mindless idiot. How many times did he need to tell her that he didn't like leaving the projector on through the night in case the thing over-heated and blew a fuse?

He walked into the bedroom, approached the crib and froze.

The baby was gone.

He opened his mouth to shout down to Sheila, to double check that she hadn't moved Summer to one of the other rooms, when a sound stopped him.

The nursery door closed. A young woman stood holding his child, cooing to her softly.

'What?' Will breathed as his eyes adjusted to the green hue of the room. This couldn't be right, could it? No.

'It's not a hallucination,' a voice from the nursery bath-room said. Will turned around and saw Francine holding the baby monitor. 'It's Autumn,' she said, and pointed. The baby monitor didn't light up when she spoke.

'What are you doing in here?' he asked, before spinning around to face this teenage apparition who looked so much like his elder daughter. 'Don't you hurt my baby,' he whispered, fiercely.

'I'm not going to hurt her, Dad. She's my sister, right? You called her Summer?' She looked past Will and smiled at Francine. 'She was born in the fall. Maybe you should've called her Autumn two-point-zero. Would've made more sense. Then again, sticking with the seasonal theme is quite good going.'

'I don't… I don't…'

'You don't have to say anything, Dad. Not yet. You just have to listen, very carefully.'

He made a sound that was something like an exhalation and something like a hiccup, then started towards Autumn with his arms outspread.

'No, I wouldn't, Will,' Francine warned.

He dabbed at his eyes with the sleeve of his sweater. 'I can't believe this. Sweet Jesus, this is a miracle.'

'No, not a miracle, Dad. Why don't you sit down over there,' Autumn said softly.

'Let me go and grab Sheila, she'll be dying to see—'

'Sit down, Will. Sheila doesn't need to hear this. This is between the three of us.'

Will's head whipped towards Francine, squinting with confusion. 'What is this all about? I don't… How…'

'Sit down, Will. We don't have long.'

In a daze, Will made his way over to the small wicker armchair and plonked himself in it. He couldn't seem to pull his attention away from Autumn, staring at her with his mouth agape and his eyes wide with wonder.

'Ten years ago, a little girl gets taken from a mall,' Autumn began, gently bouncing the baby in her arms. 'Everybody thinks it's a kidnapping, but the girl is never heard from again. Until now. You following so far?'

His mouth twitched to speak, but she continued.

'This girl is taken to a house in the woods where a bunch of other girls live. They've all been taken from their parents too. And at this house, they're raped and taken to parties where other men rape them, and then they end

307

up pregnant. You know what happens to the babies they give birth to? They're shipped off to some other place, to grow up in another house, to be farmed out to parties for a bunch of sick celebrities and important people, and so on, and so on.'

'Autumn… I… My God…'

'I told you, didn't I, Will?' Francine said, gesturing towards Autumn. 'All these years. And here she is. Our Autumn.'

He covered his face with his hands and shook his head. 'This isn't… I don't know what this is. I don't know what any of it means.' He began sobbing, stuttering on the tears, snot dribbling from his nose unchecked. 'This has to be a dream.'

'Remember what I told you about Glenn Schilling?' Francine asked. 'You didn't take me seriously, did you, Will? Now look. Biggest scandal since OJ. I'm just angry that he shot himself before he could stand trial. I would've enjoyed watching that, believe me. Your good old pal Glenn Schilling, comedian, performer, paedophile, he does it all. What was it you called him, Will? An icon?'

Will looked at her through his fingers. 'I tried to call you, Francine. But your phone…'

'Yeah, I got rid of it. I've come all this way, you think I'm taking any chances now? Not on your life. What, did you think it was a coincidence? I come to you on my knees asking for your help, and you shun me like a dog. I tell you Glenn Schilling is connected to our daughter, and you say I'm crazy. Well, the papers didn't think I was crazy when they watched his home videos, did they?'

'Francine, for the love of God, put yourself in my shoes,' he whined. 'Do you blame me? It did sound crazy at the time.'

'Do you still think I'm crazy now, Will? Because that's Autumn standing there.'

'When I saw the news about Glenn, I didn't know what to think, I didn't know what to do. I had a feeling it was you, but... I'm... What can I say that will make this right, Francine?'

'I don't need words, Will.'

From downstairs, Sheila called, 'Will? Is she okay? What's taking you so long? Your beer's getting warm.'

Very quietly, Autumn began to sing to Summer. 'If you're tired, little girl, close your eyes and go to sleep, close your eyes and go to sleep, close your eyes and go to sleep...'

Will opened the door. 'I'm on the phone,' he called back quietly. 'I gotta take this; give me ten minutes.'

Sheila grumbled something about putting the beer back in the fridge.

'What do we do now?' Will asked Francine, closing the door again. 'The police—'

'Forget it,' Autumn interjected. 'They've known all along. They can't be trusted. No doubt they're going to try to cover this whole thing up.'

Francine walked over to stand beside Autumn and stroked the baby's cheek with her finger. She pulled a silly face and Summer smiled. Without looking at Will, she said, 'Autumn and I are going on the road. We need to cover a lot of ground. It's still dangerous for us. Autumn is known to them, and they'll be holding a grudge.'

'Them?'

'It goes a lot deeper than Glenn Schilling,' Francine said as Summer grabbed hold of her finger. 'It's a whole network. There's a lot I need to figure out. But the main thing is that we will need to keep moving. For now at least.'

'And then what?' Will asked. Every time he glanced over at Autumn, he felt giddy. It made his heart bump painfully in his chest.

'Then we hit them again,' Autumn returned flatly, her face like dull steel. 'We're going to find all their nests and expose them.'

'In time,' Francine added. 'We've got a lot of planning to do first. We've made a couple of friends in the media, but we need more. And that's where you come in.'

'Will? It's Christmas Eve.' Sheila's voice drifted up the stairs. 'Call them back!'

Will strode to the door again. 'Can you just shut up and watch your movie!' he called in a fierce whisper. 'I need to do this right now!'

Silence from downstairs. Summer grumbled in Autumn's arms, but Autumn swayed her back and forth and hushed the child.

'Autumn, I...' Will began to speak and then shook his head. 'I love you. I never stopped loving you. I just can't believe any of this is happening. I don't know what to say. Maybe there is nothing I *can* say.' Very suddenly, he began sobbing again. This time he didn't try and hide his face in his hands.

'I know.' Autumn laid Summer down in her crib and pressed the button on her lullaby mobile. As it played 'Twinkle, Twinkle, Little Star', she walked over to Will and placed her hand on his shoulder. Quietly, she said, 'The time for tears has long since passed, Dad.'

Will wiped his slick, puffy face and went to clasp her hand. 'I'm sorry, Autumn. I'm more sorry than you could ever know. I want to…' He stopped when he saw her belly protruding from beneath her padded puffer jacket.

'You're going to be a grandfather,' Francine said, unsmiling. Will froze; only his eyes continued to move, darting back and forth as he struggled to make sense of it all. 'Will. Will?' Francine clicked her fingers to get his attention. 'We're going to need money. In a couple of weeks' time, I'm going to call you. We can make all the arrangements then. In the meantime, keep your eyes peeled, do you hear me?'

He was still too stunned to process it all. Francine clasped his wrist tightly. He looked up at her, confused.

'You're going to help me this time, Will. And God help you if you don't.'

He gave a small nod of his head. Autumn hugged him and whispered something in his ear that only he could hear.

And then they were gone.

About the Author

S.B. Caves was born and raised in North London. He loves crime and thriller novels, classic horror movies, Korean/Japanese thriller films and true crime documentaries. He is also a huge boxing fan.